D1548287

If it's free, I can't afford it

This book is a work of fiction. Names, characters, places, and incidents are either products of the author's imagination or are used fictitiously. Any resemblance to actual events, locales, business establishments, or persons living or dead is entirely coincidental.

Copyright © 2023 by J. Jones

All rights reserved. This book or any portion thereof may not be reproduced or used in any manner whatsoever without the express written permission of the publisher except for the use of brief quotations in a book review.

ISBN: 979-8-9854110-5-8 (paperback)

ISBN: 979-8-9854110-4-1 (ebook)

Cover and typeset by Damonza

If
it's free,
I can't
afford it

a novel

J. JONES

ALSO BY J. JONES

Ghost of the Gray
Crack in the Red Ice

To Jim and Jerry

Chapter 1

A Little Ripe

DO I SMELL urine? I looked at my front as the door to the Golden Years apartment complex closed at my back. *Whew.* Not originating from me. Ever since a recent road trip that included too many coffees and not enough bathroom breaks, I'd been a little self-conscious. I continued down the dimly lit hall to the office area where my friend, Stephanie Beckett, worked as the front desk assistant at the seniors-only complex.

"Are you ready?" I asked in the perky voice of a twenty-four-year-old anxious to cut loose on Friday night.

Stephanie whispered, "You're early, Natalie. She's still here."

I glanced down the short hallway and caught a glimpse of light emanating from the manager's office. "Can you sneak out?"

"Are you kidding? I need this job. It's the perfect place to study when I'm working the late shift." She beamed. "Only three more semesters for my master's degree."

"I don't know if it's worth it, Steph." I cupped my hand

2 | J. Jones

over my nose. "How can you stand working around the smell of urine all day?"

She tossed me a curious look. "I don't smell anything. Must be you."

I glanced at my front.

Steph brushed my arm with the back of her hand. "You get used to it. The trash bin filled up over the holiday, so people leave their garbage bags in the hall. Some of the residents wear those...well, you know, the diaper things. They can get a little ripe."

"*A little ripe.* That's putting it mildly."

"This isn't exactly a high-end complex."

"Stephanie, you can clock out now," came the grating voice of Ms. Glass, who also managed my apartment complex, the Manor, four miles down the road. "Would you take those bags to the bin in the garage on your way out?"

"Of course. Thanks, Ms. Glass," replied Stephanie, who was always much more respectful to the warden than I was.

Stephanie tidied up her desk and slipped on an orange hoodie. With me in a tangerine T-shirt underneath a floral overshirt, we were dressed perfectly for Hawaiian Night at our favorite hangout, Frozen Freddie's, celebrated on the first spring day to reach fifty degrees in Sliver Lake.

We picked up multiple garbage bags on the way down the hall, each emitting an acrid, ammonia urine smell.

"Eww! It's leaking." I dropped a bag.

"Oh, come on." Stephanie picked the bag up with the fluid movement of someone who had perfected the routine. "You know, *you* could be living in a senior center someday."

I shook my head in disgust. "You wouldn't catch me dead living in a place like this."

Chapter 2

That Was Embarrassing

THE KEYS JINGLED a little loudly for the late hour as I approached the door to my upscale apartment at the Manor. Tight security and gorgeous landscaping had made the high rent for the relatively new complex seem almost reasonable, but that was back when I was working full-time at Platform Marketing—employment conditions that had recently changed.

As I pushed the door open, the stench reached my nose before my fingers reached the light switch.

"*Moose!*"

I rushed to the side of my furry friend, who lay curled in a wet pile of excrement—which he evidently had time to track all over the taupe carpet before he collapsed. Twelve minutes later, we were sitting in the veterinary clinic waiting to pay overtime for another canine emergency health examination. Moose nuzzled his nose into my side. Glassy eyes pleaded, "Help me, Mom." I scratched behind his ear, but my go-to move for a toothy grin failed to elicit a response. Another tear disappeared into his thick black fur, already wet from the chilly drizzle outside.

When the elderly receptionist in kitten-patterned scrubs finally peered over the top of her horn-rimmed glasses, I caught her eye in an attempt to prompt some sort of status. Ten minutes? An hour? Nothing. *What is it with old people?*

"Maybe she can't see us through those thick glasses," I whispered to Moose. A glance at my large black, Labrador-Retriever mix eliminated that thought.

A few minutes later, the woman peered again, then called out in a snippy voice, possibly having overheard my whisper, "Natalie Thomas."

I patted Moose on the head. "Nobody else in the lobby, and she uses my full name. Come on, boy."

Moose shook a spray of wet droplets onto my new Calvin Kleins, further speckling the white jeans that had made their first appearance at Frozen Freddie's, though not even Steph had commented on the apparel.

"Thanks, buddy. If you survive this, I'm giving you a bath."

Moose kept his head down as we followed Cat Lady into the exam room, where I perched on the cold metal chair in the corner, leaving the wheeled stool for Dr. Dana. Moose plopped down at my feet. Sadly, we were familiar with the routine.

Waiting the federally mandated twenty minutes in an exam room before entry of a professional provided more time to stress. Moose was only four years old, but he was acting twelve. Normally perked ears drooped to the side. His nose rested on my shoe. A few rapid taps on my phone left me certain I was witnessing early signs of poisoning. I closed my eyes to hold back the tears. Big mistake. A feeling of four white walls closing in on me alone in the apartment swept in—the same feeling I had felt after...

I shook the thoughts aside and asked myself how I had let this happen again. I'd tried to be more careful with foods that Moose shouldn't eat, but my best friend Andy Michaels *just had* to bring over a box of chocolates. Nothing good ever comes from chocolate in my apartment, especially *free* chocolate. Grandpa's saying about free things came to mind.

While the minutes crawled by, I scanned the animal-themed posters hanging slightly askew on the walls. Cats outnumbered dogs three to one, suggesting the receptionist was also the decorator. An array of leaflets leaned out of the reading rack. The title of one, *Protect Your Pet*. A little late for that now.

I rubbed Moose's head again. No response. No upward tilt. No smiling "Thanks, Mom" or "Do it again." He just lay there and moaned. Any other time, that moan would sound like the relaxing exhale of a tired friend. Tonight, it turned my stomach. What would I do without my best friend? The one who cuddled with me on the couch to watch movies. Snuck popcorn when he thought I wasn't looking. Slept next to me on the bed—the only one to sleep next to me. There he lay, barely able to lift his head.

My lip quivered. "You'll be okay, buddy. I promise."

I bowed my head and uttered a prayer for pets my parish priest had provided after the service last week. The timing of such a specific prayer had my eyes toward the ceiling when the exam room door opened.

At five foot nine and slightly taller than he was round, Dr. Dana presented what Steph and I referred to as the perfect representation of a dad bod. He bypassed the stool, sat on the floor, and began looking in and around various orifices of my furry friend.

His silence brought out my loquacious side. "When I got home, I found a box of chocolates shredded on the floor. I pushed them way back on the counter when I left this morning. He's never been able to get stuff from that far back."

Ignoring my explanation, which may have sounded like an excuse, the vet continued poking and prodding. "Um-hmm."

Not exactly the response I was expecting from the highly skilled, highly educated, highly priced expert sitting pretzel-style on the floor, stroking a mound of fur.

"I brought him in as fast as I could. After the last time, I didn't want to take any chances."

Six months ago, Moose had pulled a bag of chocolate mints off the counter while I was scrolling through my phone. By the time I looked up, the bag was empty. An hour later, we were in the same office, with Moose getting his stomach pumped and me getting lectured on the importance of keeping chocolate away from dogs.

Another "Um-hmm" caused me to cringe. The vet's calm face and soothing coos provided no indication regarding the health of my smelly partner. Was Moose dying from chocolate poisoning? Did he need his stomach pumped again? Did he need some kind of medication that I couldn't afford? *Talk already!*

Dr. Dana looked up. "How many pieces did he eat?"

Nerves caused by the various lethal and costly scenarios running through my mind made me spout a reply without thinking it through. "*All of them.*"

As soon as the sentence was out, I realized how uninformative such an answer might sound to a man wearing a white coat. The response did, however, elicit a rare smile. "And how many might that be?"

"I don't know. I mean, I ate three when I opened the box and took two pieces in my lunch yesterday. Last night I had a couple."

I sensed the doctor getting impatient with the calculation. My mind jumped forward to the morning when I snuck one more piece for breakfast before pushing the box into the corner.

"*Two!*"

"Um-hmm."

*   *   *

Moose lowered his head in the back seat, but there was no place to hide.

"Well, *that* was embarrassing." My tone rightfully caused him to cower. "Two hundred and thirty-eight dollars. That's a hundred and nineteen dollars for each piece of chocolate. I hope you enjoyed it!"

The bill was only part of my frustration. More infuriating was the beady-eyed sneer of the crepe-paper-faced receptionist when my credit card was declined. My checking account wasn't an option, with a balance of twenty-two bucks, and who has a savings account these days? While I glared at the bill, the knot in my stomach was reminding me that I had known Moose needed to be fed before I met up with Stephanie. The corresponding nausea reminded me that cheese curds and frozen custard was not the best way to spend my last thirty dollars.

"And what was that lethargic act? *I* thought you were really sick!" I stared out the windshield and grumbled, "Fifteen pounds overweight. You're going on a diet."

A look in the rearview mirror revealed tear trails on my round cheeks. I grabbed my shoulder-length, light-brown hair in one hand, twisted a scrunchie around the ponytail with my other hand, then drove out of the lot into the night.

Back at the apartment, I pushed the laundry off the table to clear enough space to either bang my head or close my eyes and cry—I hadn't decided which. Two hundred and thirty-eight dollars and nineteen cents. Reading the bill over again didn't make it any less. Did they really need the nineteen cents? Not that it mattered, where was I going to get two hundred and thirty-eight bucks? I hated to do it, but I knew exactly where.

Chapter 3

It Wasn't My Fault

"HEY, GRANDPA," I said over the phone just as his antique Seth Thomas clock announced 8 a.m. in the background with a soothing set of gongs, comforting on nights when I fell asleep on his couch.

"Good morning, Natalie. Could you hold on for a second? I've got someone at the door."

His voice trailed off as he moved the phone away from his face.

"So you're offering to test my house for free?" Grandpa asked skeptically.

"That's right, sir," came an overly friendly reply. "We start with a free efficiency test to determine how much energy is being lost through your windows."

"How often does that test show the windows are fine?"

"Well, um, I'm not sure, but I can see your windows are an older style. Our advanced design is considerably more energy efficient. These new windows will provide a substantial savings in your heating and air conditioning bills. Everybody likes to save money, am I right? I can also offer a free upgrade to our window package if you schedule installation in the next thirty days."

"A free test *and* a free upgrade."

"Yes, sir."

"Sorry, young man. *If it's free, I can't afford it.*"

I shook my head. The poor guy never saw it coming, but I'd been on the receiving end of Grandpa's saying more than a few times.

"I'm back. Now where were we? I haven't heard from you in a few days."

Eight days, actually, since I asked for help with my car insurance bill. Still, the old man always seemed happy to hear from me, even when I was calling for money.

"Are you coming over for dinner?" I asked.

"Wouldn't miss our annual first-day-of-spring grilling celebration."

Annual? This would be our second first-day-of-spring grilling, and the old man already had it institutionalized.

"My weather app says it'll be fifty-two degrees from four thirty until five twenty-two."

I should have known convincing him to trade up the flip phone wouldn't end cell phone-related embarrassments. A thousand apps to choose from, and he reads the weather.

"Isn't that a little precise? I mean, the meteorologist still says 'chance of rain' when it's pouring outside."

"You may have a point there, kiddo. Need me to bring anything? I could stop at the store on my way over."

"Thanks, but I have everything. I'm making spaghetti."

He chuckled. "Don't mean to question the chef, but won't the noodles fall through the grill?"

"Ha. Ha. Like I haven't heard that one. I'll do the noodles in the kitchen and finish them in a cast iron skillet on the grill. If you behave, I may let you boil the water."

"Not sure I want that kind of pressure."

Though I preferred to blather about the upcoming

dinner, I needed to get to the point of the call. The credit card lady had said that if I made an electronic payment by 10:00 a.m., I wouldn't be charged a penalty for exceeding my card limit.

"Grandpa, I had to take Moose to the vet because he pulled a box of chocolate from the counter. I pushed it way back, but somehow he managed to reach it. The vet said he'll be fine because he only ate a little."

I paused long enough for him to offer to pay the bill. He didn't bite.

"We were lucky. Remember last year, when Moose ate a whole bag and had to have his stomach pumped? From now on, chocolate goes on top of the refrigerator."

"How's our little guy doing?" he asked through what sounded like pursed lips.

"He's fine...but the bill was more than I expected." I picked a strand of black fur off my white jeans as I prepped them for the wash—that could probably wait another day. "If they hadn't cut my hours at work, it wouldn't be a problem. I should have gotten the Cottonwood account, not Chelsea. That account would have brought me back to full time in the office. It's not fair. I've been at the company longer than she has. Nobody even calls it Cottonwood; they call it 'Natalie's account' because I rolled out the last marketing plan."

"Why'd they give the account to Chelsea?"

"I don't know."

I was pretty sure I knew the reason, but sharing details of my love life, or lack thereof, with Grandpa was never a good idea. Andy and I had stayed at the coffee shop until well past midnight a few Sundays ago while he filled me in on his recent achievements at work. Mr. Too-Shy-to-Ask-Me-Out had evidently been outgoing enough in the office to get a promotion to the Florida branch. Though I went on the occasional Grandpa-arranged date, I had always thought that Andy and I would somehow end up together. The following Monday I was so tired and upset that I wasn't paying attention in the parking lot and hit a speed bump too hard. I couldn't tell Grandpa the truth about why I wasn't paying attention without receiving a dozen relationship-related questions, so I settled for truthful enough.

"My boss insists on handing out assignments on Monday mornings. I was late a couple of weeks ago because I sloshed coffee on my blouse when I drove over a speed bump in the parking lot. I had to go home and change. What did they want me to do, attend the meeting with coffee all over myself? Dang speed bump."

"So, it's Chelsea's fault. The old speed-bump-in-the-parking-lot trick. Works every time."

He was probably kidding, but I hadn't finished ranting. "It's not just the vet bill. Andy came over this week and gave me the chocolate. He brought his little Yorkie, Jumbo, and Ms. Glass saw the dogs together. The next morning, another one of those apartment manager notes was clipped to my door. She *fined* me for having two dogs in the apartment, even though Jumbo was only here for an hour, and we spent half that time outside in the grass. It wasn't even my fault!"

"Uh-huh. Was that Chelsea's fault too?"

Okay. That was pure sarcasm, something I attributed to his age and usually ignored, but today it was a struggle.

I huffed a heavy "No."

"Doesn't your contract say something about pets?"

"It has a whole section on pets, but I didn't think it applied to visiting dogs. You saw how long that contract was. I only had time to skim through it."

"You know, it's okay to read the contract after you move in."

Instead of asking why I would ever read six extra-long pages of legal crap *after* I'd signed, I mumbled, "Uh-huh."

"You might want to give it a good review," he added without explaining how that could possibly help now.

I shook my head with an emphatic *no way*. *Who has time for that?*

"At least Andy brought food over, so dinner was free. Your saying about free things came to mind the moment I saw the note."

"Funny how that works."

"*But it's not funny.*" I could hear the stress-filled whine in my voice. It was time to place the fault where it rightfully belonged—with the apartment manager. "Ms. Glass makes me so angry sometimes."

"I'm sure she's just doing her job. It's not easy managing the Manor and the Golden Years apartment complexes."

Splitting her time between apartments was the only positive thing about the witch. I try to get along with everybody, but Ms. Glass is special, and not in a good way. A month after moving into the Manor, Andy, Stephanie, and I grilled dinner on the deck to celebrate my new place. The following morning a note was clipped to the door. Evidently, something in the contract specified that barbecue grills were not allowed on the deck. I met with Ms. Glass to see if she would waive the fine because I was new and unfamiliar with the rules. The old lady just stared at me and said, "Ms. Thomas, we must abide by the terms of the contract." Since then, I've referred to the compassionless lady as Ms. Ass.

"Sorry about Moose. Do you need some help with the bill?"

Finally. It sure took his old brain long enough to offer. "How could you tell?" I wiped a tear of frustration. "The vet was two hundred thirty-eight, and the fine was twenty-five. You know I hate to ask, but I just paid rent, and I have the car payment coming out of my next check."

"No need to apologize. I don't want you to stress over money. It's not worth it."

"Uh-huh." If he didn't want me to stress, he could have offered to pay five minutes ago.

"So, how was your date?" he asked, changing the subject from finances to the latest attempt at embarrassing his granddaughter.

Last week, Grandpa's friend had asked him if I was seeing anyone, something I needed to start lying about more often.

"Uh, yeah, feel free to turn down those requests when they come in. I'm doing okay in the boyfriend department."

"You didn't like him?"

"I never got to know him. He doesn't have a car, so I had to meet him at his place. Then he didn't want to go anywhere, because he always watches *NOVA* on Saturdays. We ate frozen pizza on his couch and watched a biology special."

"I think I saw that one." He chuckled again. "All right, I get the hint. I'll try to avoid putting you in those situations. Are you sure you don't need anything for dinner? I could bring dessert. Maybe a...chocolate *mousse?*"

Fortunately, he couldn't see my eyes roll. "That's not even funny."

"A little too soon?" Another chuckle. "I'll make a transfer for those bills before I come over. Had a hundred-dollar surprise I was going to tell you about anyway."

"A hundred bucks! What's the surprise?"

"I'll tell you when I get there."

I set my phone on the nightstand and turned around just in time to see my best friend in a sitting position, pulling himself forward with his front paws—wiping his ass on the floor.

"Moose, *no!* Stop. *Please...ahhh.* That's where I do my yoga."

Chapter 4

It's Your Funeral

BY THE TIME I had showered and dressed, my bank app confirmed that Grandpa had made the transfer plus an extra twenty bucks. *Sweet!*

I cracked the apartment window to air out the stale smell of excreted chocolate before Grandpa arrived for what he called dinner and I called a late lunch. Then Moose and I walked past the railroad tracks and up a hill that overlooked Sliver Lake. We sat in the grass and listened to a light breeze blowing through the pines that surrounded the narrow body of water. We had found this hill shortly after I moved into the Manor, and it soon became our place of solitude, where we came to think about the worries of the day.

Asking Grandpa for money wasn't weighing on my mind nearly as much as the upcoming renewal of my lease. I had lived at the Manor for almost two years and always struggled with the rent, but since my work hours had been reduced, making the rent payment was more than a struggle. The last thing I wanted to do was leave this apartment for something cheaper. My parents had helped me find the

Manor during one of the last weeks we had spent together before they...

I called Moose up from the lakeshore, and we continued our morning walk to the coffee shop to kill more time while the smell in the apartment subsided. Brisk air tingled my lungs with each breath as we passed piles of peppered snow and dodged frosted rivers of melt. The last signs of a frozen winter.

"This better melt fast, boy. We've got a canoe trip coming up."

After navigating three short blocks of icy sidewalk, I looped his leash under one leg of a cast iron chair outside my neighborhood coffeehouse.

"You can watch through the window." A lingering fog of frozen breath engulfed his head as I spoke.

Ten minutes later and twelve dollars lighter, I returned with a large vanilla latte and two muffins, one for me and one for Moose, who had lost his patience and pulled the chair closer to the door.

"Sorry, buddy, but it's your fault." The drooling backup alarm with the wispy tail had decided to sleep in. "Wake me up earlier tomorrow, and the line won't be so long."

Moose wolfed his muffin down then fixed his eyes on mine while I watched a car pull up to the Chinese restaurant across the street. Yang's was normally my Tuesday night indulgence before the weekly drive to St. John's church where Grandpa volunteered me as a way to occupy my "idle time." I was a little insulted at the insinuation that I had empty time to fill but had come to appreciate the "fellowship," another word he must have learned in his youth.

When Moose was satisfied that no errant crumbs remained, we took the back way to the apartment, where he rid himself of the last bits of chocolate in a rancid goo, much too creamy to capture with a poop bag. At the corner of the building, a large Now Leasing sign announced completion of a new apartment complex across the parking lot. The same corporation owned the Manor, but the new Legends complex would be restricted to seniors. I was already aware that leasing had begun, having received a management note instructing residents to refrain from using parking spaces designated for the Legends. The memo also mentioned a bonus for any referral—as though any of my friends would be geriatrics.

The rest of the morning was spent positioning throw rugs over stains on the living room carpet, which I hadn't had time to clean thoroughly, and decluttering the kitchen counters to limit criticism that was sure to arrive with my dinner guest. When the rooms were presentable, I threw the cleaning rags into the washing machine and stomped the trash down enough to buy me another day before having to dump it.

Moose was licking the last crumbs from the leftover sandwich I had eaten for lunch when Grandpa texted.

"Perfect timing, boy. We just finished lunch, and he's arrived for dinner. You need to wait here. He asked me to meet him next door."

I crossed the parking lot and found Grandpa in front of the new apartment complex talking to none other than Ms. Ass.

"Hello, Natalie," she said in a voice I barely recognized, probably because it sounded nice.

I pinched a thin smile.

At five foot six, the bitter old woman was my height but stick-thin compared to my more moderate body size. Her thin gray hair was pulled back in a tight teenage ponytail, forcing way too much of her pointy nose and that taut-skinned face at me.

The warden led us to a second-floor unit on the west end of the complex, where she opened the door to a luxurious apartment that welcomed us with a marble tile entry, high ceilings, and the smell of new carpet mixed with fresh-cut wood. I wanted to ask Grandpa the reason we were touring the unit, but it was pretty obvious, so I dared not speak in front of the warden for fear she might relegate him to solitary confinement in a basement unit.

The kitchen was basically the same as mine but much shinier. In the living room, I pictured myself on the couch balancing a Styrofoam food container on my lap and watching the TV mounted above the fireplace. The bathroom, slightly larger than mine, reminded me what a clean lavatory looked like.

I opened a door at the end of the hall, expecting to find a linen closet. "You're getting a *two*-bedroom?"

"I've collected forty more years of junk than you have. The space will come in handy."

"All this for the subsidized senior rate of nine-fifty, Jimmy."

My mind jumped from excitement about the second bedroom to "*Jimmy.*" What the heck? Nobody called Grandpa "Jimmy." The lady had a lot of nerve—and nine-fifty for a two-bedroom was eight hundred bucks a month less than I was paying for a one-bedroom.

"What do you think, Natalie? Should I do it? I'd be closer to you."

Closer? I can see my kitchen from your window. "You should rent two units and move me into one."

"I'm not sure you would pass for sixty. Had to use a fake ID myself." He chuckled again, then tossed a wink to Ms. Ass that curdled my stomach. "Two things you don't want to rush, Natalie—age and responsibility. They come sooner than you can imagine." He turned back to the warden. "Sounds like I'll take it. May I stop by tomorrow to complete the paperwork?"

"That would be perfect. You and Natalie can close up and walk the grounds if you like. Just drop the key off when you leave."

She placed the key in his hand, folding her hands around his in the process.

The moment Ms. Ass was out of sight, I turned to Grandpa. "So, why do you want to move? I thought you had too much stuff to downsize to an apartment."

"I'm tired of that big house. You'd be surprised how much work there is to keep a place like that up. A leak here, a squeak there, and every new sound costs money. These units are brand new, and there's that little lake down the street and the shopping center we can walk to. To tell you the truth, I've been thinking about moving ever since they started construction on this place."

"But apartments come with a lease and a lot of rules. Trust me, they sneak up and get you for *everything*."

He shot me one of his wry smiles. "I'll read the contract before I sign to make sure there's a little flexibility. Always do that with a contract. People don't like to reduce the price, but they'll often add a clause or two if it doesn't cost them anything up front. This complex doesn't allow pets, but you can bet I'll get an exception for Moose to visit. Read those contracts, Natalie. Make *them* work for *you*."

Not even moved in and the old man was already offering unsolicited advice.

He put a hand on my shoulder. "Hope you don't mind me being so close."

"Of course I don't mind," I lied. A vision of Grandpa walking in on me sitting "a little too close" to a young man popped into my head. Realizing the likelihood of that scenario was quite low, I softened my position. "It'll be great to have you next door, but aren't you too young for this place? I mean, did you see the people downstairs? I'm not gonna lie, they're old. Like, *really* old."

He chuckled again. "I'm getting up there myself."

"Seriously. The new-resident gift bag comes with a box of bran, denture cream, and a bottle of Beano." I was kidding about the gift bag to make a point. "I'm worried you'll get bored around these old farts."

Another chuckle. "Old farts aren't so bad. Not after a dose of Beano."

"More jokes like that, and I'll believe you belong here." I shook my head with reluctant acceptance. Maybe having Grandpa nearby would be a good thing. If I needed a cup of sugar or a couple of T-bone steaks, he would be right across the parking lot. On the other hand, he'd probably insist on sharing the steaks. "Okay. At least you'll be close enough that I can drop off my laundry on the way to work. Blouses lightly starched, please."

We left the unit and toured the downstairs area, passing the office and a small exercise room that had fewer weights and more elliptical machines than the Manor, evidently catering to the older clientele. At the end of the long hall, a single glass door opened into a large room that had a dozen circular tables in the middle and a few two-tops next to the windows. Glass double doors on the opposite side of the room exited onto a patio where two chrome-plated gas grills glistened in the sunlight.

I made a beeline to the gas grills, weaving between tables of old people where an almost rhythmic *tsit...tsit...tsit* caused me to stop and investigate. Snow-white heads surrounded the table on my left, not a single black hair in the flock. Playing cards were fanned out in wrinkled hands that looked barely strong enough to carry the weight. Players' faces were as etched as their fingers, and each person had a clear plastic hose looped from their nose down to a small oxygen tank on their hip—the source of the symphony.

Outside the double glass doors, my mind shifted to the evening menu and Italian sausage sizzling over ceramic coals.

"Welcome," said an old lady sitting with perfect posture on a white wrought iron bench. "It will be nice to see a young person in the halls."

"Oh, I'm not moving in, my grandpa is. I'm Natalie."

The gray-haired woman exhaled a thick stream of smoke and replied in a soft, raspy voice. "Of course you aren't. It's nice to meet you, Natalie. I'm Thelma."

Grandpa eventually made it outside, no doubt having given the phone number of his single granddaughter to everyone in the room.

"I'm going to drop the key off with Christine and set a time to meet her tomorrow. Need to do it soon, since this is her last week. I want to remind her that you referred me for the unit." He smiled. "Get you that hundred-dollar bonus."

"What do you mean, *her last week?*" I focused my question on Ms. Ass, whose departure would have an immediate and positive impact on my life, but the bigger concern was "*Christine.*" How could he call that witch by her first name? He knew how miserable she made my life at the Manor. He paid half the fines she gave me—more than half.

"I thought you knew. She's taking over a larger property across town. I want to work out some contract details with her before she leaves. See you in a little while."

As he walked away, I shouted, "We're cooking on these grills tonight. Get that in the contract!"

* * *

After a dinner that tasted wonderful, having been cooked on a shiny new stainless-steel grill, I went straight to the front office of the Manor to get the scoop from Stephanie, who, like Ms. Ass, also alternated days between the Manor and the Golden Years complexes.

"Is this really her *last* week?" I asked excitedly. "How come you didn't tell me when we were out last night?"

Stephanie extended her long thin fingers and blew lightly

on freshly painted nails. I glanced at my stubby nubs. The polish was good for another week.

"I just found out." She nudged a letter with her elbow. "This memo was on the desk when I got in. Sounds like her new job is a promotion and closer to where she lives. I was going to text you earlier, but I got busy."

I glanced at her nails again.

Stephanie's confirmation was all I needed to release the squeal that had been building up since Grandpa gave me the news. "I can't believe that witch will be out of my life."

"Yep. A couple more weeks, and she's out of here. Are we grilling on your balcony to celebrate?"

"You bet we are, if we survive our canoe trip on the Saint Croix."

Chapter 5

Hello Jimmy

RAMEE ULRICH AND DeAndre Lewis, friends of mine since our sophomore year in college, met me at Grandpa's house to help with the move. DeAndre is six foot three and thin but not skinny. Ramee is a wisp taller than I am and ten pounds lighter—maybe twenty. Her butterscotch hair hangs just past her shoulders and is two shades lighter than my brown mane.

With Moose on our heels, we walked past a large moving van on our way to the front door.

"Good morning," said Grandpa, his arms loaded with kitchen items.

Moose barked once in reply.

"Nat, your dog barked at me again," said DeAndre, continuing our never-ending game of "who does Moose like the best?" He scratched Moose behind the ear. "How come you never bark at Ramee? Every time I—"

Grandpa interrupted before DeAndre could get into one of his rambling rolls. "I was thinking of you girls when I hired these gentlemen. Sorry, DeAndre, maybe one of them has a sister. This is Dave and Robert. I've informed them that you're both single, successful, and looking for handsome young men to take you dancing tonight."

Dancing? I hope you didn't mention those "sock hops" with Grandma that you like to talk about a little too much.

Without fail, anytime a cute guy was around, there was no filter between Grandpa's mouth and my humiliation. Ramee, on the other hand, was never embarrassed. In an exaggerated sultry voice, she said, "Hi, Dave, I'm Ramee. That's with two Es...and one arm." She swung her empty sleeve forward to emphasize the one arm. As with every other guy I had observed in that situation, Dave and Robert were at a loss for words.

"Good morning," they finally replied, not quite in unison.

DeAndre picked up a box and carried it out while the movers lifted the couch and shuffled to the door, which I happily held open. My eyes were mere inches away from chiseled arms as they negotiated the leather-backed frame through the narrow doorway. Cute, rock-solid, and just a little sweaty. What more could a girl want?

While they manhandled the oversized furniture, Moose licked up a few rogue Cheerios, then slid butt-first across the carpet, an action that seemed appropriate for the last day in the house.

DeAndre returned and caught me ogling the muscular movers. "I think they got it, Nat. You can let go of the door."

I held my ground.

"They got nothin' on me, girl. Look at these guns." He flexed thin muscles, dropped to the floor, and started counting push-ups. He stopped at four, scrunched his nose, and glared at the carpet. "What's that smell?"

"Problem?" I asked innocently.

He sniffed the air. "Something stinks."

"Moose just wiped his ass on the carpet. He still has the runs from that chocolate."

"*Nasty!* And you let me put my nose in it?"

I was doing well not to allow my muffled giggle to burst into an all-out laugh. "Right. Like I had any idea you were going to show off to Ramee with four push-ups. A little jealous of the hunks, are we?"

He flexed again. "With guns like these, I don't get jealous."

While DeAndre kissed his biceps, I wrapped the mantel clock in a thick towel and carried it out, careful not to let the pendulum fall off. With Grandpa nearby, it would be nice to hear the rhythmic ticking and hourly gong more often.

"These are full of books," said Grandpa, warning the chiseled helpers about the final load.

The weight was reflected in swollen biceps when the movers each picked up a box. *Showtime.*

Hmph! Ramee beat me to the door.

I gestured to the movers' bulging muscles and whispered to DeAndre, "You may want to do a few more push-ups."

Standing in the entry one last time, Grandpa draped an arm across my shoulder. The small house looked big now that it was empty. Memories flashed through my mind of game nights at the kitchen table, movies on the big screen, and all the restaurant take-out containers that had passed through the door. We each released a reflective sigh. Both of us had faced dramatic changes in our lives since he had moved into that house, but since he was across town, we were still mostly on our own. Now that we were going to be neighbors, we would have plenty of opportunities to spend quality family time together.

*   *   *

The drive to the Legends was filled with Grandpa interjecting parental advice between suggestions on things we could begin doing together. Each mile closer to the apartment complex had me second-guessing whether the move was a good idea.

"Have you considered delaying your canoe trip?" he asked as we skirted a wilting pile of snow on the side of the road.

"I would, but Andy can only go on Saturday. He's moving to Florida next week, so this is the last time we can go canoeing together." I glanced out the window and crossed my fingers. "We'll be fine. It was chilly this morning, but every day is getting warmer."

"Chilly down here. It'll be a lot colder on the Saint Croix."

I tugged at my sleeve. "There's no such thing as bad weather, only bad clothing. An old man taught me that."

"Learned that saying when I traveled to Norway," he replied with a nostalgic gleam in his eye. "We're not Norwegian, you know."

"I'll wear my cold-weather gear, and it's not like we're going to get wet. We've done that river a bunch of times." Well, we had done it twice before, and one of those trips was cut short when Moose jumped out near the shore to chase a squirrel.

Grandpa pulled into the apartment parking lot, which moved the discussion to which items should be carried inside first. We each picked up a box and carried it into the Legends through the door nearest Grandpa's second-floor unit. Two ladies, much older than Grandpa, were standing next to a round table near the entry.

Synchronized voices, one perky and the other timid, said, "Hello, Jimmy."

There was that "*Jimmy*" again.

"Good morning, ladies," said Grandpa, giving each a much-too-generous hug.

Those were the only words he got in before the perky-voiced woman went on a roll, filling *Jimmy* in on everything that had happened at the Legends since she arrived on opening day two weeks prior. Though some of her casserole dishes sounded appealing, when she started rattling off her list of aches and pains, I slid my phone from my pocket and caught up on a few texts. She finally stopped for air, giving Grandpa an opportunity to introduce us to Gladys Dawson and Angie Chambers.

"I'd like you to meet my granddaughter, Natalie, and her dog, Moose. They live next door." When he pointed toward the Manor his sleeve crawled up the outstretched arm revealing age spots I hadn't noticed before. "You'll be seeing a lot of them around here."

"A *dog*," huffed Angie, a tall, grayish-blond woman who was wearing way too much jewelry for an afternoon conversation around an entry table. She took a half step back.

The lady was tall enough to sport the long necklaces intertwined around her thin neck, one of which was made of large copper balls. Too much for me, but I had to admit the ensemble went well with her lemon chiffon blouse and lavender elastic-waist slacks that hung loosely on bony hips.

"My daughter has a dog, but she knows better than to bring *it* to the apartment. Can't have all that fur and filth in the carpet, you know."

"Filth," repeated Gladys, who was half a head shorter than Angie and stood a step behind the domineering woman.

Moose sniffed Angie's ankle and withdrew, probably sensing, as was I, that the lady might not be a dog lover.

DeAndre and Ramee arrived, somehow taking longer than us even though they had left first. Good timing, because another dog comment and I might have asked Moose to fetch one of the copper balls around Angie's neck.

Ramee pasted a full cheek on the outside of the locked

glass door and pleaded "*help me*" to get my attention. I moved to let them in, happy to distance myself from the bitter woman.

"Serena is history!" exclaimed DeAndre in an overly animated voice.

Grandpa looked a little less confused than the two ladies. "Who's Serena?"

"The voice in his cell phone," said Ramee between laughs.

"She used to be my girl, but we're finished. We followed her directions all the way to the railroad tracks. Then she had the nerve to tell me..." He raised his tone to that of a snippy female. "*You will have to find a place to park and walk from here.*" A tone not a lot different from that of the stone-faced woman on the other side of the entry table.

Crusty makeup on their cheeks or a lack of knowledge regarding cell phone assistants prevented Angie and Gladys from cracking a smile. Thankfully, the moving truck beeped a backup warning, which refocused our attention on the door.

"Gotta go, girls," said Grandpa to the ladies. "If you have some time, stop by and help me arrange the place. It's going to need a lady's touch."

I gave Ramee a "*what are we*" look.

While Grandpa instructed the movers on where to place the furniture, Moose scoured the apartment, nose to the floor, in search of the most expensive area to destroy when no one was watching. DeAndre, Ramee, and I brought in items from the cars and began unpacking the breakables. On one trip, DeAndre filled my arms with a heavy load and placed the mantel clock carefully on top then took his sweet time selecting a perfect bundle of items for himself. I left him to his indecision and carried my load inside, where I placed the clock prominently on the mantel above the fireplace and wound it with the circular key. With a flick of the pendulum, the steady cadence of the aged timepiece mesmerized me once again.

"How'd you get back inside?" I asked DeAndre, having heard the entry door lock behind me.

"Yeah. *Thanks* for that. A little hunchback guy held the door open. Well, he was either holding it open or stuck trying to get out. I couldn't really tell. Bald dude with pants pulled up to his chest. Pull those babies up any higher, and he wouldn't need a shirt."

Grandpa chuckled. "Sounds like Mr. Orval Gray. He wasn't stuck. It just takes Orval a little longer to get through."

DeAndre shrugged. "Might still be there."

He and Ramee performed another rendition of "Serena" as they left together with the movers, and unless Grandpa needed his clothes piled high on the table, I wasn't going to be much more help either.

"See you in the morning." On the short walk home, I thought about how to keep cougars like Angie away from Grandpa. As aggressive as she seemed, I would need to start early, before the big cat could pounce.

Chapter 6

Knocked My Head

GRANDPA'S EYES NEVER left the cup in my hand when I entered what he and I were now calling the "great room" at the Legends. The old man went to bed when the sun went down, of course he didn't need a caffeine boost. At twenty-four, I had to scroll through my phone until midnight to catch up on everything important. My double-espresso vanilla latte was the only way to keep me from falling asleep at work—something I learned the hard way. Thankfully, the disapproving look was interrupted when an old couple entered the room and introduced themselves to Grandpa, but no doubt a lecture was forthcoming.

His "fiscally irresponsible" lectures were usually short, but the month before, he had created a spreadsheet that listed coffee as my third-highest expense behind rent and my car payment. He must have done the math wrong, because coffee doesn't cost *that* much. When I promised to cut the vanilla from my lattes, he acted like that wasn't a sacrifice, which turned into a separate lecture on sacrifice and how hard it used to be for him to scrounge two bits for a cup of joe. I was still confused over that speech.

To avoid being pulled into conversations and introduced as Grandpa's "single granddaughter," I slid casually to the side and leaned against the wall. A quick scan of the room had me reasonably comfortable as I noticed that most of the old women were paired with their husbands. Only two women sat alone. The first lady was sitting tall and proper at the front of the room. Her silver hair gleamed compared to the luster-lacking white hair on most of the other ladies. She was properly dressed in an alabaster long-sleeved blouse with creases sharp enough to cut. Her pale skin had fewer wrinkles than others in the room, though I had a feeling she was older than most. I sensed no threat.

When Grandpa finished his latest attempt to influence my love life through arranged dates with grandchildren of people he had just met, he joined me next to the wall. "That's Mrs. Barrington," he said, catching my gaze. "Angie introduced me yesterday."

Aha. The cougar was already making her move.

"I mentioned that you and Moose live next door. She used to see moose around their family cabin up north. Do you know how big those get?"

I heard him but wasn't listening. A second woman sitting alone had caught my eye. Small and wearing a faded green blouse under a fully buttoned beige cardigan, the lady was a little unkempt, as though her clothes had been left in the dryer overnight. Her deep-set eyes maintained a steady gaze upon the teacup vibrating ever so slightly in her hands. Boisterous people were making introductions all around the room, yet this woman was alone. Though Mrs. Barrington also sat by herself, she didn't appear to be alone at all.

"According to Angie, who seems to know everyone, that's Gwen Baker, but I haven't met her yet. Let's say hello." He tugged my elbow and pulled me over to the woman's table.

"May we join you?" he asked.

The feeble lady offered a warm smile and a warbled tone. "Please do. I just moved here and don't know anyone."

Her faded blue eyes blended into pale pink skin that was accented by red hair dye, which was so fresh I could smell the fumes.

"I guess none of us really know anybody since the place is so new," said Grandpa with a soft chuckle. "I only moved in yesterday and still have a dozen boxes to unpack."

Gwen spoke slowly, enunciating each word as though it carried special meaning. She used to live up north until her son moved her to the Legends to keep a closer eye on her.

"I was alone there, but not really. I had a routine that served me well over the years. The pharmacy delivered my pills, and on good days, I would scoot to the market down the street. When I didn't feel like getting out, which seems more often now, the market delivered. My son would drive up and take me to the doctor on occasion, but mostly I used the senior van for appointments." She looked up at Grandpa. "I saw a store nearby when we arrived. They don't deliver, and I don't want to go to a new place alone. It looks so big compared to my corner market."

"Natalie would be happy to take you to the store."

I knew you would collect on that vet bill.

"Could we go tomorrow, please? I'm running out of a few necessities."

Grandpa's pinched grin said, *"I'm sure that's fine."*

"Uh-huh," I replied with a discreet roll of my eyes. "Tomorrow works."

While Grandpa and Gwen talked about the challenges of moving, I sulked at the thought of spending half an hour at the grocery store with an old woman I didn't even know—until loud voices at the next table interrupted my self-pity. I wasn't trying to eavesdrop, but the larger of the two men evidently lacked an inside voice, and his wife was almost as loud.

"We raised chickens in the backyard," said the wife of the loud man in a voice that was crisp with a hard edge. "Those birds are mean. Chased me all over the yard. Come dinnertime, my brother would grab one by the neck and swing it around until the head popped off." She glanced my way. "Plucking a chicken—now, that's a chore I don't miss, but we were happy to have those birds." She then added a little too much detail about beheading, defeathering, and deboning the fowl.

Her large husband gave my coffee cup the same look I had received from Grandpa. "Four bucks for a cup of coffee. It's free on the counter, dontcha know."

"Oh, this isn't coffee," I replied, recalling when this size latte was only four bucks. Clearly the man had not visited a coffee shop recently. "It's a vanilla latte with a double shot of espresso. I get these when I need an extra boost. Besides, this one was free."

"Uh-huh. And how might that have come to be free?"

"With my club card. I get one free drink after every tenth cup." I spread my best "*smart businesswoman*" smile.

He offered another "uh-huh" accompanied by a placid look that suggested my math was wrong.

His wife nudged his shoulder. "Why can't you mind your own, old man?"

"Maybe I should at that." He released a soft chuckle. "We was talking chickens, right? Well, let me tell you, meat was scarce around our place too. Bread and beans at our table. Cheap and filling." He rubbed his stomach. "Course, now we got a grandson who won't buy dog food if it has grain in it, dontcha know. What the heck is wrong with grain?"

His wife reached over and patted the large man's stomach. "That's what's wrong with too much grain, Louis Hansen."

He bellowed a laugh that caused folds of skin around

his neck to ebb and flow like waves on the Saint Croix, then he continued describing to the second lady at the table, who by now I gathered was Millie Hymer, how sparse their dinner table had been when he was a child.

Millie sat low in her chair and wore a natural smile that was barely noticeable with her tiny frame sandwiched between Louis and Glen, her tall, pencil-thin husband, who was not an active participant in the conversation. Dressed entirely in tan velour, Glen sat quietly, his face taut, much like his wife's, with purple veins exposed under transparent skin. A wisp of hair was combed over in an attempt to cover a receding hairline that had made it all the way to his crown. Glen's eyes were directed at the window while he sucked his lips in and pushed them back out with no regard as to whether anyone was watching. He sucked in a little too much and released his lips with a pop, flashing a glimpse of toothless red gums that caused my stomach to flop.

Louis caught my expression and tossed me a wink.

"Pay him no mind," said Louis' wife, pulling me into their conversation. "He ate plenty well." She patted his gut again.

"I'm just funnin' ya," said Louis. "But it's true. Meat was scarce back in the day, except the now and then when Pop would bring home a bag of pigeons. He worked at the rail yards not more than a mile from here."

"They sell pigeons at the train station?" I asked, my experience with urban fowl limited to the infrequent washing of my car.

Louis slapped his leg and broadened the smile. "Not the train station, little lady. Pop worked at the rail yards as a machinist. Made new parts to fix old parts that broke."

"And Pop never paid for a bird in his life," said Louis' wife, whom I now knew as Patti Jane, a pleasantly plump woman about my height and the same age as her husband—old. "That man could stretch a dollar clear across this table."

Stretch a dollar? I'd have to search that phrase when they weren't looking.

"*That's* the truth." Louis' eyes connected with Patti Jane's long enough to exchange a visual kiss. My eyes zeroed in on the bushel of hair in the man's ears, thick enough to impede hearing and possibly a contributor to his loud voice.

"He throwed rocks at birds until he had enough for dinner. Cleaning pigeon is the same as chicken, dontcha know. But it's more work for less meat." He leaned back and allowed a deep sigh to take him to a childhood that I couldn't even imagine. "We sure ate a lot of pigeon."

I looked from one person to the next, each of whom had their own stories about what it was like to have nothing, yet none of their stories hinted of want or complaint.

"He may not have had much meat when he was younger, but he's made up for it over the years." She rubbed his gut again.

Louis covered his wife's hand with his own. "I got no complaints."

"You'll like it here at the Legends," said Millie, studying me carefully. "Though I'm not sure how you qualify as a senior."

I provided an obligatory smile and gestured out the window. "I live at the Manor across the parking lot." As the words came out, a chill crawled up my back, reminding me there was no possible way I could make next month's rent. "That's why Grandpa picked this place. Everything is so close. There's even a lake a couple of blocks past the grocery store. You can rent canoes there and everything." An unnecessary point, as nobody at our table, or in the room for that matter, was likely to climb into a canoe. Grandpa was the lone exception.

"Did you hear that, Louis? We can rent canoes at that lake we walked to yesterday."

He adjusted an imaginary hearing aid in his hairy ear. "Did you say canoe? What would we do with one if we rented it?"

"Come now. You used to be pretty good in a canoe."

"I had my fun in a boat." He rubbed a scar above his left eye and chuckled again. "Knocked my head pretty good a few years back. Keeps me from remembering all the other times I banged myself up on the water."

I found it hard to imagine the heavy man in any type of watercraft that had less than twelve decks and a forty-foot buffet. "Did you ever canoe on the Saint Croix? Some friends and I are going up there Saturday."

"Made my way down that river a time or two." He raised an eyebrow. "Seems a little early to be out on the water. Still pretty cool up north, dontcha know."

"I'm not worried about that," I replied, blowing off geriatric advice on boating safety for the second time in as many days. "I've got a good jacket, and we won't be getting wet. Besides, I canoe a lot. I'm not gonna lie; I'm pretty good at it. My friend Andy and I have done the Saint Croix twice and a couple of other rivers too."

"Well you be careful, little lady. Just when you think you know everything about canoeing, that dang boat will reach out of the water and crack you in the head." He pulled his hair back to expose the full length of the ragged scar.

"Be careful up there," said Patti Jane. "Louis knows a lot about the water."

I offered an understanding nod, though the old man would barely fit in the canoes we were renting. No wonder he fell out and hit his head. Probably at the dock, before he ever got to the open water.

* * *

Grandpa put his arm on my shoulder as we walked down the hall. "Thanks for taking Gwen tomorrow."

"I'm off work anyway, so I've got time."

"Again?"

I finished a text to Ramee before answering.

> Taking one of these old people shopping tomorrow. Will be quick.
> Meet you for lunch at 11:30 ☺

"Yes, again. You know how much I like my job at Platform Marketing. I used to work directly with customers laying out marketing strategies and everything, but lately it seems like more companies are closing than expanding. It's not just me, we've lost half our clients in the last two years, so everyone's hours have been cut back. It's starting to hurt, but no worries. I'll get it together."

I typed a list of items for the river trip into my phone while Grandpa mentioned something about getting a second job to fill my spare time. We split at the door, and I headed home to the Manor, checking my bank balance on the way.

Maybe I should have told Grandpa the truth about my finances.

Chapter 7

We Can Use These Next Time

I HAD JUST stuffed the last afghan into Grandpa's spare bedroom closet when Seth Thomas announced the ten o'clock hour and my dreaded appointment with the tiny stranger.

"Come in, dear," came the oddly trusting voice of a woman I'd met only yesterday.

Unsure of the proper protocol, I took a half step inside Gwen's apartment and stood like a mannequin, hands folded at my front. No sign of the woman who had seemed overly excited about a trip to the store.

A loud crack reverberated from the hallway.

"Oh, dear!"

A second smack was followed by another elderly exclamation.

I made my way toward the source of the sound and found Gwen engaged in a futile attempt to muscle her scooter through the bedroom door.

The pale woman looked up with pleading eyes. "I

thought better of it last evening, when I scooted into the room, but I was so tired."

Somehow, she had made it through the doorway and then wedged the scooter in the gap while trying to turn it around. Scuffs on the doorjamb indicated she was familiar with the routine.

"Let me give you a hand."

I grabbed the front end of the three-wheeled conveyance and pulled with all my strength. The heavy unit didn't budge, but a touch to the Forward button shot the scooter into the doorjamb with a *thwack*. After three attempts, I successfully maneuvered a five-point turn and positioned the scooter in the hallway.

"Thank you, dear."

Gwen adjusted her blue floral blouse that was wrinkled just enough to be noticeable, then tugged the elastic waist on white pants that ballooned at the hip.

I rolled my eyes when I noticed the circles of red blush she had applied in a shade slightly brighter than her home hair-color treatment. I was about to go shopping with a life-size Raggedy Ann doll.

I grumbled under my breath. *"Thanks, Grandpa."*

She rolled into the living room where she evidently felt the need to describe each piece of furniture along with its origin. Her son had given her the tufted green couch and matching chair—vintage furniture that paired well with a bulbous television that was as wide and fat as it was tall. A blue-light special, she exclaimed proudly. *Whatever that was.*

In what appeared to be a mechanical sequence, she moved to a large oxygen tank next to the television, refilled the portable unit on her hip, untangled the tubing, touched the dual ports to her tongue to verify oxygen flow, and inserted the nasal cannula into her nose.

I scratched an itch on my nose.

Gwen dragged her purse off the counter, dropped it into the scooter basket, and said, "I'm ready," in a voice much too enthusiastic for a short trip to the grocery store.

My five-foot-six frame, supplemented with lattes and cheese curds, has never been mistaken as athletic, so I found it awkward having to shorten my stride and slow my pace to stay alongside the red scooter, which was clearly stuck in low gear.

The sloth-like speed gave my mind time to wander. What if she has a heart attack? What if she has to go to the bathroom? What if the battery dies? What if *I* have to go to the bathroom? A vision of me desperately needing to pee, pushing a red scooter down the road with an old lady grasping her chest, forced me to cut diagonally across the parking lot to conserve precious battery life.

As we rolled up to the storefront, Gwen's scooter triggered the automatic doors, releasing a blast of chilled air that might have blown the tiny woman into the parking lot had she not been strapped to the seat. I grabbed a shopping cart while she made a surprisingly direct path to produce. One bag of salad, two bananas, and three Honeycrisp apples.

I texted Ramee.

> Will finish shopping early.
> Lunch 11:15 ☺

In the meat department, I found that having a choice complicated things. From the vantage of her scooter, Gwen couldn't see over the freezer bins, the first of which contained pork. She wanted some "*chops.*"

"What size package would you like?"

"Just enough for me, dear."

Not a helpful answer.

"Most of these packs are two or three pounds," I offered suggestively. A size that seemed about right for a single individual.

"Three pounds sounds like a lot of *chops*." She emphasized *chops* as though it were an elderly joke.

Executive decision. "Two pounds."

"Do you think that will be enough?"

*Enough for what? Are you planning a party? Do you
have a dog you forgot to mention on the twenty-minute
walk that I make in five? I have no idea if it's enough.*

"Definitely," I replied in my most convincing voice.

"Okay, dear. I like pork, you know."

I know now.

"My brother raised chickens and hogs on a farm. He
made the best maple sausage."

She licked cracked lips while I made a mental note to
ask Grandpa if everyone from his generation used to own
chickens.

"We gathered eggs every morning, and I cooked breakfast for the two of us. His wife passed when he was quite
young, you know."

I didn't know and didn't really care.

She gazed up at the ceiling, forcing my eyes to follow.
"Acres of corn on that farm. Have you ever eaten corn right
off the stalk?"

No, but I picked a piece straight out of the can once.

"Fresh, without cooking." She licked her lips again.
"Tastes just like candy."

Not any candy I would eat.

Having no desire to learn her family farming history in
the meat department, I led Gwen from the pork bin to the
beef, where her eyes lit up like those of a child.

"I haven't had a good steak in years. Do they have
round steak?"

The grill master in me cringed at the implication that
round steak was *good* steak.

For fifteen minutes, I shuffled plastic-wrapped Styrofoam
packs, all leaking watery red fluid, until we found the

perfect steak; a steak that looked exactly the same as a dozen others we inspected. I had talked her into flank steak as a better cut only because it was on sale. The thought of her choking to death on a tough bite of leathery meat had directed my hands to hide anything labeled "round steak," though by the end of the process, I was reconsidering.

We then selected two whole chickens, each weighing slightly less than three pounds. I've never bought a whole chicken in my life, preferring to let somebody else cut the bloody bird into bits. But Gwen wasn't going to pay an extra fourteen cents a pound for something she had been doing for eighty years—I had no reply. I had to dig to the bottom of the pile to find those special birds. She passed on four others that were exactly three pounds because she couldn't imagine eating three pounds of chicken. I, on the other hand, was able to imagine stuffing the extra few ounces down the woman's throat.

I set the second chicken in the cart and took a step forward. Gwen didn't budge. Her eyes were locked on the display sign listing the price.

"One is probably fine," she said quietly.

I tossed one bird back in the bin, then pulled a hand wipe from the pole-mounted canister. Though Gwen never touched a pack of meat, she too pulled a wipe and in the process ripped a machine-gun fart that would make my friends proud. Any friend who wasn't standing next to her. I, however, was stuck in a rancid olfactory plume while she tugged on a wipe that refused to release, each tug generating a staccato toot. When the thin wipe finally let go, she sat back down as though nothing out of the ordinary had occurred.

Rounding the endcap and heading toward dairy, I began to notice how the weekday-morning crowd differed from the crowd on a typical Saturday afternoon when I shopped. Most of the shoppers were elderly and seemed to be walking at the same speed as us—not fast. More elderly men than elderly women were shopping alone, and one old man in thick cotton jogging pants raced by at twice the age-appropriate speed. Two young mothers with children in tow rounded out the crowd.

The young mothers moved briskly up and down the aisles, grabbing only those items on their lists, clearly on a mission to load up and get out before the child of the day decided to have a breakdown on aisle four. With more time on their hands and no threat of a toddler tantrum, the elderly shoppers had a more leisurely approach, shuffling a few steps from one item to the next and comparing prices on everything. A glancing thought passed through my mind of how my parents might have aged, if only...

An elderly couple in front of us looked to be in their seventies—young compared to Gwen, old compared to the rest of the world. They shuffled from one item to the next, squinting to read the nutritional value, studying the price, then returning the item and repeating the process a few steps down the aisle. I wanted to pass on the left but wasn't certain the scooter's top speed would get us around the inquisitive couple. Thankfully, Gwen stopped at the cheese bin, where I hoped we would fare better than we had in meats because the bins were lower.

No luck. Gwen could see the items, but she couldn't make out names, weights, or prices.

Together, we peered at yellow blocks, white circles, and red rings beneath a sign emblazoned with the word "cheese."

"We have cheddar, Swiss, Muenster, and any other type you like. Do you have a preference?"

"May I see the yellow one, please?"

I passed the cheddar. "They have slices, or you can get a block of this."

"May I see the white one?"

I handed her the Swiss and Muenster. With one cheese in each hand and one on her lap, she either studied the labels intently or took a quick nap.

When her mind returned to the store, she said, "I like the yellow. This white one has holes in it."

"That's just the way they make Swiss," I replied matter-of-factly.

"They're the same size, but this one has holes in it," she repeated. "I don't want to buy something with holes."

"You pay by the pound, so you're not really paying for the holes."

"But I can't eat a pound." Her face slumped with exhaustion at the thought. "Can you find one of these that doesn't have the holes?"

While I contemplated a reply, she said, "Is this cheese, dear? I don't eat cheese. It binds me."

I should have snuck some into her snack before the wet-wipe incident. My fingers relayed our status to Ramee.

> Bogged down in Brie.
> Lunch 11:45 ☹

Though frustrated over having to delay lunch, I was fascinated with the way Gwen rationalized every decision and a little concerned over how frequently she mentioned that a particular purchase could wait until after the first of the month.

It took twenty minutes to cover the next three aisles, where we added pasta, rice, soup, and canned vegetables to the haul. Vegetables were the easiest because she only wanted the Jolly Green Giant brand. With each can I placed in the basket, she uttered a catchy, "*Ho, ho, ho, Green Giant.*" Everything else was a comparison of ounces, prices, and size of the box. The ounces didn't matter if the box looked too big, and more often than not, the color of the package was the deciding factor. Finding the right toothpaste proved challenging because her home store had evidently never delivered the same toothpaste twice, so she didn't know what brand or color she preferred.

"I like the red box," said Gwen. "And the green box with sparkles is pretty."

I handed her both colors.

She squinted to read the text. "Does this say 'baking soda,' dear? We brushed with baking soda when I was little, and every year I got a new toothbrush for Christmas."

My mouth fell open. I would be *pissed* if anyone gave me a toothbrush for Christmas.

"So...do you want the one with baking soda?" *It's just toothpaste—pick one already!*

"Never liked the taste, dear," she replied flatly.

After listening to the history of baking soda to clean teeth, why the tube with three colors tasted funny, and how cinnamon burned her mouth, we settled on the red box without cinnamon—the first box I had picked up when we entered the aisle.

Another text.

> Tangled in toothpaste.
> Lunch 12:00 ☹ ☹

The next aisle dedicated 90 percent of its shelf space to babies. I started to pass, but Gwen turned the scooter. She stopped at the adult diapers and pointed a crooked finger mostly upward.

"The green ones, please."

"I'm not sure, Gwen. These say extra-large."

"That's good, right?"

I hoped she wasn't thinking in terms of loading them up.

"The pack says, 'one hundred and seventy-five pounds.'" I smiled down at the tiny woman. "You're a little less than that."

She returned the smile as though we had started a new game. "That would be two of me. But I always get the green one."

I grabbed the smallest size available. Anything smaller would have put us in the section with bottles and pacifiers.

Satisfied with the selection and evidently finished shopping, Gwen beelined to the nearest checker. *Finally! A light at the end of the long shopping tunnel.*

I unloaded while Gwen scooted in front to pay. When the checker scanned the last item, Gwen reached for the hobo purse in the scooter basket. The soft leather collapsed just out of reach with each sloth-like, bony-fingered attempt to hook the strap. With no room to squeeze by and help, I was forced to watch the slow-motion effort until she eventually looped the strap and pulled the purse to her lap. Bag in hand, she fumbled with the zipper.

That she might need help with such a routine activity had never crossed my mind. I mean, how long could this really take?

As I was about to find out, it can take way too long.

Gwen was in her own little world, oblivious to the frustrated line of shoppers behind us while her arthritic fingers tried and failed to grab the zipper. She eventually pinched the tab and pulled three times, opening the purse a third of the way with each tug.

Success! Let's pay and get out of here.

Her hand disappeared inside the bag, reappearing with an overstuffed envelope of coupons for every product imaginable, except those in our cart.

The fed-up checker gave me a disgruntled *"what am I supposed to do with these?"* look.

Three coupons cleared, saving a whopping ninety cents.

"We can use these next time," I growled through gritted teeth as the checker totaled forty-seven dollars and change.

Again her hand disappeared, this time reappearing

with a checkbook. My checkbook was covered in dust on the dresser. Everyone was paying online now with a debit or credit card, or just tapping their phones to the card machine. Some people even used cash. The only people who still wrote checks were those in front of me when I was in a hurry, like now, with Gwen asking for a pen.

A final text.

Exhausted. Some other time? ☹

Back in Gwen's apartment, I put away the dry goods while she placed perishables in the refrigerator and casually set the flank steak in a drawer with the dish towels, as though she always kept her steak and towels together. I moved it to the freezer, then checked my phone. Twelve-thirty.

"I'd be happy to go with you anytime," I said on the way out, though I wasn't entirely sure I meant it.

I had missed lunch because it had taken two and a half hours to walk down the street, buy five bags of groceries, and endure the most painful shopping spree I'd ever experienced. If this was any indication of life at the Legends, Grandpa would never survive.

Chapter 8

First Impressions

THE FIRST TIME I cooked on the glistening gas grill at the Legends, Grandpa and I had the outdoor area virtually to ourselves, partly because it was still a little cool outside and partly because Grandpa had yet to befriend every single resident in the complex. When I fired up the grill a couple of weeks later, half the residents who were sitting in the great room migrated outside, possibly drawn by the mouthwatering aroma wafting through the courtyard but more likely because I provided the only entertainment for the evening.

With Grandpa supplying the groceries, I was able to attempt a new recipe. Mouths watered when I removed the appetizers from the grill and loaded the *kofta* kebabs onto the glowing surface followed by the eggplant a few minutes later. After giving the eggplant four minutes on each side, precisely the time specified in the five-star recipe video on my phone, I moved the perfectly grill-marked slices to the top rack to keep them warm while Grandpa went upstairs for the chilled basmati rice side dish I had made earlier. As soon as he returned, I prepared our plates, then cut the remaining eggplant and kebabs into bite-size pieces and set that plate in the center of the table for everyone to sample. One kebab still needed a few minutes, so I moved it to the middle of the bottom rack.

"George used to do all of the cooking," said Thelma, perched on the same bench where I had seen her a couple of times. "He was an excellent cook, but I don't remember eggplant on the barbecue."

"Would you like a plate?"

"Heavens no," she replied. Smoke dribbled out of her mouth as a cigarette bounced with each word. "I grabbed a sandwich at the Shamrock when I filled up with gas."

Eww.

She exhaled a thick plume. "Well, maybe just a taste."

Yellow-stained fingertips reached in for a piece of eggplant.

"You're down the hall from my grandpa, right?" I asked.

"Next door, actually."

"I don't see you—I mean, we don't see you very often."

"My hours are a little different than yours. Thank you for the taste." She snuffed out her cigarette, slipped the unused half into the pack, and went inside, holding the door for Gwen, who scooted to a seat next to Millie and immediately began talking about homegrown food from her brother's farm.

I snapped a few food photos and texted Ramee a set of emojis that provided an animated illustration of the sizzle, grill marks, and aroma.

With my photo documentation complete, I sat next to Grandpa at the table, with Gwen and Millie on the opposite side. Moose lay quietly to my left.

A moment later, Grandpa's face tensed. His eyes shot from left to right. I glanced at the food for an errant dog hair before realizing the problem was elsewhere. The *tsit...*

tsit that had accompanied Millie outside had turned into a constant hiss.

"*Moose, no!*" Too late. My furry little angel that everyone cooed over had chewed through Millie's oxygen hose.

"Think we got ourselves a leak," said Glen, picking up two ends of the clear tubing. "Let's get you upstairs and take care of this, dear."

"Will she be okay?" I asked.

"Oh, this is nothing to worry about. We have a repair kit with all kinds of neat stuff. Won't be the first time I fixed a hose."

Grandpa held the door and followed Glen and Millie inside to help.

Glen's assurance did little to ease my tension. The last thing I needed was for someone to complain about Moose and get our visitation rights revoked.

I bent over to better secure the leash just as a roar of flames engulfed the lone kebab remaining on the bottom grill.

"*Shoot!*" Not my first word choice. I had planned to pull it off sooner, but the hissing hose had distracted me.

Angie and Gladys, who had been sitting on the far bench, joined us and sampled the eggplant morsels.

"Your dinner looks wonderful," said Angie. "Almost as good as my daughter makes."

She had obviously missed the flame-up. "Thanks, Angie. I don't get many opportunities to grill at the Manor. Three of the grills over there don't work, and the other one is usually dirty."

"I never used an outdoor cooktop," she replied. "My late husband did all the outdoor cooking, but he wasn't very good at it. He would burn everything." Her giggle sounded more like a sarcastic snicker.

Gladys mimicked the sound.

I had tried not to allow my first impression of Angie to bother me, but in the last few days, she had cornered me in the hall to babble about her daughter, complain about dogs, and talk about her late husband, who evidently bickered about everything.

Where on earth would he have learned to bicker?

"That man was always underfoot in the kitchen. What business did he have at the stove?" Another half laugh. Another mimic by Gladys.

Maybe her generation did things a little differently in the kitchen, but I didn't need or want an explanation. "I better get this food up to Grandpa before he comes looking for me."

"You tell Jimmy I expect to sit with him on movie night."

"I'll tell him," I said with a smile as fake as her giggle. *Like that was going to happen.*

Chapter 9

If It's Free, I Can't Afford It

FOUR LARGE TURKEYS strutted across the road, forcing me to slam on the brakes. A blast of the horn only made them march slower, their glaring eyes warning me to turn back. This particular bunch was a nuisance, especially the ringleader of the flock, who often pranced out into the road when I least expected it—or when I wasn't quite paying the necessary attention to my driving. I set my phone in the console and swung into the coffee shop drive-through to pick up four coffees and an equal number of muffins. A quick stop for gas, and Moose and I were at Stephanie's, who sensed something was wrong when I stepped from the vehicle.

"Problem?" she asked.

"I just maxed out my credit card again. I'll tell you, Steph, this free canoe trip is costing a lot more than I thought it would."

She hip-checked me. "That's what happens when you live life on the edge...of a credit card."

"You don't understand. This is the worst it's ever been, and I hate to ask Grandpa for money again, because he just covered the vet."

She tossed me a curious look, having been with me multiple times when our first stop was at Grandpa's house to pick up forty bucks for a Friday night.

"Okay. Maybe I don't hate it, but I don't like it."

"He's got your back. That's a good thing."

"But do you think I'm taking advantage?"

Another head tilt suggested the question required no reply.

"Well, I've got thirty days until my lease is up. I can't commit to this apartment for another year unless I get back to full-time work." Something I probably should have mentioned to Grandpa *before* he moved in across the parking lot.

Andy and Rob Orendarfer stepped up behind Stephanie. "Don't worry about that stuff today," said Rob, Steph's longtime boyfriend. "We've got a river to run." He waved the gift certificate he had won in a raffle.

An hour later, the four of us were at the boat rental shop on the Saint Croix. Rob handed the gift certificate to the old man behind the counter, signed us in, and provided a contact number. Though we considered ourselves experienced on the water, the old man still felt the need to give his obligatory boring safety speech, which emphasized the importance of wearing life jackets and not losing his paddles.

I was only half listening to the gravelly voice while I fought to connect a stiff clip on my life jacket.

The old man pointed to a map under the glass-covered countertop and continued his routine talk. "The entire route is smooth water…"

I pinched my finger in the clip and turned around to mouth a few choice words. My back was to the old man when he said something about staying along the bank and we would be fine. I didn't catch which side of the bank or where exactly we would encounter that part of the trip, but

I'd heard it all before. When I turned back around, my eyes zeroed in on a prize wheel tucked back on the counter.

"What's this?" I moved to the three-foot-diameter colorful wheel near the wall.

"Sumpin' new we're trying," replied the old man. "Get a free spin with any boat rental. Paddle lands on a winner, you get a prize."

He spun the wheel to demonstrate.

I studied the eight possibilities. Three slots were labeled "maybe next time." Two offered a "free pop." Two offered a "free snack." One slot was surrounded by gold stars and labeled "free rental."

"Give it a spin," said Rob.

The flapper sang like a playing card in bicycle spokes until it slowed to a *click, click, click.* It looked like it was headed toward a "maybe next time" but stopped abruptly on "free rental."

"*I won!*"

Stephanie jumped almost as high as I did.

"Does this work for today?" asked Rob. "I could save my gift certificate for some other time."

"Only good on the next visit," replied the old man.

We bagged our stuff, and the old man handed me the coupon. "Has to be used in the next three weeks."

I passed the coupon to Rob, who glanced at Stephanie.

"Don't look at me. I'm not coming back. I told you, one trip on the water. Keep it, Nat."

The old man led us out the back door to the riverbank, where his boots sank in the mud as he stood with hands on his hips at the launch site. "Two canoes, four people, four paddles, four life jackets, and one dog." He pushed each canoe away from the muddy bank.

With a river as smooth as glass and barely a breeze in the air, the only sound was water lapping gently against the side of the canoe and the occasional fish breaching the surface to snag an insect. Up ahead, Rob commanded his canoe with authority. From the rear seat, his strong arms pulled the paddle gracefully through the water, angling the paddle left or right as needed to keep the canoe centered in the middle of the river. Stephanie sat in the front pointing to various birds in the tall grass, squirrels in the trees, and the occasional frog that jumped from the bank into the river.

Andy and I had a slightly less efficient approach to canoeing. He sat in the back and slapped the paddle at the water, steering us in more of a serpentine movement than a straight line. His less than fluid strokes required changing the paddle from one side of the canoe to the other in an attempt to keep the zigzagging to a minimum. Adding to our less than leisurely float was his propensity to hit the side of the boat with every third stroke, which rattled my nerves and evidently attracted black flies.

After forty chilled-to-the-bone minutes of swatting flies, Andy splashing water on my back, and Moose drinking from the bottom of the canoe, I was ready for our Saturday fun to end when a small, tree-lined island came into view. Rob yelled at us just before his canoe disappeared on the left side of the islet. Andy tried to follow but wound up steering erratically to the right side of the grassy islet—directly into rapids that were moving much faster than either of us had ever encountered.

Turbulent whitecaps pushed and pulled us into peaks and pools. When we exited a large pool, the bow rose so high that it blocked my view. A nauseating scrape of the hull against a boulder stopped us with a jolt and tossed Moose and I over the side.

As I hurtled headfirst into the water, important details I had skipped in preparing for the trip flashed through my mind in a whitecapped blur. In anticipation of a routine float down the river, the only dry clothes I had were those I was wearing; the emergency kit with bandages and matches lay safely under the seat in the car; and the old man's instructions to stay on the left side of the island resonated clearly. A final insult brought forth by the icy dunk was a reminder that I might have exaggerated my canoeing experience when I was talking to Louis.

I held tight to Moose's collar and we swam to the shore of the island where I helped him up through the high grass along the bank. Andy yelled something about getting help and continued downriver, not that he had any choice; turning around in the rapids was well beyond his ability.

Moose and I shook ourselves off and walked along the water's edge for a couple of hundred feet until we met up with Rob and Andy who had anchored their canoes at the end of the small island to wait for us.

*   *   *

Sunday morning my wet footprints were still visible on the lobby carpet at the Manor. To avoid any confrontation with Ms. Ass that would surely result in a fine for some obscure contractual clause about not removing wet shoes, I made a quick exit to the Legends.

Grandpa had given me a set of keys to his apartment, so I had been coming and going frequently and was fairly comfortable among the seniors, many of whom had already started treating me like a regular, with frequent "hellos" and "good afternoons," typically followed by a geriatric "dear."

Though they were old and slow, I found the elder crowd to be more engaging than my age group at the Manor, who were wrapped up in their phones and video games. It was oddly refreshing to use my voice to speak rather than my thumbs and my ears to listen rather than my eyes. I did, however, frequently imagine colorful animated emojis hovering above gray-tufted heads. Thelma's character was an intellectual cigarette smoker; Louis' character had a round, jolly face; and Angie's character had suspicious eyes under a poop hat because she had been getting much too cozy with Grandpa.

Grandpa had already poured me a cup and was sitting with Patti Jane and Louis when I arrived. Fortunately, Louis was in the middle of another boisterous story, which I hoped would keep him from asking about my river outing.

"Patti Jane answered the phone," said Louis while I shook water from my ear as discreetly as possible. "Someone on the other end was explaining that we won a free trip to Las Vegas. That was before everyone knew those calls aren't all they appear, dontcha know."

"Used to be you could trust people," said Patti Jane.

"She was holding the phone out so I could hear the conversation." He mimicked a phone being held a few inches away from his bushy ear while the shar-pei wrinkles on his round face bounced in sync with another chuckle. "I looked at PJ and shrugged, like, *why not?* Couple days later, we had a coupon in the mail for three free nights at a hotel in Las Vegas. It was real. You betcha," said the native Minnesotan, who had a strong command of the vernacular. "PJ was excited 'cause we never been to Las Vegas. I'm looking at the coupon, and I see that we got to get ourselves to Nevada. Can't hardly drive there for a weekend. So we bought ourselves some plane tickets, which weren't cheap, dontcha know, and we flew down for the trip."

PJ slid her hand over Louis' forearm. "Used that travel bag I got with my green stamps."

Green stamps? I thought stamps had the American flag on them.

"We had a wonderful time," continued Louis. "The hotel was free, sure enough, but I spent our savings on those tickets, so we had to be real careful with our other expenses. Went to some place where they gave free hot dogs

to people sitting at them slot machines. We plopped ourselves down at a nickel machine and had our dinner right
there."

He rubbed his belly and I scrunched my face, each of us
thinking about processed meat in a tube.

"We made do. Point is, be careful with those free trips,
Natalie. They're not really free."

"*If it's free, I can't afford it*," I said, quoting Grandpa's
oft-employed phrase. He's tried to explain that cost is not
always money, but as an economically challenged twenty-
four-year-old, I lose interest in that part of the conversation.

Louis bellowed extra loud and slapped his thigh. "You
betcha! How'd you come up with that?"

"Not me. That's something Grandpa says."

"It's been some time now," said Grandpa. "But way
back when, I just started noticing that every time something
was free, it cost me something that I didn't have. Might cost
time or stress or something else, but usually it cost money."

"If it's free, I can't afford it," repeated Louis who looked
back to me. "I got my own saying about boats—any trip
you don't drown is a good trip."

I pictured the old man sitting in a flat-bottomed boat
four feet from the shore, hugging a life jacket.

"Are you gonna tell us about your river adventure?"
he asked.

Grandpa had already provided me an earful of constructive ridicule about the outing, so I kept my reply brief.
"It was okay. I got to explore an island in the river."

Patti Jane's eyes lit up. "What a good idea. Did you
pack a picnic lunch?" She turned to Louis. "Remember
when we used to picnic along the riverbank?"

The truth was out. The closest Louis had ever gotten to
the water was sitting on a red-and-white checkered blanket
near the shore. It was pretty clear the jolly man had par-
taken in many of those lunches.

"Um, we didn't picnic."

Louis gestured to the back of my wrist. "See you got a little scratch there."

Before he could say "I told you to wait until the weather was better," a tube of cream magically appeared in Patti Jane's hands.

"Looks like impetigo."

"It's not *impetigo*, PJ. Every time you see a red spot, it's impetigo." He glanced at Grandpa. "I think she's got stock in that cream."

PJ leaned into my ear and whispered, "Don't listen to them. It's impetigo. Here, rub this on your hand."

I was ready to rub cream on anything if it would stop the onslaught of questions about my trip.

Chapter 10

Senior Drug Trade

THE FOLLOWING FRIDAY, without any prompting from Grandpa, I took Gwen to the grocery store again. A little smarter this trip, I avoided cheese, remembered the preferred colors of most items, and sorted coupons before we entered the checkout line. Forty minutes later, when we were unloading the groceries, Gwen placed the milk on the pantry floor. I moved it to the refrigerator while she microwaved a snack made with the apples we had picked up at the store the previous week.

While Gwen prepared the dish, she talked about her life up north. "Every summer my Robert picked apples from our tree." Her voice was distant, as though she were watching her husband pull each apple from the branch. "We planted that tree the summer we moved into our house. Every day, I would sit on the porch and watch it grow. When Robert came home from work, he would sit with me." She closed her eyes and repeated in a whisper, "Every day."

She removed the ceramic dish from the microwave, then searched for a serving spoon.

"You should see it now, Natalie. Our tree is as big as

the house, and so many apples. We would sit on the back porch when the blossoms were in bloom and smell the sweet scent of spring. He built that porch by himself, you know, and he screened it in to keep the mosquitoes away. A soft breeze and the scent of apple blossoms was all I needed. I can't wait to smell those blossoms again." Her eyes drifted back to the porch, and she released a sigh that sounded as though it had been building since her husband died. "It's hard sometimes when you miss someone so much."

The story about her husband, a tree, and a porch, was touching, but I was focused more on whatever had released the buttery cinnamon aroma that was quickly filling the kitchen. When she finally placed a bowl in front of me, I slid an oversized heap into my mouth, chomped once, and stopped. She hadn't mentioned any crunchy ingredients. Apples, sugar, butter, and cinnamon. Evidently, Gwen had forgotten to remove the core and seeds, which were not going down without a fight. She had put so much effort into the dish and was so excited to share it with me that I couldn't very well dribble the contents back into the bowl with her watching, so I moved to the stove to put on a pot of tea, discarding my bulging napkin in the process.

Filling the teakettle was easy enough, but moving her crusty cast iron skillet out of the way was real work. "Do you want me to put this into the dishwasher?"

"Heavens no, dear, skillets aren't to be washed. Just wipe it clean. That keeps the pan seasoned, you know."

It's also a great reason never to lift the thing.

Gwen turned around with a pack of thinly sliced ham in one hand and a jar of mustard in the other.

"Does this smell good to you?"

I studied the options. "The mustard or the meat?"

"The meat, dear. You should always smell your meat."

Smell my meat? The thought alone turned my stomach. Thankfully, the kettle whistled.

"Where do you keep your tea bags?"

Gwen handed me a saucer that held three damp tea bags. My thirst quickly diminished.

"I still have the full set of these saucers," she said proudly. "They were a gift from the gas station."

The only gift I ever received from the gas station was when they lowered the price—a rare gift, indeed.

We sat at the window with our tea and snacked on finger sandwiches while Gwen continued talking about her home as though she would be visiting soon.

*   *   *

I left Gwen upstairs and cut through the great room to grab a cup of coffee before returning to the Manor. While I stirred in two sugars, Orval smacked his walker into the door, prompting me to open it for him.

Most of the less ambulatory residents used scooters at the Legends, but Orval relied on his trusty aluminum-frame walker, complete with faded yellow tennis balls on the front legs. With his pants pulled up to his chest, he inchwormed his way to a window table, pushing the walker forward, taking a step to catch up, and pushing the walker forward again—an action that created a sound much like zombies pursuing their victims in one of DeAndre's video games.

I found myself mesmerized by the methodical movement as he maneuvered the walker in a six-point turn, plopped into the chair, and poured the contents of his tote bag onto the table. His wallet tumbled out first, followed by a wad of used tissue, multiple tubes of cream, a square pillbox, and a bottle of water that immediately rolled to the floor. He organized the items in a deliberate but not obvious pattern, then turned his head to the window, gazed a thousand miles into the distance, and began talking to his reflection—or the glass, I wasn't sure which.

I picked up the bottle of water and set it next to his

pillbox. Only then did I notice that colorful plastic pill-boxes decorated most tables in the room. Residents, with extreme care and trembling fingers, were removing pills from amber plastic bottles and placing them into tiny pill-box compartments.

I joined Patti Jane and Louis, both of whom were filling their own plastic boxes. "What's with all the pills?" I asked PJ, whose pink strip of cubes had letters for each day of the week.

"Prescriptions are refilled on the first of the month, dear. Louis made the pharmacy run this morning and picked up everyone's medication. Blood pressure, cholesterol, heart, and anything else you can imagine. At our age, we're all on one pill or another, you know."

Actually, I didn't know. Grandpa had never mentioned any regular medication.

"The doc adds another pill every time I visit," said Louis as he loaded pills into a colorful container that resembled a small board game.

"Maybe you shouldn't schedule so many appointments."

"Now there's an idea." He chuckled and pinched a purple pill that shot across the table to me. "You won't like that one, but I got a green one here that'll clean your pipes."

"Oh, stop that, Louis," said Patti Jane.

I rolled the pill back to him.

"Come on, PJ. They always give me extras, dontcha know. I got something here for everything."

"Everything but pain," said PJ sternly. "That's the one he needs the most."

"She could be right, but the day something ain't hurting, I'll think I'm dead."

He chuckled again, but Patti Jane didn't enjoy the joke.

"Hey, PJ, I'll trade you two of my yellows for one of them red ones you got there."

His wife smiled politely at what was obviously a monthly joke.

Having learned more about the senior drug trade than I ever wanted to know, I moved on to Grandpa and Mrs. Barrington.

Mrs. Barrington lived in the top-floor corner unit and had her own rooftop garden. I had come to know her as a proper woman who employed a British etiquette not often observed in the Midwest. "It takes a lot to get into that unit," Grandpa had told me. "And it takes someone special to do it right."

I rested my hand on Grandpa's shoulder as I sat down. "Good morning, Mrs. Barrington. You look nice."

"Thank you," she replied with a hint of a nod. "How is our friend Gwen coming along today?"

"It's hard to tell. We did great at the store, but she slowed down when we got back to her apartment. She's knitting a scarf, and it sounded like there was some rush to get it done, and she was talking a lot about her husband again. But this time she was saying weird things like she'd be meeting him somewhere."

Mrs. Barrington donned a grandmotherly look of all-encompassing knowledge. "She's having a difficult time. For the last seventy years, Gwen lived in the same house up north. Most of that time was spent with her husband. Her son thought it would be better if she were closer to him, but that required moving her away from the only life she knew. I worry about her too." She smiled and asked, "Did you enjoy the baked apples?"

I carefully considered my reply because the apples were tasty, but the crunch was not good. "They were... mouthwatering."

"Now there's a proper description."

"You ate them too?"

"I pop in on Gwen now and then to see if she needs

anything, and I'm grateful you have been doing the same. She enjoys your visits."

"She kind of grows on you." I glanced back at the pill festival. "Do you guys play the pillbox game? I don't think I've ever seen you take medicine, Grandpa, even when you're sick."

"I sort mine out on the kitchen counter," said Mrs. Barrington. "Occasionally a tablet tries to make a run for it. If one jumps to my floor, I don't mind picking the little rascal up and putting him in his rightful place. If I were to drop one on this floor, it would surely be a lost cause."

"I'm getting close," said Grandpa. "The doctor suggested a cholesterol pill at my last visit, but I promised to exercise more and improve my diet."

That explained the tofu in his refrigerator and his desire to go kayaking.

"And my blood pressure has been bouncing a bit. If I can't get regular in that department, he's going to put me on something." He looked at the table next to us, then tossed a reassuring smile. "But I shouldn't need a container anytime soon."

The conversation turned to small talk, mostly about how quickly the weather had changed from piles of snow blocking our cars to rivers of melt to the sunny spring that was quickly turning into a pleasant summer. I glanced at Orval on the way out; his eyes were still focused on something in the distance.

Chapter 11

My Robert

AFTERNOON VISITS WITH Gwen had become routine, with her sharing stories of a Norman Rockwell childhood and me soaking in every word. She had grown up on a small block where neighbors knew one another and kids played in the street until dark. A gas lamppost in her front yard served as hide-and-seek home base for the entire street. A street Gwen seldom left, because an internal voice constantly told her that the world was too big.

She met Robert at a job her mother had insisted she take to force her out of the house and off the block. An old-school, tough-love approach to a problem that nobody understood.

Robert, who was two years older, and Gwen were pin-setters at the local bowling alley. They worked behind the lanes, where dim light and isolation from other employees made the job tolerable for her reclusive nature. After each bowling ball crashed through the pins, she in one lane and Robert in the adjacent lane picked out the fallen pins and straightened those still standing. It was love at first sight.

"I was his girl," she said with a timeless gleam in her

eye. "That's how he introduced me, and I cherished those words every time he said them. Always praying it would not be the last time."

They were inseparable until Robert was drafted into service and sent to Korea. Gwen's father had died in World War II, and the fear of losing Robert and being alone again was more than she could handle. An eating disorder ensued, something not recognized as a medical condition at the time. She also developed what sounded like severe anxiety. A combination of cold climate, lack of nutrition, and never leaving the house opened the door to a variety of illnesses.

"He sent me a letter every week, but I worried until the day he returned." Another sigh of contentment, as though she were in the moment.

"I was in pretty rough shape by the time he came home. He was so handsome in his uniform, and I was less than a shadow, certain he would want one of the pretty girls. But my Robert came straight to me and gave me the biggest, warmest hug. We were married a month later, and life was just the way I had dreamed."

I had gathered from various conversations that Robert was a hard worker who arrived home to find dinner on the table at five o'clock every day, typical of midcentury Midwestern American families. They raised one child and retired in the house they had shared for decades.

"After he retired, we would have our morning coffee together on the porch. The newspaper was never between us. Do you know what I mean, dear? Today when you see couples having coffee, they're always reading something."

I silenced my phone.

"Robert and I would read each other's eyes while we listened to birds in the backyard and looked out at our tree." She released a long exhale and then said matter-of-factly, "Until the cancer took him."

My eyes welled at the unexpected turn in the story.

"One day he came home from the doctor. Cancer. You couldn't tell at first, because nothing slowed my Robert down." A tear pooled in her eye. "But I noticed he was finishing all the little jobs around the house. He organized our insurance and bank files because he knew I would need to start doing those things on my own." The tempo of her voice slowed. "During his last six months, I had help from a home nurse, and our friends would come by now and then, but it was hard."

I wanted to tell her that she didn't need to share so much, but my throat was too choked up to get the words out.

"I would roll his chair out to the porch, and we would look at our tree. He had spent his life being my rock, and when he needed me, God gave me the strength to be there for him. I took him to his appointments and stayed with him in the hospital."

With tears in my eyes, I listened to the last days of a lifelong romance.

"But the hardest thing..."

The hardest thing? Everything she had just said was the hardest thing.

"The hardest thing," she repeated, "was watching him die and not being able to do anything to help. My Robert never complained. He never mentioned the pain, but I could see it in his eyes. He passed on our sixty-fifth anniversary. That man held on long enough to share our special day with me one more time. Our anniversary was my favorite day of the year, and for that reason alone, it was his favorite day too. He'd dedicated his life to taking care of a feeble old woman when he could have done anything."

"It sounds like he did exactly what he wanted to do," I said quietly, eliciting a soft smile.

"I kept his ashes in a wooden box for a long time because I couldn't think of a place special enough for him. Then it came to me."

I know this. "You buried him under the apple tree."

Another soft smile.

"That's so perfect."

"I've never told a soul. Our son never asked, and I don't like to bother him with such things. He's so busy all the time."

Gwen closed her eyes and muttered faintly, as though she had forgotten I was in the room. "Soon, Robert. Soon."

Her story forced me to think about how Grandpa must have felt when Grandma died. How I felt when my parents...

A tear rolled down my cheek as my mind carried me back two years. Had it only been two years? It seemed like a lifetime since Mom and Dad had been packing for a working vacation in Brazil, a trip sponsored by one of Dad's clients.

Two weeks before their trip, they attended my college graduation. While they were in town, they set me up at the Manor and took me shopping for clothes to replace my college wardrobe with "attire befitting a young professional," as Mom had put it. Their visit was unusually pleasant because I had just graduated, so there was no nagging about grades or homework. I had introduced Andy to them as my boyfriend, and though he was a little uncomfortable playing the part, he cleaned up nicely, which satisfied Mom, and he had a job, which satisfied Dad. They only stayed a few days because Dad had to prepare for the South American business trip.

Dad traveled so much that I never kept track of his departures or arrivals, but Mom was so apprehensive about flying on a small plane that she called me daily to share her concerns, including the night before they left. The following morning, Grandpa informed me the plane had disappeared. An investigation revealed the plane had been on course when it vanished. There were no storms in the area and no trace of wreckage. Everyone involved said it would be impossible to find the small aircraft in the vast rain forest. What little search was conducted ended quickly.

It took days for me to realize they were probably dead and a few months to accept it, during which time Grandpa moved from Texas to the house across town to be near his only granddaughter, but not too close. The whole process was oddly surreal, and it wasn't lost on me that the trip had been free.

Chapter 12

Fun to Try

"GRANDPA, THERE'S SOMETHING I need to talk to you about," I said after I received the smallest paycheck of my career. "They cut my hours at work a couple of months ago, and they'll be cutting some more starting next week. It's getting hard to make my rent payment."

"I see."

As usual, he allowed the word to linger.

"We'll get by. Are you looking for that second job we talked about?"

We never talked about a second job. *He* had not-so-subtly lectured me about responsibility and how it was up to me to work enough hours to pay my bills—a conversation that included references to his working multiple jobs when he was younger in order to save for the unexpected.

"Um. I haven't found anything."

I hadn't actually looked, though I had mentioned to a few friends that I was interested in a change. None of them had called back with any prospects. "I think it would be better if I just quit and got a new job."

"Quit?"

Ugh. Here comes the lecture.

"May want to hold off on that until you line something else up."

That was less admonishment than I expected. "Well, I made rent this month, but next month will be impossible. The thing is, my lease is ending, and the rent will be going up a hundred and fifty bucks, plus they're adding a hundred-dollar-a-month pet fee. I don't know how they get away with that."

He gave me one of his looks that are hard to interpret. "I recall you being in favor of higher wages."

"Of course I'm for higher wages, but not if the price of everything is going to go up."

"I see."

Ugh. I wished I did. "The thing is, I can't afford to live at the Manor, and you can't keep paying my rent."

"You like the area, don't you?"

"It's great. The problem is the cost not the apartment."

I braced myself for another *I-told-you-so* lecture about money management.

"Well, you're right. I can't afford to pay your rent every month, and signing a new lease is risky when you don't know your job situation. I have an idea, though. I've got two bedrooms. Why not move in with me until you get another job? Then you can get an apartment closer to wherever the new job is."

"That would be great, but I'm not quite sixty, and there is Moose to consider. The Legends doesn't allow dogs." Not to mention that this was clearly an attempt to punish me for not getting that elusive second job.

He spread one of his sly grins, which made me think this wasn't entirely a punishment. "It's pretty obvious that you haven't been working. My Legends contract allows Moose to visit, and you're both over so often that the residents are comfortable seeing you around the place. If we're careful, it could take a few months before anyone figures out you're living at the Legends and not just visiting. That should be enough time for you to get through your employment slump." He chuckled. "And wouldn't it be fun to try? If we get caught, we'll deal with it."

The thought of free rent, free utilities, and a loaded refrigerator was definitely appealing, but memories of being admonished for leaving dirty dishes in the sink and laundry on the floor, along with his unhealthy obsession for the bed to be made *every* day, haunted the back of my mind. Living with him would be difficult under the best of conditions and being surrounded by old people would make things even harder. But one thing made the offer appealing—the lack of *any* other option.

We discussed logistics and timing for my move and agreed I should give my notice at the Manor. I would start looking for a new job rather than a second job, and since I would have no rent to pay, there would be no immediate pressure on finding that job.

* * *

By the time I got home, Moose was more than ready to go outside.

"Sorry I'm late, but look what I have for you." He pulled the plush stuffed dog from my fingers and shook it rapidly.

"Let's go, boy."

With the new stuffed toy in his mouth, I unleashed Moose just outside the back door where he trotted a few feet, dropped the toy, and did what we had come out to do.

While I bagged, he nosed around a shrub and rustled a rabbit out of hiding.

"Sit, boy. Sit," I begged in my calmest, firmest voice as I reached out to clasp his collar with the leash. An inch from success, he pounced into the shrub. The rabbit shot out the other side and ran directly toward the train tracks with Moose hot on his heels.

Where's Mr. Lethargic today?

I yelled my four often futile "S" commands: "*Stop! Sit! Stay! Shit!*" Commands he ignored anytime a live animal was in the vicinity. "*Come back here!*"

I hurdled the bush in pursuit, but much like my high school phys-ed days, I didn't quite clear the obstacle and found myself tumbling down the incline. From my prone position, I recited a thankful prayer for residents who picked up after their pets.

As usual, Moose came to a stop at the edge of the tall grass near the train tracks after he lost sight of the hurried hare.

My anger vaporized when he returned with a smile that said, "*Did you see me, Mom? I almost caught him.*"

"It's a good thing you have me to feed you twice a day."

We continued on to Yang's with a fresh twenty-dollar bill courtesy of Grandpa. The owner, Wi Yang, whom I'd come to know well, and I chatted about our recent escapades while Moose, securely leashed to an outside table leg, lapped at a bowl of water. On the way back to the Manor, I couldn't seem to shake a chill that I must have picked up from tumbling in the damp grass.

"Hope I'm not coming down with something, boy, or you'll have one grumpy mama hanging out at the house."

Grandpa was waiting at my door when we rounded the corner in the hallway.

Chapter 13

You Have Your Mother's Eyes

"LET'S GO INSIDE, Natalie. I have some bad news." His voice trembled in a tone that I'd only heard once before. I steeled myself for the worst. "There's no easy way to say this. Mrs. Barrington just told me that Gwen passed away." He wrapped his arms around me. "I'm sorry. I know you were close to her."

"What happened?" I asked, so choked up I could barely get the words out.

"She didn't come down for coffee this morning. When Mrs. Barrington noticed that Gwen also missed lunch, she got worried. Older people seldom change their routines. When there was no answer at Gwen's door, Mrs. Barrington asked the manager to check on her. They found her in bed." He released his grip and stepped back. "She was ninety-three years old, Natalie. It was just her time."

I wiped my eyes, and we sat in silence.

"Oddest thing," he continued, "she had an apple in her hand."

I couldn't help but smile between the sniffles.

"Are you going to be okay?" he asked. "You and Moose can stay with me tonight if you like."

Though I dreaded being alone, it didn't feel right going to the Legends.

"I'll be okay," I replied, my voice barely audible. "I need to do this on my own."

After he left, I sat in the corner of the couch next to Moose and pulled my knees up. A steady drip in the kitchen sink put a dreary rhythm to my memories of Gwen. On our last trip to the store, she had only picked up a few things, including one apple. Moose nuzzled his nose into my leg as though he too had lost a good friend.

*   *   *

The following morning, Moose and I walked to the grassy hill overlooking Sliver Lake. We took our positions sitting in the grass, gazing at ripples in the water, and thinking about Gwen. The light breeze was just chilly enough to make me want my jacket, so we headed back. As we neared the Legends, a powerful feeling of loss pushed me to enter. I took the elevator to the second floor and walked down the hall to Gwen's door, which stood partially open. Management at the Legends must be as heartless as at the Manor if they were showing the unit already.

I peeked inside to grab a last glimpse and find out who had the nerve to show the apartment so soon. An old man sitting in Gwen's favorite chair was staring at the floor.

"Yes, come in." He gestured to boxes along the wall. "Those should go first."

"You have your mother's eyes," I said, surprising myself with such a direct remark.

His features were too obvious. He had a round face with close-set eyes that hinted of blue. Probably sky blue when he was younger, just like I pictured Gwen's. Who he was didn't occur to me when I first walked in, because I had always pictured Gwen's son as being much younger, but if she was ninety-three, her son must have been around seventy.

"Are you Natalie?"

How do you know my name? I had never seen this man visiting his dying mother. He was never in the great room, never at movie night, never involved in anything.

"Your mother spoke of you often," I said as more of a jab than a compliment.

"Mom left this for you."

He handed me a flowered gift bag closed tight with a yellow ribbon. Yellow. The color of spring flowers blooming around the complex that only days ago Gwen and I had admired from her tufted couch at the window. The yellow flowers had rekindled memories of her home up north, and she described a flower bed that her Robert had constructed in the backyard; yet another labor of love that gave his wife something to occupy her time at the home she scarcely left.

I untied the ribbon and looked inside the bag, finding the scarf that Gwen had been working on for the last two weeks. She never mentioned the scarf was for me, when I was watching her meticulously knit each stitch. I imagined she could have whipped the scarf together in an hour when she was younger, and knowing Gwen, she would have stitched just as much love into the pattern.

"Thank you. It's beautiful."

"She told me about you and your dog." He glanced at Moose but refrained from petting him. "You know, Mom never liked dogs much until she met yours." He gestured to the boxes again. "I just moved all this a few months ago. I don't have the time to be moving it again."

Are you trying to say that your mother's death is inconvenient? "I was told there wouldn't be a service."

"She didn't have any friends down here, and those up

north are too old to make the trip. I had her cremated. I think that's what she wanted, since that's what she did with my dad. Now I have these ashes and no idea what to do with them."

It's a good thing my mind was winning the battle with my mouth, or I might have said some things Gwen would not have appreciated.

"I have an idea if you're interested. We could take them up to her home and bury them with your dad's ashes under the apple tree in the backyard."

"So, that's what she did with his ashes. That would be nice. Thank you."

He handed me a lacquered wooden box, having evidently missed the "we" part of my suggestion. He then went to the refrigerator and removed a package of gourmet cheeses.

"I sent this to her last week. You're welcome to it."

With Gwen in my right hand and cheese in my left, I thought of the conversations she had shared about her son. Anyone else might have been disappointed in such a child, but she always had pride in her eyes whenever she spoke of the man. I thought of a time when I was younger and had slipped up so badly that I expected my mom to be severely disappointed, but Mom had simply said, "The view of a child through her mother's eyes is nothing less than miraculous."

So instead of criticizing him for shirking his last duty, I took the opportunity to be selfish. I *wanted* to take Gwen home, and I didn't care if Mr. Always Too Busy went along or not.

"I'll be happy to take Gwen home." I glanced at the lacquered box in my hand. "Your mother was a wonderful woman."

I turned in a circle to soak in memories of the room one last time. The oxygen tank in the corner, the vintage television, and the sofa where we had shared many cups of tea. The window shades were up, and the glass pane, warmed by the morning sun, wept with humidity. Even the apartment was sad to see her go.

It occurred to me when I was in the elevator that I never got his name. She had always referred to him as her son, and he hadn't introduced himself.

*　　*　　*

A few hours later, Moose and I pulled to the curb in front of a light-green Victorian with white trim and a large front porch that sat unimposingly back from the street. The quaint little house that Gwen had described so many times still had a For Sale sign in the front yard. If Gwen hadn't been forced out of her home, she would be doing just fine right now, sipping tea on the back porch. Who am I kidding? She had been missing her Robert since the day he passed away. At ninety-three, she might not have lived much longer even if she had stayed at home.

I walked to the side of the house and pulled on a thin nylon rope to unlatch the gate to the backyard. In the center of the yard, the apple tree stood as stately as Gwen had described. Its wide trunk supported a canopy of leaves that reached well above the house. Moose darted to the tree and circled it a few times to release pent-up energy from the drive. While he sniffed and marked multiple spots, I made my way to the porch and sat at the small cast iron table that was just large enough for Gwen and Robert. Having finally exhausted himself, Moose nosed his way through the door and curled at my feet.

The sun was low in the sky when we went back to the tree to accomplish our mission. The grass around the trunk revealed no indication of where a hole might have been dug years ago, but a small heart with "G and R 4 EVER" carved in the base of the trunk told me all I needed to know.

I had to dig only a few inches before my garden spade hit something wooden. I carefully enlarged the hole to one side of Robert's box to make room for Gwen, then set her beside him, their boxes touching—holding hands forever.

"You're home, Gwen, together with your Robert. May God bless you both."

I picked an apple from the tree and smiled all the way to the car.

Chapter 14

That Woke Me Up

A RESTLESS NIGHT had me in the great room early Sunday morning, where I wrapped my arm around Grandpa's shoulder and let out a yawn before taking a seat next to him and across from Mrs. Barrington.

"Good morning, Mrs. Barrington."

"Please, call me Bea. My given name. Short for Beatrix."

That woke me up. "Uh, thanks...Bea."

"It's been a difficult week for you, and we appreciate everything you've done. Of course, it is hard for all of us, but we've come to accept the passing of friends. Sadly, it does not get any easier as one gets older. Possibly harder, because the occurrences are more frequent, the friendships are often much longer, and, of course, it is a reminder that our turn will come."

"Did everything go okay?" asked Grandpa.

For the next hour, I sat glassy-eyed, talking about Gwen, her quaint little house, and the apple tree. What had started as me doing a little charity work for an old woman had become a symbiotic friendship, with each of us benefiting, me more than her. Gwen had been in a hurry to finish that scarf because she knew she was going home. Maybe her son had made a good decision by moving her to the Legends, where she was able to make new friends. Had she remained in her house for the little time she had left, nobody would have known to bury her next to Robert.

Throughout the week, I found myself sharing stories of Gwen with other residents at the Legends and was amazed at how many people were fond of the tiny woman.

"Had lunch with her twice a week in the garden," said Patti Jane. "Sat with her while she was knitting your scarf."

Louis looked at his wife. "You've done a lot of those scarves yourself, dontcha know. Lord knows they come in handy in the winter. Mom still uses the ones you gave her."

The sound of my chin hitting the table when my jaw dropped could have woken the dead—a poor choice of words considering recent events.

"Your *mom?*"

"Mom's in an assisted living place not far from here. I pop over there every day."

"Dang," I said reflexively. "She must be a hundred."

"Hundred and three. She and Gwen were friends for eighty-some years, if you can believe that."

Angie stepped up behind us. "I know how hard it is to live alone. You never get used to it."

I let the self-absorbed comment slide, having gone through my own all-about-me phase the night before, feeling sorry for myself because I'd never again get to shop or sit or talk to Gwen.

"I have to get back to my apartment, Grandpa. DeAndre is on his way over to help me...organize things."

With a full cup of coffee in hand, I turned around and nearly bumped into Orval, who had snuck up behind me in his khaki shorts and knee-high compression socks, his hands anchored to the walker. I leaned back just fast enough to divert the slosh of my coffee away from his pale, bald crown. At five foot six, I seldom have an opportunity to study a cranium from above, but I was fairly certain I could make out a map of Australia and parts of Indonesia in the age spots covering the man's scalp.

Though Orval was in the great room often, I seldom said more than hello to the little man because he was always in the middle of a conversation—sometimes with another person. As I steadied my cup, I realized he was speaking to me in what must have been his library voice.

"...faster than you would think, but I was pretty quick myself," he said with a quivering lip. "Never want to be in that situation again. Saw one around here. Black as coal. Quick as a cat. Disappears in the grass and returns in the morning before dawn. Be careful in the tall grass, Natalie. Nothing good happens near the railroad tracks."

What the heck was he talking about? I had clearly missed too much of the story to understand any relevance.

"Scary in the dark, but you know that. Wonder if I'll be alone when we meet again. As long as you're there, everything will be fine."

"If I'm where?" I asked.

Orval tilted his head up and said, "My ankles are starting to swell. I'm going to sit down."

Before he could start another conversation with me or with the cup of coffee in my hand, I gave him a quick "See you later" and darted out the door just in time to see DeAndre sprinting toward a car in the parking lot.

"*Get out!*" he shouted. "*Get out!*"

DeAndre grabbed the handle on a large sedan and pulled repeatedly, but the door refused to open. I arrived in time to see movement inside the smoke-filled interior but couldn't make out a face.

"Find a rock!" he yelled. "I'll bust the glass."

As I reached for a small boulder, the car window rolled

down with a calmness neither of us shared. A cloud of smoke spewed out, revealing the occupant.

"Oh no you don't," said Thelma in her raspy voice.

DeAndre pulled his head back and regained his composure surprisingly fast. "Uh, I thought the car was on fire and you were stuck inside."

"I'm trying to have a cigarette in peace."

She rolled the window back up, and the car refilled with smoke.

I dropped the stone and nudged my shoulder into DeAndre. "That's Thelma. She's a bit of a smoker."

"Ya think?"

"Come on. We've got some packing to do."

Over the past few weeks, Gwen had taken up so much of my time that I had put everything else off, including household chores and packing for the midnight move—at least that was the excuse I gave DeAndre when we entered my messy apartment.

To keep residents from figuring out what we were doing, we made multiple trips with small loads and entered the Legends through different doors. Shortly before midnight, DeAndre left, and I carried one more bag to Grandpa's unit.

Halfway down the hall, the click of a doorknob stopped me in my tracks. Most residents retired to their unit before eight o'clock, and few were awake past nine. The last thing I expected at the late hour was someone entering the hallway.

A head poked out from the unit next to Grandpa's.

"Productive night?" asked Thelma.

"Uh, good evening," I sputtered with the anxiety that accompanies nefarious activities. "Sorry about the fire thing. See you tomorrow." I dropped the bag inside Grandpa's apartment and left.

What kind of eighty-year-old monitors the halls in the middle of the night—and what had she seen?

Back in my apartment, I reviewed social media to catch up on the important events of the day, then drifted into a restless sleep. I woke up Saturday morning tired and late because Moose had again blocked my view of the alarm clock. Today was the day that Grandpa was using Rob's coupon for a free rental on the Saint Croix, and I wanted to see him off.

After Rob had given me the coupon, I called all my friends, but none of them could join me on the river. As a last resort, I asked Grandpa to go with me, but when he found out that I had double-booked myself with a commitment to volunteer at the church rummage sale, he guilted me into keeping the church commitment since I hadn't found another job "as of yet." With a free coupon he suddenly had a desire to go kayaking on the same river he insisted was too cold to get out on only three weeks earlier.

"Eat up, boy, so we can go out and see Grandpa before he leaves."

I placed a bowl of brown pellets next to Moose's water bowl and popped a coffee pod into my espresso machine. The loud machine kick-started Moose into hyper mode. He dashed around the living room, back to the bedroom, and repeated the route while tossing high-pitched yaps to count off the laps. When he zipped between me and the wall, his foot flipped the food bowl into the water bowl.

Ugh. "Stop right there, mister!" Moose pressed his front paws forward and put his chin on the floor. "*Have you had your fun?* Look at this mess!"

I stormed out the door to say goodbye to Grandpa.

"Good morning, kiddo. Where's our little guy?" he asked through the open window of his midsize SUV. I had the same make but the smaller model.

I handed him the certificate while grumbling about Moose making a mess in the kitchen and how that made me forget my keys, so now I was locked out. Grandpa mentioned something about "fault," but I was preoccupied with thoughts of soggy dog food scattered about the kitchen floor and the dreaded encounter with Ms. Ass to unlock my unit.

An hour later, the floor was mostly clean, Moose was somewhat settled, and I was frustrated, grumpy, and late when I arrived at St. John's Catholic Church to help with the rummage sale—all because Moose wanted to play.

* * *

Four hours later, I lugged a bag of rummage-sale items that were too cheap to pass up over to the church courtyard and sat alone on a concrete bench. Though I had stayed busy enough throughout the morning to keep my mind occupied, a number of parishioners had asked if I was okay. Polite replies satisfied their concerns, but the parish priest, who seemed to have been studying me over the course of the morning, was now making his way to my bench.

Father Diamond sat next to me, his eyes focused on the grass at our feet. After a few moments of silence, he said, "Isn't God amazing?"

I was pretty sure the question was rhetorical.

"This grass has been trodden upon by a hundred people today, yet each thin green blade stands strong, having withstood more weight than we can even imagine." He released a concerned sigh. "I sense a weight on your shoulders, Natalie. A heavy burden that feels like too much to bear. At times like these, we must put our trust in the Lord." He gestured to our feet. "Look again at the grass. He has refreshed each blade that was tamped down. Know in your heart that God will do so much more for you than He has for these blades of grass. The burden you carry is a heavy load for someone so young, but it is not so much that you can't handle it. Such burdens often increase before they are lightened, but they *will* be lightened, and you will be better for it."

He left me to ponder his words. Had I been angry this morning because I still missed Gwen, my friend, who had not once exhibited anger in the time I knew her? She must have been frustrated often—when she got her scooter stuck or realized she had put perishable groceries in her pantry. She couldn't leave her apartment without her oxygen tank and was always having to refill it, which was cumbersome to say the least, yet she never got angry or upset.

I tossed my cup into the trash and headed home with a new resolve to tell Grandpa more often that I loved him. The most important thing I had learned from Gwen was that life is fleeting. To show Grandpa just how much I loved him and appreciated everything he did for me, I would prepare his favorite meal and have it ready when he walked in the door.

Grandpa was in for a surprise tonight!

Chapter 15

You Never Get Used to Eating Alone

GONG! WITH MY back to the mantel clock, the first of four gongs nearly scared me out of the chair.

If my estimate was right, Grandpa would have finished his river run around three o'clock. It would take another hour for the rental shop staff to load the kayak and drive him back to his SUV. The drive home to the Legends would take about two hours, which gave me until six o'clock to have everything ready—a late dinner for him, perfect for me.

Eighty-two degrees outside and just enough breeze to keep the humidity at bay made walking to the grocery store an easy decision. I had an extra hour to kill, so I stopped to catch up with Stephanie, who was working her weekend shift at the Legends instead of the Manor.

A ten-minute onslaught of each of us talking excitedly over the other in an attempt to cover every detail ended with "I better go. This dinner isn't going to cook itself."

I threw my hands to my face. "Did I just say that? I sound like these old people."

"I'm not gonna lie, Natalie. You're more stressed than usual. Maybe when you're all moved in, you can try to relax and enjoy the peace and quiet around this place."

"Enjoy it? No way! I'll be lucky if I can tolerate it. I was just in the great room getting coffee, and Orval was there. That guy is always in the middle of a conversation with the window or his shadow or something. I can never tell."

"Orval's harmless, and you know it."

"Yeah, but I feel like he's telling stories that I'm in. Not stories about me, stories *with me*. Like I'm on vacation with him or something."

She gave me the same motherly look I'd received from several old ladies around the complex.

"Maybe you are. Some of these people don't have it all together upstairs. I can tell you this, Orval doesn't have a granddaughter visiting once a week. He hasn't had a single visitor since I started here. Try talking to him next time."

I rolled my eyes and turned toward the door, smacking directly into the side of an aluminum walker.

"I'm so sorry, Orval. I didn't hear you come in." I turned back to Stephanie and mouthed, "*Did he hear us?*"

She pinched a grin and shrugged.

"Because I'm leaving," replied Orval with a wheezy chuckle that sounded as though it would benefit from expectorant.

I mouthed to Steph again, "*Is he allowed outside?*"

She tossed another grin followed by a head nod suggesting that I help the man.

"I am so sorry," I repeated. "Let me get the door for you."

I opened the inside door of the entry and stood like a sentinel while the little man took a full minute to maneuver his walker far enough over the threshold for me to close the inside door and open the outside door. After three attempts, the walker cleared the threshold just in time for us to catch a soft breeze carrying the fragrance of asters and hydrangeas blooming around the complex.

Following Stephanie's suggestion to talk to the man, I said, "It smells nice today."

Orval replied by oscillating his chin faster than normal.

So much for talking to the man. How was I supposed to make conversation with a round-headed relic who wouldn't reply? What were his interests? What on earth could we have in common?

"Where are you headed?" I asked, cringing the moment the words left my mouth. My slower-than-normal brain, which had struggled to come up with a question to ask Orval, immediately knew his reply.

His chin stopped quivering long enough for him to say, "Shopping. And you?"

My inclination was to tell him that I wasn't going anywhere, walk back inside, exit the rear of the complex, drive to the store, and be back before the little man made it to the end of the block. Just then, a gust of wind whipped across the lawn, causing the blades of grass to bristle. I glanced up and caught sight of Stephanie through the window, waving her hands in a spasmodic sign language, instructing me to converse with the man. *Ugh.*

"Me too. Want some company?"

With that, the two of us started a painfully long journey to the neighborhood grocery—a store I could see from the front step of the complex.

The entire way, Orval was walking, wheezing, and reciting cryptic vignettes that seemed to include me, though the stories had such large gaps I questioned which of us was more confused. The pleasant breeze disappeared the second we stepped onto the sidewalk, leaving us drenched in sweat from the muggy heat by the time we arrived at the front of the store, having made our way at a speed that hovered between slow and sloth, with his aluminum walker scraping the pavement with each push forward.

We stepped inside the entrance, where he stopped to either remind himself we were at the grocery store or to marvel at the opening and closing of the motion-activated doors. My *"ahem"* was promptly interpreted as a request. He handed me his ragged cotton grocery bag, which was half-filled with personal items, then shuffled over to the store scooter. With steadfast determination, he completed an eight-point turn, positioning the walker perfectly askew in the corner. I caught a gleam of success in the man's eyes when he accomplished the feat and moved to assist him in getting up on the scooter. As he lifted a leg, his shirt crawled up, revealing a white plastic trim. The accompanying crinkling sound left no doubt what was underneath.

My chest heaved. "See you later."

I pitched his bag into the scooter basket and darted off in the opposite direction of the bald little man and his diaper. I had smelled a faint scent of urine along the entire walk. No way was I going to accompany a hairless urine factory through the store on a shopping venture that was sure to take longer than any trip I had made with Gwen.

The trek to the store had begun with me trying to kill an hour. Now I was officially in a hurry, with a throbbing pulse in my temple providing a countdown to Grandpa's arrival. I rushed through produce and meats and quickly had most items but couldn't find pine nuts anywhere. I gave up the search and was making a beeline to an open register when I saw the elusive nuts on the bottom shelf of an endcap. My time in the store could not have been more than twelve minutes even with the delay in finding the nuts.

I rushed to the nearest register, rewards card and credit card in hand, only to find Orval in front of me with a full basket. The option to back up and pretend that I hadn't seen him was eliminated when a large woman with an overloaded cart sandwiched me in place. Dejected at the thought of a slow walk back to the apartment, I reluctantly helped Orval place his groceries on the conveyor, patiently waited as he handed over an envelope of coupons, then gritted my teeth when he pulled out a checkbook and asked for a pen.

Two bags for me, three bags for the little man, and one item too large to sack and too awkward to suspend from the walker crossbar: adult diapers.

I settled in for the slow, miserable walk back to the Legends, my arm wrapped around a pack of thirty-two medium-sized pull-ups that looked like something Stephanie's nephew would wear. The entire way, Orval continued telling stories that made absolutely no sense but included attributes to which I could relate. Hair color, toothy smiles, a black dog, and a dozen other tidbits could apply to me if I didn't know better.

We entered the Legends the same way we had left, with me holding the door for Orval and a half dozen other residents who felt the need to squeeze by while the old man shuffled and shifted through the narrow entry. After carrying Orval's groceries to the third floor, I was finally back in the apartment, where I half expected to see Grandpa eating Yang's at the kitchen table.

The room was quiet, the stillness broken only by the loud tick of the Seth Thomas clock.

I glanced at the mantel just as the clock struck six with a gong so loud that I dropped the groceries and Moose yelped.

"I need to have Grandpa lower the volume on that thing."

The meal I had conceived would take forty minutes to prep and thirty minutes to cook, and thanks to Orval, there was no chance of me finishing the elaborate dinner in time to show Grandpa how much I loved him. He would walk through the door any second, starving after an exhausting day on the water, and I had nothing prepared, not even a decent excuse for why I hadn't finished cooking.

As I unpacked the groceries, the bag of pine nuts fell onto the granite countertop, reminding me why I had selected the menu for the evening. I had been angry for no reason this morning, and Grandpa acted like he didn't even notice. He was letting me move into his apartment, which was sure to cramp his lifestyle, yet he never hesitated in the decision. Everything Grandpa did was centered around me, and I couldn't even control my grumpy mood long enough to tell him goodbye or that I loved him before he left. *Am I the grass in Father Diamond's story, or is Grandpa the grass and I the one doing the trampling?*

I studied my glum reflection in the glass front of the microwave. Not the look I needed if Grandpa was going to get the best meal he'd had in months, albeit a little late. I drew in a deep breath, pushed it out with resolve, and went to work.

With the speed of an Iron Chef, I organized the pans, bowls, and knives, then pounded the flank steak into thin flat squares, and cut a lemon in half. I carried the butternut squash and corn ears downstairs to the grill to get a good char started, then returned to the apartment and put together the rest of the ingredients, which I layered onto the steak, then rolled it into tight logs. When I stepped back to admire my work, I caught sight of the mantel clock. Six-thirty.

Where is he?

I carried the food outside, removed the butternut squash, and placed a cast iron skillet on the grill.

Louis came up from behind and peered over my shoulder. "Whatcha got there?"

"Toasting pine nuts, then I'll sear the beef. Grandpa's in for a treat tonight."

"Tell the old man to stop by. I won another meat raffle at Big Jake's. Got some steaks for him."

"I'll tell him. Hey, would you watch these steak logs for a minute? I need to get this squash and corn inside."

"I can handle that. Not my fault if one's missing when you return."

I offered the obligatory smile I reserved for senior citizen humor and ran the roasted vegetables upstairs.

No shortcuts tonight. I was going to prove to Grandpa how much I appreciated everything he did for me the one way he understood—with extra effort. This dinner would be nothing less than a tribute to all his motivational sayings. I was walking the extra mile, carrying the extra load, bending over backward, putting my best foot forward, and his favorite, *doing my best.*

At six forty-five, I deglazed the pan, which wafted an aroma of charred beef toward Thelma, who had stepped in for Louis.

"Hey, Thelma, how are you doing?"

"Very well, thank you." Her cigarette hissed as she pulled a long breath. "Quiet evening."

"Yeah, I'm waiting for Grandpa. He must have had a good time." I flashed a confident smile, reflective of a dish coming together perfectly. "But he's got twenty minutes before I start without him."

She exhaled a plume of smoke that drifted upward. "It's been fifteen years, and I'm still not used to eating alone. George did the shopping and the cooking. I worked graveyard most of my life. Sleeping during the day never gave me much opportunity to get out."

"You worked in a *graveyard*?" I knew the woman was a little different, but that was creepy.

"Graveyard is the midnight-to-eight shift," she replied with a familiar "*you'll learn*" look that probably had something to do with twenty-somethings and work ethic.

Midnight to eight? That explained why she monitored the hall at all hours. "You don't go out at all?"

"I'm not a hermit. I simply prefer to stay in." She glanced at my new shorts. "Like you, I have my indulgences and do some shopping, but at my age, I have everything I need." She pulled another drag on her cigarette, which was now little more than a nub. "When it's a little too brisk to sit outside or when somebody has occupied the bench, I smoke in my car, but you already know that. Don't mention this to management, but I've been known to sneak one on the balcony now and then."

"What do you do to stay busy? I mean, with nobody around."

"I read a lot and play a little Scrabble to keep my mind sharp."

"I'll play you sometime."

"That would be nice. I play my grandson now and then. Quick as a whip, that one. A game often comes down to who's holding the last letter."

"I should warn you, I know a lot of words," I said, realizing instantly how much my reply sounded like that of a nine-year-old—who had no idea how quick a "whip" was.

Thelma turned to me as she opened the door to go back inside. "You never get used to eating alone."

*　　*　　*

The sun had long since set, dinner was finished, the dishes were clean, and Grandpa's plate had been moved from the table to the refrigerator. Still no sign of him. No reply to the multiple texts and phone messages. To kill time, I organized things in the spare bedroom that I would soon be sleeping in.

My cell phone rang at eight-thirty with "Unknown Caller" on the screen and a familiar voice on the other end.

"Is this Natalie?"

"Yes."

"This is Asa Olsen from Mountain River Rentals. You've been here a few times, probably know me as 'the old man.' That's what everyone calls me."

"Hi, Asa. My grandpa was there today for his free rental, right?"

A wave of nausea coursed through my body. It was a *free* rental. It was eight-thirty.

"He was here this morning. Put your name down as a contact in case there were problems. I don't know any other way to say this, but we can't find him."

My stomach lurched. A cold sweat broke on my forehead. "What do you mean you can't find him? Did he miss the landing?"

Someone in the background asked for the phone.

"Ms. Thomas, this is Deputy Marshal Peterson. I'm here at the shop with Mr. Olsen. It appears there was an accident on the river. Your grandfather's kayak was pulled ashore near the landing, but he wasn't in it. We have a lot of people looking for him. I'm sure he's just wet and cold somewhere on the riverbank."

My gut clenched tighter. "The kayak was empty?" I repeated meekly while half my brain reminded me that Grandpa was great in a kayak, swam well, and still worked out at the gym. The other half of my brain was telling me how cold that water was, how hurt he could be, and how dark it was outside.

"We talked with other boaters and pieced the events together. Your grandfather took to the water at about nine o'clock this morning. When he reached the island, he steered himself down the right-hand side where the rapids are Class III."

I had been on that stretch. I had been in that water. Grandpa could easily handle a Class III.

"A group of boaters a few hundred feet behind him saw

your grandfather's kayak roll. When it turned back upright, it was empty. We focused our search on that stretch of river and farther downriver. I'm afraid that's all I have right now. Twenty officers and volunteers were searching the water and both banks all afternoon. We stopped because of darkness, but we'll be back out at first light."

The deputy asked about Grandpa's health and physical abilities, then gave me his phone number and promised to call me in the morning with an update.

I slid off Grandpa's couch and wrapped my arms around my knees. Moose circled once and lay down next to me. He knew.

Chapter 16

Colder on the Saint Croix

MOOSE AND I awoke on Grandpa's couch to a hard gong and the soft light of an early dawn crawling through the window. My morning brain didn't know what to do first. Drive to the rental shop? Wait by the phone? Call the deputy? A glance in the mirror helped prioritize activities. My oily face, sticky teeth, and matted hair were in desperate need of attention.

I cleaned up, showered, and prepared for the unknowns of the day. Every move was mechanical. I selected clothes with no concern whether anything matched and brushed my hair with an unconscious stroke.

The long night had been spent worrying about every possible scenario, with the silence interrupted hourly by that damn mantel clock. Grandpa was as tough as nails, but it had been cold last night, even colder on the Saint Croix. If he was wet and hurt on the riverbank, he might have…If he hit his head on a rock when the kayak rolled, he might have…If he never made it out of the river, he might have…

I muttered, "It could be worse." A phrase Grandpa liked to say. I wrapped Moose in a hug and whispered,

"I'll bet he's huddled under a tree somewhere, saying, 'It could be worse.'"

Tired of waiting, I called the deputy, who agreed to meet me at the rental shop.

I found Asa sitting slump-shouldered on a varnished tree stump just inside the door. With heavy eyes, he repeated the events of the previous day.

"The sheriff called after he received a report about an empty green kayak that had our company logo on the side. James, your grandpa, was the only one who rented a green kayak yesterday. A few red and a couple of yellows went out, but James had the only green one. Loaded the green kayak myself."

Filled with anxiety-induced energy, I considered asking him the color, but genuine concern in the man's voice had me feeling sorry for him.

"My boys pushed James and some others off, then watched the boats float downriver until they were all out of sight. Said he was handling the boat just fine."

The bell above the door jingled. A young man entered and removed his circular-brimmed hat. "I'm Deputy Marshal Peterson. You must be Natalie."

The officer was in his mid-twenties, with short brown hair and a deep dimple in the middle of a square chin. He was wearing dull green pants and a tan short-sleeved shirt with a badge above his heart. His voice was strong and crisp, but obviously he hadn't found Grandpa, or he would have said that first.

"Asa told me about the rental and the green kayak, Mr. Peterson. I mean, deputy. Have you found anything else?"

"Most folks call me Marshal or Deputy Peterson."

He then repeated almost verbatim what he had said on the phone. Some kayakers behind Grandpa saw him enter the rapids. His kayak flipped. When it turned back upright, he was gone.

"Did they look for him?" *A dumb question.*

"Yes, ma'am. The boys on the water at the time had two kayaks and were fairly experienced. They circled the area, then pulled to shore and scoured the bank. Didn't find any sign of him."

"Can I follow you there?"

"I understand you want to help, but we have twenty experienced people out again this morning. We're checking the water, both banks, and the islet. We're doing all we can."

Before I could say "I'm going anyway," he added, "But I can see you're determined, so yes, ma'am, I'll take you to the search area."

Moose and I followed his truck downriver for over an hour until he turned onto a dirt road that led to a clearing along the riverbank. Grandpa had flipped very near the spot where Moose and I had fallen into the water. I had been able to swim out with one hand holding on to Moose. Grandpa could easily have made it to the shore—if he was conscious.

Marshal led us to the bank and looked out over the water. "His kayak rolled just upstream there." He pointed north past the islet, toward the bend in the river. "We checked the island. No sign of James, and nothing appears disturbed. Would you like us to check it again? I could arrange that."

I shook my head. "I've been on that island. If your people searched it, they would have found him. I'll take Moose downriver first, then we'll turn around."

"You'll find me somewhere around this clearing if you need me," said Deputy Peterson.

Moose and I followed a river trail that ran along the water's edge, neither of us having any idea what to look for. I tried to identify things that were out of the ordinary, like crushed grass or broken branches or any sign that might indicate he had crawled out of the water. In the first twenty feet, I realized the futility of my effort. Hundreds of footprints from various search teams had trampled the path, leaving no way to distinguish whether Grandpa had come ashore.

A group of three kayakers came toward us. One stopped his kayak dead in the water in front of me.

"Have you found anything?" I asked.

"This is our fourth run this morning. Haven't found anything new, but yesterday Chip pulled a stuffed black dog, about two inches long, out of the water." He gestured to the blond kayaker to his left. "It was maybe a hundred feet past the island."

"That could be my grandpa's keychain. It has a small black dog on it."

"Gave it to Marshal. We'll be out here as long as it takes. Don't worry, we'll find him."

Comforting words that I repeated to myself on the walk back to the clearing where Marshal was on the phone directing the search. The words "a few more hours" hung in the air.

"Marshal, can I see the keychain that Chip gave you? It might be Grandpa's."

With the phone stuck to his ear, he reached inside his truck for the keychain and handed it to me.

"This was his," I whispered then quickly corrected, "I mean, this *is* his." *Why am I talking about him in the past tense?*

"Confirmation on the keychain," said Marshal into the phone.

Moose and I then headed upstream, where the path was farther from the edge of the water. Tall grass with fuzzy hayseed tips covered half the trail, destroying my hopes of finding anything that other searchers wouldn't have already found. The reality of the situation was beginning to set in.

We returned to the clearing and talked to Marshal a little longer.

He lifted his boot to the bumper and tied the lace. "It's getting late, Natalie. Since we found the keychain, I was able to convince my boss that we should spend another day on the river."

"How long do you usually look?"

"For a drowning...I mean, a missing person, a day, maybe a day and a half is about all we can afford. They usually...turn up somewhere downriver within a few days."

"He didn't drown," I said firmly. "I know my grandpa. He could take these rapids in his sleep. He's tough, Marshal. Grandpa is really tough."

"We'll be back out tomorrow. Chip and his buddies said they'll make as many runs as we need. I'll have them search farther downriver."

I handed Marshal a key to Grandpa's SUV, which he offered to drop off at the apartment, then said, "I guess I should get home. There are a few calls I need to make."

Chapter 17

Does He Polish That?

MOOSE AND I stopped at Yang's on the way home. I wasn't hungry, but Marshal had insisted that I eat something. Wi's husband, Li, was working the register, thank goodness, because I didn't feel like talking. Just as I turned around with a small white cube of spicy sustenance dangling from my fingers, I bumped into Orval. The white take-out box smacked the top of his shiny scalp. Oddly, the first thought that came to mind was, *"Does he polish that?"*

"I'm so sorry, Orval." A phrase I'd been using much too often. "I didn't hear you come in."

The little man didn't acknowledge my apology, because he was wholly engaged in a quiet conversation with me—a conversation that I wasn't even aware was taking place. He stood there, rambling, wearing khaki shorts, with one compression sock on his left leg and one on his right arm. *An accident or doctor's orders?* With Orval, either was possible.

"…following you like a shadow. Quiet and close, but not always there. Scary in the dark. He blends in well. Don't go near the trains. Marion wants me to tell you, and she wants me to keep quiet, because I talk too much. I know I do, but there are so few minutes in a day, except for the long days, when there are too many minutes."

His eyes remained fixed on the white container while he spoke. The poor guy wasn't trying to be creepy, but if I didn't know him from the Legends, I'd be a little freaked out.

"Trains are dangerous. Stay away. Stay away." He turned toward a booth. "My ankles are starting to swell. I need to sit down. Remember what I said, Natalie, and pat him on the head for me."

Moose? Had he been talking about Moose all these times? Thankfully, my phone buzzed a text message that Marshal was waiting in the parking lot at the Manor.

"Gotta go, Orval. Can we finish this conversation later?" *Or you can finish it by yourself after I'm gone.*

On the walk back, I stopped on the train tracks next to the apartment and looked both ways down the long empty rail corridor. I had never seen more than one freight train a day come through Sliver Lake, and when they did pass through, they moved very slowly. What on earth would cause Orval to be so fascinated with the trains?

Marshal was waiting at the front door, and luckily, nobody was in the hallway when we walked inside. The last thing I needed was rumors of an officer of the law escorting me home.

I offered him a diet soda, and he took a seat on one of the barstools. The table wasn't an option with my laundry still piled in the middle.

"Nice place." He gestured to the clothes on the table. "That's convenient, having the laundry room so close to the kitchen."

"I meant to finish that before you arrived." I always *mean* to finish it, but the pile is there so often that it's become more of a centerpiece than a chore.

We talked for a long time, initially about the search and then about our college experiences and work history. Marshal Peterson lived in a small town not far from the boat rental shop and described what sounded like a peaceful rural life. I mostly talked about Grandpa and how he had just moved into the complex next door.

After Marshal left, I called Grandpa's brother.

"Hi, Uncle Jerry."

"Uncle Jerry? That's *great*-uncle to you, young lady." He snickered a little too loud for the phone.

"Uncle Jerry, hey, I'm sorry to bother you, but something happened to Grandpa."

His voice transitioned to concern. "What's going on?"

"Grandpa went kayaking yesterday. His kayak flipped over, and they haven't been able to find him."

"Did you call the police?"

"Some people saw his kayak roll over and called the sheriff right away. A lot of people were searching yesterday and today. Deputy Peterson checked all the hospitals, and the search team will be back out tomorrow. I don't know what else to do. I feel like he couldn't have drowned. Those rapids are only Class III, and you know how good he is."

"He's pretty good on the water. I'll be there tomorrow, and we'll figure this out."

That was exactly what I had expected him to say and what I needed to hear.

"Thanks, Jerry. Just come to my place. I'm only here two more days before my lease is up. I'll explain everything when you arrive—and don't drive too fast!"

"*Me* exceed the speed limit? Not likely, Ms. Thomas." He snickered again. "I'll be careful. You try and get some sleep. We may be busy for a few days."

Next, I called Ramee and DeAndre, who had both known Grandpa for years. By the time they arrived, my description of events sounded almost mechanical. An empty kayak, Deputy Peterson, the keychain.

"A *free* rental," I said to Ramee after she pushed my laundry to one side of the table. "I gave the certificate to Grandpa and watched him leave—alone. I should have gone with him."

"Don't blame yourself. You couldn't have known this would happen."

"But you know Grandpa's saying. The kayak was free. He and I both should have known better."

Ramee shook her head. "It's just a saying, Nat."

"It's just one of those things," said DeAndre. "I'm sure he thought it was cool to get the free rental and get out on the water again."

DeAndre was right. Grandpa had been excited about the trip. He loved being on the water more than I did and had even owned a bass boat when he lived in Texas. When he wasn't canoeing or kayaking, he was fishing. He was at home on the water.

A couple of hours later, Moose and I were alone again. The mood was very different from the previous evening. Last night, there was a chance that Grandpa would walk through the door or that someone would find him shivering in the grass on the riverbank, but those feelings of hope had dwindled with every minute of the day. My stomach was nauseous when I climbed into bed, Moose at my side.

The hour was late, but neither of us could sleep. I stared at the ceiling. Images of the riverbank, the grassy path, and the icy rapids passed through my mind. A feeling of hopelessness enveloped me. A feeling I'd had once before.

Chapter 18

Uncle Jerry

UNCLE JERRY ARRIVED just after lunch on Sunday. By my calculation, that meant he had basically hung up the phone after talking to me and climbed into his car. I didn't ask how fast he drove.

Jerry was Grandpa's younger brother, and like Grandpa, he was five foot ten and about 150 pounds fully wet. Too much sun from a landscaping career had aged his skin with the wrinkles and liver spots typical of many residents at the Legends. Before he even sat down, I was filling him in on the empty kayak, the old man, and Deputy Peterson. I followed that with a tearful description of my eye-opening walk along the riverbank, where the roar of the rapids had drowned out my hope. He cringed when I told him the kayak trip was free.

The first thing he wanted to do was drive to the rental shop, where we found Deputy Peterson and Asa cross-checking search areas on a large map.

Marshal brought us up to date, repeating most of what I had already told Jerry and finishing with an explanation of activities that were currently underway. The search team was down to four crews totaling nine people. Chip and his friend were searching farther down the river, and other searchers, including Asa's teenage boys, were scouring the banks.

Jerry seemed to understand better than I that at some point they would have to shut down the activities.

We spent a few minutes talking to Asa, then drove to the clearing where the kayak had washed ashore. Uncle Jerry and I walked up and down the river, but there was little we could do other than stare at the water. On the drive home, Jerry fell into a well-deserved sleep.

When we returned to my nearly bare apartment at the Manor, I told him about my lease situation and Grandpa's plan for me to move into his unit. The few items that remained in my place were all large—not that it mattered, because moving to the Legends was no longer an option with Grandpa gone.

I shouldn't have been surprised when Uncle Jerry took a more hopeful approach and viewed the move as an opportunity to occupy our minds on a physical activity. He suggested DeAndre come over to help with the heavy stuff.

"I passed the little bald dude on the sidewalk," said DeAndre when he arrived a couple hours later. "Is he allowed outside after dark?"

"Can you grab that end?" I asked, ignoring his attempt to delay physical labor.

He wriggled his fingers. "I make my livin' with these babies," he said in reference to his computer programming skills. "And you got me haulin' tables and chairs. How come you never ask me to move the pillows?"

"Quit your whining. If it's any consolation, we tried to get more people to help with the big stuff."

"But the girls down the hall were busy," said Jerry, picking up one end of the futon while DeAndre picked up the other.

"And don't forget, I hauled twice this much when we moved you into your apartment. You had four computer monitors! Who needs *four* monitors?"

DeAndre pulled his head back. "I got the heavy stuff then too, while you and Ramee carried one dish at a time and stopped to talk with every trip into the kitchen." He set the futon down and mimicked carrying a single dish.

"Sure, I got this," said Jerry, holding the other end of the futon. "You girls want to stand and gossip or give me a hand?"

DeAndre picked his end back up. "You owe me some serious grillin', girl."

We finished in forty minutes. DeAndre went home, and Uncle Jerry, Moose, and I slept at Grandpa's.

* * *

The red number eight was the first digit I saw on the clock when Moose licked me awake. My body was still tired from the long night, but keeping busy had kept my mind off other things, which was exactly what I needed.

Uncle Jerry had already gone downstairs for coffee by the time I showered and dressed. I joined him in the corner of the great room, where he was nursing a cup.

"Left my big cup in the car," he said, referring to the quart-size coffee cup he carried everywhere. "I suppose it wouldn't be very nice to empty the pot with each refill. Not that I care, I'm leaving later this week. You gotta live with these old farts."

He would give any one of these "old farts" the shirt off his back if he thought they needed it.

Coffee in hand, we headed back to Grandpa's unit to discuss details of my situation in private.

"Good morning, Jimmy," said PJ with barely a glance when we passed her in the hall.

Jerry returned a reflexive "Good morning."

Based on my precarious financial situation, which I had told Jerry about in a tear-filled confession the night before, Jerry suggested I keep a very low profile to extend my stay at the Legends as long as possible. The only way the plan would work is if I could convince residents that I lived at the Manor and was only visiting. I would also need to convince residents that Grandpa was still living at the Legends, though his whereabouts remained unknown.

I walked Jerry to the car when he left for his appointment to complete some forms at the sheriff's office, then I returned to Grandpa's unit as stealthily as possible, taking the stairs, peeking around corners, and listening for conversations in the hallway. I was so paranoid about someone seeing me in the hall that I opened the door without any thought to what might be lurking inside—Moose wearing a devious grin. He shot into the hall at full speed. Thank God no aluminum walkers were blocking the way, or he would have bowled them over.

Moose would never bite anybody, but when he was releasing pent-up energy, he could easily knock one of these old people down. I chased after him, turning the corner to see an even more horrific sight: my furry delinquent sprinting directly toward Angie at the far end of the next hall. She crossed her arms over her chest and shook in fear while Moose dashed around her and sprinted back.

"*Stop! Stay! Sit!*" From the end of the hall, Angie's seething eyes halted my fourth futile S command.

Moose zipped past me and didn't stop until he was back inside Grandpa's unit—not the low profile that I needed on our first day at the Legends.

An hour later, I was walking out as Gladys was coming in.

"Hello, Natalie."

"Uh, hi, Gladys." I kept my head down and my pace

up. The last thing I needed was an admonition for Moose's antics.

"Saw you and Jimmy leaving the room this morning. Will you let him know I baked some cookies for him?"

I stopped short. PJ had mistaken Jerry for Grandpa, and now Gladys thought she had seen Grandpa.

"Uh, sure, I'll leave him a note. I'm on my way home to the Manor."

"And in case you haven't heard, be careful in the hallway. Angie had a terrible fright this morning when a big dog attacked her. She has a weak heart, you know."

Ugh.

Later in the day, I stopped by Gladys' apartment with an excuse that I had spent way too much time fabricating. I've never been good at lying. Even childhood offenses that I had long since reconciled in the church confessional still haunted me now and then. I could only imagine the penance coming my way for the whopper I made up about Grandpa going ice fishing. My facts were terrible. Most lake ice was no longer suitable for ice fishing, so I created a fake lake and told her it was six hours away. If she had done the math, she would have realized that driving six hours in any direction puts you in an entirely different state. Not to mention that nobody in their right mind would drive six hours to fish for an hour. Still, she accepted the excuse and handed me a plastic container of cookies wrapped with a red bow, the curled ends of which dangled over the sides. She had gone to a lot of trouble—for Moose and me. I thanked her and promised that Grandpa would return the container. Another lie.

* * *

Jerry left on Wednesday, having completed everything that could be done, including convincing the sheriff to treat the case as a missing person. We were both surprised to learn there were no other official reporting requirements.

Evening arrived to find Moose and I alone on the couch and a single light on in the kitchen. We had a full supply of groceries courtesy of Uncle Jerry, but cooking was the last thing on my mind, as life at the Legends was beginning to feel confining.

A knock on the door brought a growl from Moose and a cringe from me. Did someone want to talk to Grandpa? Had a resident seen Moose running at Angie? With nauseating apprehension, I opened the door.

"Maybe this will help." Thelma handed me a single cup of hot chocolate and returned to her unit before I could say thanks.

Chapter 19

What Did You Do?

I SET MYSELF up in the guest room, still hopeful that Grandpa would walk in at any moment, though inside I knew that wasn't going to happen. A dozen bags and boxes scattered about reminded me of all the work that was not going to get done with me lying on the bed next to Moose. A discomforting quiet set in. The only sound, an irritating ticking from the mantel.

"I have to get out of here, boy."

I snuck out the back side of the complex, walked along the train tracks to the Manor, and cut through the parking lot, taking a very long path to Yang's. The mid-June evening was still cool enough that I wished I had worn one of the sweaters that was piled on the kitchen table.

I ordered a bowl of egg drop soup and sat in a booth.

Wi came over and sat across from me. "You look sad, Natty."

"Long day." I was not ready to share my situation.

She offered a consoling nod, then spent fifteen excited minutes describing her son's scholastic accolades and his acceptance into a prestigious music camp.

Listening to Wi's rapid rhapsody about her son provided a welcome distraction from my problems. I returned to the Legends a little less downhearted and was able to enter through the back door without being seen outside by anyone.

Ugh. Movie night in the great room had just ended, and residents were swarming the hall, albeit slowly. I slipped inconspicuously into the flow and took the stairs to the second floor. When I turned down Grandpa's hall, Angie and Gladys were at Thelma's door.

"Did Jimmy like the cookies?" asked Gladys. "They were butterscotch ripple. My own recipe."

I put on a confident smile and nodded lightly. "I think he liked them. I just stopped by to pick up something for work tomorrow. Then I need to get right home and into bed." *Bed? Ugh.* It was eight o'clock.

"You didn't tell me you made cookies," snipped Angie.

The ensuing argument allowed me to slip inside, where a rancid smell almost knocked me back into the hall. An odor that was occurring way too often in the confines of my dwellings.

"*Moose,*" I shrieked in a whisper. "*What did you do?*"

He grinned and pleaded to go outside where he could play with his new toy—the mangled plastic cookie container dangling from his teeth. Behind him was his version of a butterscotch pile. I quickly locked him in the bedroom to keep him from spreading the mess, then rinsed the container, which had been chewed so much it was nearly in two pieces.

I stepped back into the hall and handed Gladys the ragged piece of plasticware. "He said thanks." I glanced at the dish. "Um, we, I mean he, hasn't figured out the dishwasher yet. I think this got caught in it." The multiple lies I was tossing so freely prompted me to wonder whether Father Diamond would still be talking about grass the next time I was at church.

The cookie encounter was a clear warning that I needed to be more careful. If Gladys and Angie had not been arguing, they might have realized that I was arriving after eight, at a time when visitors would normally be leaving. Not to mention the noise Moose must have made scampering around the apartment.

I turned on the fan and opened the door to the balcony, then cautiously returned to the scene of the crime. A few minutes of scrubbing the carpet, a skill I had oddly mastered, and the place looked as good as new.

Fortunately, the cookies were butterscotch. Had they been chocolate, Dr. Dana would not have been pleased.

Chapter 20

Craig's List

THE NEXT MORNING, Mr. Slobbers woke me at eight twenty-eight with a wet tongue that still smelled of cookies. I had planned to get up at the seven o'clock gong in order to leave the apartment before the neighbors started moving about, but the antique clock had been oddly quiet. I donned yesterday's clothes, which were piled at the foot of the bed, and took Moose out the back door. With nobody around and Moose moving in a slow morning trance, I unleashed him to do his business. He moseyed a few feet away and did his job, at which point I bent over and did mine. When I looked up, bag in hand, he was gone. *What the heck?*

I called out in a hushed tone. "*Moose!*"

Nothing. I scanned every direction, then took off in pursuit when I located him halfway across the parking lot, sprinting toward the open pool gate at the Manor. The only thing Moose loved more than a good rabbit chase was a swim—but dogs aren't allowed in the pool, a point Ms. Ass had made very clear, twice fining me for "bringing a pet into the pool area." *Like I had any say in the matter.*

When I heard the splash, I slowed to a walk. My canine

Phelps would do at least two laps before he would even consider getting out of the water. On the way back to the Legends, he showered me twice with full-body shakes, leaving me soaking wet by the time we entered the same door we had exited.

Angie, wearing her emotionless face, stood at the end of the hallway. "My, you're here early today."

My, you're being nosy today.

"Do you and Jimmy have special plans?"

"Good morning, Angie. Just took Moose for a swim at my apartment. See ya!" I slipped inside the unit but couldn't shake an eerie feeling that she had been waiting for me.

Ugh. "Why is she following us, boy?"

Moose tilted his head.

"You can't go swimming whenever you feel frisky." I shook my finger at him as though he were a toddler. "Only at the lake—which we'll go to soon. I promise."

To keep people away and hopefully put an end to Angie's questions about Grandpa—at least for the time being—I decided to spread a rumor that he had caught a cold. If my plan worked, Grandpa being sick would make me feel a lot better.

I headed to the great room the following morning, where a dozen chairs were occupied. No sign of Angie or Gladys. I filled a cup and sat at a table near Patti Jane and Louis who were in another one of their Depression-era conversations. Stories they must have told each other a hundred times, but neither seemed to tire of listening.

"You look like a young lady with a lot on your mind," said Louis, turning my way.

My hand twitched so fast that my coffee sloshed over the edge.

"Care to join us? Where's James this morning?"

I gathered myself and feigned a sigh. "There's just so much to do taking care of two apartments. With Grandpa not feeling good, the chores add up."

Patti Jane's ears perked. "Be sure he gargles with warm water and salt."

She had the solution before I explained his illness.

"What's the old man got?" asked Louis.

"He's coughing a little and had a low fever all night."

PJ patted the back of Louis' hand. "Pick up a chicken when you go out, dear. I'll make the poor man some soup."

Pick up *a chicken?* Having waded through the bin of chilled featherless fowl with Gwen, the thought of one of those three-pound birds bobbing in PJ's pot turned my stomach—but not Louis'.

"Bowl of your soup sure sounds good about now." He closed his eyes and sniffed the air. "All those exotic spices you and your mom use. I can almost taste it."

"A bay leaf is hardly exotic." She turned to me. "He always makes it sound like my family was rich."

Louis winked. "That's 'cause her family had new furniture all the time. Now, if you ladies will excuse me a minute."

"Were you really rich?" I asked as he left looking a little uncomfortable.

"By no means, dear. Louis is just being Louis. I was born in a shotgun house, same as he was."

Images of houses and shotguns passed through my mind, but nothing connected the two.

"What did Louis mean about the furniture?"

She shook her head and slid me a sly smile. "It's true. My dad was known to buy furniture now and then. So, yes, Louis is correct; we often had the nicest furniture in the neighborhood—for three months at a time. What Louis leaves out of the story is the part about my father buying on credit and the store taking everything back because Dad never made a payment. Dad was shrewd all right, but raising all us kids in those days, he did what he had to do, and that was one way to make us all feel better for a few months or so at a time."

"So you grew up poor?" I asked, totally confused at this point.

She shrugged. "When everybody is poor, dear, you don't really notice."

Louis returned, his discomfort replaced with a cheeky smile. "Just taking care of business."

"I was going to tell you before you left that when I first started college, I got a dresser on Craigslist for ten bucks. It was a lot of work to refinish it in the apartment, but hey, it was cheap."

They both responded at the same time, with Louis saying, "You *refinished* a dresser in your apartment?" and Patti Jane asking the more obvious question, "Who's Craig, dear?"

I spent the next twenty minutes impressing Louis with the detail I had put into refinishing a four-drawer dresser in the confines of an apartment without disturbing the neighbors or getting paint on the carpet. But I had no luck explaining Craigslist. Either they couldn't grasp, or I couldn't convey the concept of shopping for used items on the internet. Louis left the room twice during my explanation, each time saying he'd be back in two shakes—a unit of measure with which I was not familiar.

"I think Angie's got some kinda list like that," offered Louis. "She's sitting right over there. If you ever have a run-in with that Craig fellow, maybe Angie could help you out."

She was the *last* person I wanted to talk to about anything.

"Now, Louis, don't go pushing your nose into this girl's personal business. Craig sounds like a nice boy, so leave her be."

"I'll be right back." He pushed himself up from the chair, looking as though he had strained his lower back, then walked awkwardly to the door.

"Is there anything you would like to tell me about Craig?" asked PJ before the door had fully closed. "Does James approve of the young man?"

Evidently, only Louis had to keep his nose out of my personal affairs. I had started to explain one more time when Louis returned. He wiped his forehead with a white handkerchief that looked exactly like the ones Grandpa used.

"Just taking care of business."

"What business are you in?" I asked, thankful to change the subject to anything other than men in my life.

"There you go, old man." Patti Jane spread a sardonic smile. "Let's hear you explain this one."

Louis chortled. "Now, PJ, there's no secrets among friends."

There was at least one secret, but I wasn't about to tell.

"Thought my colonoscopy procedure was scheduled for this morning," said Louis. "Woke up before the sun and started drinking that yellow laxative mix. Takes two hours to drink all that down, dontcha know."

I didn't know and wasn't about to ask for clarification on any statement with the word "laxative" in it.

Patti Jane put her hand on my arm and grinned. "His appointment is next week. I told him to check the calendar."

"She's right about that. It's not that I didn't believe her, but I wrote the date wrong." He slapped the palm of his hand to his forehead. "Uff-da. PJ came in just as I swallowed the last gulp of poop juice."

"*Poop juice?*"

Another disapproving glance from PJ.

"Let's just say the laxative works fine," he replied with a more restrained chuckle than usual. "Now, if you'll excuse me again."

"Ooh." I grimaced. "Now I get it."

"At our age, it seems like we have some kind of

procedure every month. Like I tell Louis, we have to take care of ourselves because nobody else will."

"Like the little problem that Grandpa is having this morning," I replied casually. "I thought it was something he ate, but his temperature is a little high, and the cough just started, so I'm making him stay in."

"Be sure James gargles with warm water and salt," she repeated.

"Does that really work?"

Her eyebrows shot up as though she could hardly believe the question. "Absolutely."

Louis returned to the room, stopping at the coffee counter for a jelly doughnut.

"You put that right back, mister," ordered Patti Jane.

A sneaky grin spread across his round face as he downed half of the circular cake in a single bite.

"You aren't supposed to eat those."

"Gotta live a little, PJ," he said, the words muffled by a full mouth.

"His doctor told him to stop those things altogether." She shook her head in disgust. "But look at this man acting like his health doesn't matter. We have sugar-free doughnuts upstairs."

"*Sugar-free* doughnuts?" He gave me a wink. "Now, PJ, doesn't that kinda defeat the whole purpose? I gotta put something back into my stomach. One of these treats every now and again isn't going to kill me."

"That's not what your cardiologist said." She looked back at me. "After his bypass a few years ago, he was ordered to stop eating those things, but the man is incorrigible."

I'd heard that word but tapped it into my phone to be sure while she continued her loving berating.

"That's not even the half of it." He chuckled again. "Had a couple of skin cancers removed a while back, a little bout with leukemia, and the prostate cancer. Like I tell PJ, it ain't the doughnut that's gonna kill me."

My jaw nearly hit the table. Nobody in my family had ever been that sick. *Nobody reaches the age of seventy*, but they're always healthy when they go.

He noticed my shock. "Now, don't get all worried about me. The skin cancer was benign, and they got the other one before it spread."

Benign is good, right? I tapped my phone again.

Other than having my wisdom teeth removed, which DeAndre often reminded me had an irreversible effect, my experience with medical conditions had been limited. Skin cancer, prostate cancer, *any* cancer scared me.

PJ lifted her oversize handbag to the table. "If you're going to eat that, then we need to check your sugar."

"I'm not diabetic, dear," he replied with his loving smirk. "Not since they changed the A1C levels."

"Once a diabetic, always a diabetic." PJ pulled out a pink oval glucose meter.

Louis slid an open hand toward his wife. "Hardly seems fair. My A1C has never hit seven, but I'm labeled for life."

He didn't even wince when she poked his finger.

"The number will be fine. Always is, but she insists on poking that finger twice a day."

PJ studied the reading. "It's fine."

Louis tossed me an *I-told-you-so* wink and left the room again.

As inconspicuously as I could, I moved to other tables to spread further word of Grandpa's not feeling well. In half of my conversations, somebody suggested he gargle with warm water and salt. In the other half, chicken soup was the sure cure—a dish that would never taste the same, knowing the history of these people and their chickens.

*   *   *

Grandpa's illness worked almost too well. A dozen cas-seroles were dropped off in the first week, and every time I stopped by the great room, a resident handed me chicken soup in what they called a "thermos." Though I was grateful for the kindness and the free food, casserole for breakfast, lunch, and dinner was more than I could handle. In three days, the kitchen counter looked like a buffet line, with large casserole dishes containing cabbage, noodles, and rice mixed with chicken, beef, and tuna. Someone had even delivered a hard-boiled egg casserole made with the eggs cut in half, their rounded white ends sticking up. The baked penne pasta with Italian sausage was my favorite, though for the life of me, I couldn't remember who had delivered it. Some residents had taped their name on the side of the dish, and some used disposable aluminum pans, but that still left a number of rectangular, square, and oval dishes with no designated owner.

I organized the meals by size, type, and taste. Casseroles that tasted the best went into the refrigerator and freezer. Anything that tasted worse than it looked went into the garbage disposal, which was working overtime. Anything that wasn't loaded with vegetables went to Moose along with a couple of pans he had pulled down from the counter on his own. Even after my sorting, there were still too many dishes, so I called in reinforcements.

"Yuck. Tuna," said DeAndre. He pushed his chair back and rushed to the sink to deposit a mouthful of fishy noodles.

"I told you to smell it first."

He skewed his face. "I trusted your sorting system."

"Slide the tuna this way," said Ramee, sitting at the end of the counter with her fork at the ready.

Even with help from Moose and my friends, I still had to give three pans to Stephanie.

*   *   *

It had been three weeks since Grandpa's kayak was found empty. Moose and I returned to the clearing every Saturday and Sunday and a few times during the week. We walked up and down that desolate path with nothing to show for it but muddy shoes and blisters. Deputy Peterson kept in touch, but his calls were less frequent and his news less promising. My little game of faking Grandpa's illness had begun with a level of excitement that distracted me from the seriousness of the situation, but as the days crawled by, a dark reality crept in.

Chapter 21

Bring Out the Girls

IT HAD BEEN three months since Grandpa disappeared and I was more nervous than ever that I'd be kicked out of the apartment the instant management realized I was living at the Legends. One other thing had become clear: Grandpa was not coming home. With work barely providing enough hours to keep me busy, I couldn't risk getting caught, so DeAndre and Ramee came over one Saturday, after the residents had left for dinner at the senior discount buffet, to help figure out a longer-term plan and finish off another casserole—something I hadn't warned them about for fear they might not show. Our objective was to keep me at the Legends long enough to find a new job and save enough to move into a cheaper apartment. Getting my life back into some sense of normalcy and routine was secondary.

I opened a notebook to capture our thoughts. "Telling residents that Grandpa isn't feeling well worked great, but if he doesn't get better soon, somebody's going to call an ambulance."

"And I am *done* with these casseroles," said DeAndre, shoveling a last spoonful into his mouth.

"I need another excuse that these old people will believe."

"We could bring out the girls," said Ramee.

"*The girls?*" DeAndre's eyes lit up.

"Some lady friends Natalie and I called upon in college when we needed an excuse for a late assignment. Miss Direction, Miss Informed, and Miss Understood."

I clicked my tongue. "A little Miss Direction can go a long way."

"I thought you meant real girls, girl." He shook his head. "Why don't you just tell some of these people they sat with him at breakfast? Modo wouldn't have any idea who he had breakfast with. Dude's missing it upstairs." He swirled a finger around his ear.

"And...which one is Modo?" I asked.

"The little bald dude who wears his pants too high." He rolled his shoulders forward. "Has a hunchback."

"Orval?"

"That's the guy. I call him Modo, as in *Quasi...modo*."

Ramee scowled. "That's not nice. These people have feelings too."

"Eh, they're so old the only feeling they have is numbness in the legs and maybe a sharp pain in the chest once in a while. I got names for all of them." He held up his fingers and counted off. "You got a Sneezy, Sleepy, Cleany, Diapey—"

"Cleany and Diapey?" Names I hadn't heard before.

"Yeah, the guy who sprays his table and wipes it off before he sits down. And Diapey is that lady who doesn't tuck her diaper in." He twisted his face. "Always sticks up in the back."

The descriptions were spot-on and brought to mind images of each resident he described.

"You're sick," said Ramee.

"Diapey is Gladys," I said. "She's pretty nice when she's not with Angie, and she can't help it with her clothes. These people are weird that way. For some reason, they don't like to buy new stuff, even though they're all pretty well off. I've seen elastic waistbands so slack they could stretch across the room. Honestly, it's kind of surprising their pants stay up as well as they do." I reached for the sheet of paper and wrote "job" at the top. "What do you think about telling people that Grandpa got a job?"

DeAndre raised an eyebrow.

"Yes, I'm aware that I need another job too, but let's focus on Grandpa for now."

"We'll need a good reason for him to want to go back to work," said Ramee. "Maybe he got bored or something because he's so much younger than most of the residents."

"I talked to my granddad about this," said DeAndre. "A job is good, but you could also put him on a cruise. Granddad likes to go on cruises to pick up chicks. It made me throw up a little in my mouth when he said it."

"They'd never believe Grandpa is *picking up chicks*, but the cruise could work. We could send him on a cruise where he meets a lady from out of town or something. That would give him a reason to leave for a few days at a time. Throw in a job, and he'd never be home." I leaned back and interlocked my fingers behind my head. "The first thing I have to do is get him well enough to go on a cruise. Your other idea is good too, DeAndre. I'll start telling people they saw him in the morning. A couple of residents are perfect for that."

"Make it a three-week cruise," said DeAndre. "That seems long, but just say he likes to travel and hasn't been anywhere for a while."

I released my first relaxed sigh in a long time. "I could sure use a three-week break."

DeAndre leaned forward. "There's one element of the plan that we haven't discussed. You're not gonna wanna hear this, girl, but six is the new nine for you. If you're going to last at this place, you gotta walk Moose early in the morning, before these geezers are up, especially if you think some of them are watching you."

As the thought of waking before sunrise was sinking in, a light knock on the door spooked us. I glanced instinctively at the mantel clock, but it had stopped two weeks ago. Tired of the symphonic reminder that Grandpa was missing, I no longer wound it.

"Who could that be?" whispered DeAndre.

"I don't know."

I crept toward the door as though something sinister were on the other side.

"Good evening," said Bea. "I heard that James hasn't been feeling well. Do you need anything?"

I had avoided Bea since she returned from her extended vacation to London, because I didn't know what else to do. She and Grandpa had become such good friends and she had treated me so well. I stood there with my mouth gaping open but not saying a word. A flushed feeling flowed through my entire body. All my emotions seemed to come together in full force, ready to burst out.

"Uh...James—I mean, Grandpa—should be back in an hour, right, DeAndre?" Ramee's voice was not convincing.

"Yep. Back in an hour," replied DeAndre as though they had rehearsed the scene, but not very well.

"Come in, Bea. We need to talk."

My tears flowed as I filled her in on the kayak trip, the sheriff, the search, Uncle Jerry, and the apartment. I explained that I had started moving in before he went missing because my job had cut my hours, and that he and I had planned to live together for as long as we could get away with it.

"I'm so sorry. I had no idea." She wrapped me in her arms and held tight.

"We were sitting here coming up with ideas to keep residents from figuring out that Grandpa is missing. I can't be kicked out. I know it's selfish, Bea, but I don't have anywhere to go."

"We'll get to that. How are *you* doing?"

"I'm not gonna lie; it's hard. I stay awake thinking of all the things Grandpa and I did together. I wonder where he is and if he is alive and hurt, or if he drowned, or if...I don't know, Bea. I just don't know."

"It's good for you to think about things you did together, dear. Do that as often as you like. It's also natural to wonder where he is. He was a strong man, and if anyone could make it, he could." She looked directly into my eyes. "But it has been a long time. I'm sure you realize that. Now, how can I help?"

DeAndre explained the cruise, the girlfriend, the job, and how we hoped people would get used to not seeing him around.

"Excellent ideas. I'm not one to fib, but for select individuals, it may be possible to bend the truth." She clasped her hands together and sat up straight. "You've covered James, at least for now, but what about Moose? We have a winter inspection next week when maintenance turns on the heating units. Obviously, you'll be the one to schedule this for James since part of your assisting him includes taking care of his appointments. That is how you can explain your involvement to management when they ask why you are making the arrangements. Bring Moose upstairs to stay with me until they finish."

I rubbed his tummy while he listened to the conversation. "Thank you, Bea."

We agreed to set the plan in motion the following morning in the great room. Bea gave us each a hug and told me to knock on her door at any hour. Ramee and DeAndre walked out with her.

Knowing I could call on Bea at any time was a huge relief and helped me to sleep soundly for the first time since Grandpa had gone missing.

Chapter 22

Cutting It a Little Close

RESTED AND RELAXED, I awoke to a faded red 6:42 on the clock that was barely visible through the bushy tail resting on my face. Not quite the 6:00 a.m. that DeAndre had suggested, but close enough for the first day of our new plan.

I passed Patti Jane and Louis in the hall and told them Grandpa was feeling better. Residents of the Legends might only be able to walk a half mile an hour, but gossip traveled at the speed of light.

Inside the great room, I poured a coffee and glanced at Bea, who was in conversation with Glen and Millie. Angie and Gladys entered together as I pulled a chair out at the nearest table.

"I'm happy to hear Jimmy is feeling better," said Angie.

Wow. News travels fast.

"Happy to hear he's better," parroted Gladys.

"Will he be down this morning?" asked Angie.

"I'm sorry, you just missed him."

"I saw him," said Gladys, drawing a glare from Angie and raised eyebrows from me, but I couldn't waste the opportunity.

"Did you notice he has his color back?" I asked.

"It sounded serious," said Angie. "Almost as bad as my bout with pneumonia last year."

Uh-huh. Make this about you. "You must have been *misinformed*. Antibiotics and chicken soup fixed him up. He's keeping to himself for another day or so, but he needed a little air, so he slipped down here for a cup."

"The apartment can be so confining," said Gladys.

More than you know.

"We appreciate his consideration." Angie gestured to a tissue on the floor, next to a full table. "Some residents have little regard for others when it comes to illness."

Our eyes shifted to five residents who were alternating tissue retrievals from a single box at the next table. I was mesmerized by the next sport sure to be included in the Senior Olympics—the Tissue Tango.

I studied the players' movements as each shaky hand reached for a tissue but struggled to secure the flimsy edge drooping from the box. Once a tissue was secured, the player tugged until it released. In my imaginary game, scoring was based on time, the distance the box traveled toward the player when they pulled, and the number of tugs required to free the fluff. A deduction was applied for using two hands.

A new round began with Ms. Feeble Fingers tugging the tissue three times, but it refused to leave the box. She tugged again, pulling the box close, then used a second hand to secure the prize. Low score.

The next lady was starting her turn with her eyeglasses so fogged that she could barely see the target. Ms. Foggy Glasses reached out quickly, snapping her wrist like a pro, but she missed the tissue entirely. On her second attempt, she grabbed the box rather than the tissue and pulled it her way, then used two hands to pull. Lower score.

Surprisingly, the next two players both took longer

than Ms. Feeble Fingers. Last up was a large man with a square body and long arms. I picked him as a ringer hiding athletic prowess under a sweater that must have been an inch thick.

He interlocked his fingers to stretch arthritic joints, adjusted the thick sweater cuffs, and focused on the box. The elderly jock made his move with a tremble twice as jumpy as any other player. His long reach exacerbated the vibration and caused his fingers to bump the box farther away. On his fourth attempt, he pinched a tissue. With a heavy tug, the box lifted from the table, releasing the tissue one second too late, giving Ms. Feeble Fingers the win.

I balled a fist and yanked my arm back. "Yes!" The elderly jock then blew his nose so hard the tissue tore in the process. *Eww.*

"Word is getting around that James is better," said Bea when I sat down at her table. "I've casually brought it up in conversation. I find it interesting, the illnesses residents so willingly share when the subject of medical conditions is introduced."

"Good morning, little lady," said Louis as he and PJ joined us. "Shouldn't you be gettin' to work about now?"

"Um, well, my work has been a little light lately, and I needed to take something upstairs this morning anyway."

"If work is a little light, you could always get a second job," said Louis, sounding a lot like Grandpa.

"Louis worked two jobs for most of his career," added PJ.

"Maybe that's not a bad idea," I replied. "You know what they say about idle hands." *Ugh.* Now *I* was sounding like Grandpa.

Louis rubbed his large hands together. "From an early age, Pop taught us to work when there's work. Never know when that gravy train is gonna dry up."

He had often talked about his dad working on trains at the rail yards, but this was his first mention of gravy.

"I'll start looking for another job today," I said with more confidence than conviction.

Louis and PJ left the great room, he satisfied that I would be looking for a second job and she satisfied that Grandpa would continue to gargle with warm water and salt for the rest of the week.

"I'm getting a lot of questions about James," Bea whispered when Louis and PJ were in the hallway. "It might be a good time to put him on a boat."

"Yes, today *is* the day," I said loud enough for those with weak batteries in their hearing aids to hear. "He'll be on a plane in an hour and on the ship tomorrow afternoon."

"That was cutting it a little close," exclaimed Bea, also louder than normal. "I'm certainly glad he's well enough to make the trip."

Angie and Gladys were tableside in an instant.

"Did you say Jimmy is going on a cruise?" asked Angie. "I would have loved to talk to him about the Alaska cruise I took with my daughter. Such an amazing trip. So many shades of white and blue and..."

I spread a slight grin. Enduring her self-centered conversations was going to be necessary to achieve our objective.

Ten minutes later, Angie finished talking to herself, and Gladys stopped saying, "That sounds wonderful."

We now had three weeks to find James a job and a girlfriend.

*   *   *

During the next coffee shop planning session with Ramee and DeAndre, we considered various types of employment that fit Grandpa's personality and skill set. To jump-start our brains, Ramee bought us each a large vanilla latte, the millennial fuel DeAndre needed for his fingers to burn up the keyboard.

"I've got two here," he said. "A retail electronics

corporation and an agriculture company. What's your poison?"

"Grandpa is more of a tech guy than a gardener. Do the electronics."

He typed while he talked. "Does your grandpa have a social media page that I can update to show him as employed?"

Most residents of the Legends had no understanding of social media, but Angie and Gladys were avid users, with their tablets open in the great room almost daily.

"He doesn't do that stuff, so you'll have to set it up. Ramee and I will send links to people on our sites. The trick will be to get all this on his social media while making it look like it's been there for a long time. A page that lists everything as updated today won't get past nosy Angie."

In less than an hour, DeAndre had Grandpa's social media profile complete, including information on a prospective new job at a company called Digitronics Plus 2, where he hoped to start work as soon as he returned from the cruise.

With multiple phases of our plan successfully deployed, I was breathing a sigh of relief when I returned to the Legends—until I saw the violation notice clipped above the peephole.

Chapter 23

Fur Everywhere

AS I NEARED the apartment door, an intermittent beeping told me the smoke detector battery needed to be changed. *Why couldn't it have gone off at three in the morning like a smoke detector is supposed to?*

I read the violation notice. Three sentences curdled my stomach. "Maintenance arrived but was unable to enter. A dog was reported barking inside the unit. Please come by the manager's office to discuss this incident."

The last thing I needed was an appointment with the apartment manager.

When I opened the door, I could hear Moose barking inside the bathroom. He must have panicked when the smoke detector went off and closed the bathroom door behind him, like he had done previously at the Manor. To prevent such incidents, I usually closed the bathroom door whenever I left the apartment—something I had evidently forgotten to do.

My stomach dropped to my knees when I let Moose out. In his frenzied panic, he had shredded the rugs, eaten the tube of toothpaste, and destroyed the shower curtain.

At some point in his struggle, he had tangled with the toilet paper, making the room look much like a high school prank that I might have been involved in some years ago.

Ugh.

He had created a mess that couldn't be put off, given the impending meeting with the manager, who would likely want immediate access to replace the battery in the smoke detector, which was beginning to irritate me as much as it did Moose.

I plopped down in the pile of paper and grabbed a handful to wipe my tears. Moose panted from the doorway but refused to enter, though his minty-fresh breath wafted into the room.

"This mess isn't going to clean itself," I said with pursed lips, followed by a grunt directed at yet another phrase that sounded so much like Grandpa.

I gathered the torn rugs and the shredded toilet paper. When I reached for the wastebasket I noticed deep scratches all the way up the back side of the door to the height of a scared black dog standing on his hind legs trying to free himself from the confines of a small room. Hair on the floor, grime along the edge of the tub, and brown crust around the faucet gave me a similar urge to flee.

This apartment was brand new. Grandpa had kept it spotless, until... My eyes followed a trail of fur out the door, down the hall, and into the living room. Dog hair coated every inch of the baseboard, and tufts of black dotted the carpet throughout the entire apartment.

When was the last time I cleaned the bathroom? When was the last time I cleaned anything?

I moved to the edge of the tub and sighed. Keeping Grandpa alive in the minds of the residents had taken so much effort that I'd neglected everything else, especially cleaning, which was never my favorite chore.

Moose pushed his wet nose into my lap, sensing my

dispirited state. The poor little guy must have been scared out of his mind, locked in the bathroom with the smoke detector beeping while Ramee was treating DeAndre and me to a latte—a *free* freakin' latte.

I cleaned the tub and scrubbed the floor, sink, and toilet, then stood in the doorway to look over the effort. Not a bad day's work. A glance down the hall at the clock on the microwave revealed the cleaning had taken a mere twenty minutes.

Fixing the chipped tile in the shower and painting the back side of the door would have to be done later because the warden was awaiting my presence. Though Ms. Glass was long gone, I had no desire to meet another set of pursed, leathery lips and had successfully avoided the manager for weeks. In fact, I had steered so far away from the office area since Grandpa's accident that the young Spanish lady who greeted me with big brown eyes and a friendly smile caught me by surprise.

"*Natalie?*" she said in an excited, heavily accented voice. "From St. John?"

"Estrella!" The last thing I expected in the manager's office was a friendly face. "I didn't recognize you. How have you been?"

"I have been well, *gracias*. It is wonderful to work here at the Legends."

Estrella Contreras and her aunt were at the church almost as often as I was. I had met them last year during one of the parishioner support sessions where my job was to translate government forms and other documents for people who need a little help. For Estrella, my translation was more for insurance than necessity, because she was fluent enough to read and comprehend everything on her own. Through my contacts in the congregation, I had sought out jobs for both of them.

"I had no idea they placed you here. That's wonderful. How is your aunt?"

"She is fine since we no longer worry about rent with our new jobs. It is all because of you."

I squared my shoulders, but slumped them back quickly as I recalled something about not being prideful. "I'm just part of the team."

"Let me get Mr. Brooks. You will like him. He is a very nice man." She disappeared in the back.

Him? I thought apartment managers were all snippy ladies who studied contractual clauses just to harass tenants. Not that it mattered; I wasn't going to like any manager today, even if he was nice. Moose being found inside the apartment was the nightmare I had tried so hard to avoid, and if they conducted any inspection when they fixed the smoke detector, the bathroom and stains on the carpet would be a *dead* giveaway that I was living in the unit.

While I waited for Estrella to return, I leaned against the desk and watched one maintenance man put Halloween decorations up in the window while another placed an unopened Christmas tree box in the lobby. Overlapping holiday themes was normal to me, but Grandpa had told me of a time when the holidays were separate and distinct. A time when Christmas was celebrated for what it was, the birth of our Lord.

The maintenance man stacked a few fake presents on top of the boxed tree. The presents reminded me of the gifts under Grandpa's tree last year. I had counted them multiple times, and after church on Christmas morning, I tore into them like an overanxious five-year-old. Twenty presents for me, two for him. Two! A shirt and a coffee cup. *Had I really been that cheap? That thoughtless?*

Estrella returned with a thirtyish, dark-haired man who was about six feet tall. His lightly puffed cheeks accentuated a pear-shaped body that hinted of someone comfortable in an office chair. I had seen this man around the complex, usually going into or coming out of the underground garage, and had assumed he was a son or nephew of one of the residents because of how friendly and animated he was in conversations I had observed. It now occurred to me that most of those conversations had been with the yard workers or other staff who also frequented the garage, where landscape equipment was stored in the maintenance rooms.

"Ms. Thomas, I'm Wayne, Wayne Brooks," he said in the least threatening voice I'd ever heard from an apartment manager. "Please, come on back."

I followed slowly, still more than a little fearful about what lurked in the new warden's office.

"So, you're a friend of Estrella," he said, impressing me with an expertly rolled "R."

"Um, I've known her for a while."

"I heard you mention working at the church, right? That's so great. I've often thought about volunteering, but I'm not sure I have the time."

I didn't have the time either, but Grandpa found it for me.

I described my volunteer efforts, which had somehow expanded over the years, and then I tossed in a compliment on his Spanish pronunciation.

Mr. Brooks was a welcome change from what I was used to with regard to overseers of tenants, who, like me, were sometimes less than compliant. He had a genuine pleasantness in his voice, almost as though he liked his residents, unlike my past experience with Ms. Ass.

"About this letter," he said, holding up his copy. "I expected Mr. Thomas to stop by."

"He's on a cruise," I replied with no hesitation. Lying about the apartment and Grandpa had become almost second nature. "I'm taking care of things while he's gone."

He flipped through Grandpa's contract then looked up. "I'd like to meet James when he gets back. Part of the job is getting to know all my residents."

Well, you just got to know one of them pretty good.

"Can you send him over when he returns? Until then, of course, we need to get into the unit to change the battery in the smoke detector. Is there a convenient time we could come by? This afternoon would be best. We try and replace batteries within a day of being notified."

"Um. Yeah, that would be great."

"Well, okay then. I'll have maintenance stop by within the hour."

I thanked Estrella and made a hasty exit to put distance between me and the office before the unusually nice manager remembered the canine issue in the note.

Moose had destroyed the bathroom, probably howled because he couldn't get out, and barked at maintenance when they tried to get in. At the Manor, Ms. Ass would have fined me and lectured me on every broken rule. Mr. Brooks had basically said, "No problem. We'll come right over."

Another of Grandpa's sayings rang in my ear as I entered the apartment: *"It's never good to press your luck."* A barking dog was one thing, but more than just the carpet needed to be cleaned. I grabbed a bath towel and crawled over the kitchen floor, swooping up everything from green beans to coffee grounds to black fur. I shook the towel over the balcony and dashed back to the bedroom, where I stripped the fur-coated comforter and put it into the washing machine. Back on my hands and knees, I picked the largest clumps of fur off the carpet, then vacuumed twice while alternating between desperate requests for help from above and uttering not so nice words at the beige carpet that couldn't conceal black in the dark. If I could get through this maintenance visit unscathed, I might have to accept Father Diamond's invitation to be a lector at Sunday service.

After the maintenance man replaced the batteries in each smoke detector—the bathroom door closed during that activity—I finally had time to take a breath and admire the clean apartment. With Bea babysitting Moose, the entire unnerving process had turned out to be no big deal, and as an added benefit, the apartment was spotless.

Next on the to-do list was repairing the bathroom. I took a picture of the tile pieces that had been damaged when the shower rod fell, then cut a small sample of paint from the wall for the paint associate at the hardware store to digitally match the color—another process with which I was all too familiar. Grandpa had taught me that preparation was half of any job, and it began before the shopping. A mere twenty minutes inside the hardware store once again proved him right.

"Hi, Angie," I said as pleasantly as possible, standing in the hallway an hour later with a hardware store bag dangling from one hand and a gallon of paint dangling from the other.

"Are you and James making repairs? Surprising, considering the apartment is brand new."

"We're adding a skylight."

"A *what?*" she asked as the door closed.

An hour later, the bathroom looked as good as new—well, it looked good enough.

Chapter 24

New to the Legends

WITH GRANDPA ENJOYING the sun and sand of the Caribbean, a nonthreatening manager in the apartment office, and Angie having been quiet for a few days, life at the Legends was becoming routine. Envious residents drooled over carefully photo-shopped pictures of Jimmy windsurfing the tropical islands and hiking forested paths. In comment fields, Grandpa frequently asked how I was doing and thanked me for taking care of the apartment. Words that warmed my soul, though I knew they were posted by DeAndre. Further stress relief came from conversations with Estrella in which I learned that all of the apartment costs, including rent and maintenance fees, had been paid three years in advance. As great as that sounded, I would be happy to pull off the charade for another three months.

A downside to knowing the apartment costs were covered was a further lack of enthusiasm for that second job, but luckily, work had picked up enough that I was back to half-time, which was enough to cover utilities and food provided I cut out all weekend splurges and most lattes.

Still, I needed to get back to full-time employment if I had any hope of saving enough money to get a place of my own and forever shed the feeling that Angie was stalking me, ready to pounce the second I let my guard down.

* * *

Friday morning, Bea was engaged in a lively conversation with three ladies I hadn't seen before. She motioned me over and introduced me to Jamie, Janie, and Jane, friends she had known for sixty years who had just moved into the Legends.

"Did I hear sixty?" asked one of the Js, a hand cupped to her ear. "It's been longer than that, Bea, but if we get any more specific, she'll figure out our age."

I glanced around the room. "At this place, I just round to the nearest hundred."

"Oh, we've got a live one," said the second J. "You don't look much beyond puberty. How'd you get in the front door, dear?"

I held up my keys. "I'm older than I look."

"Wish I could still say that," replied a J.

"And a smart one too," said the tallest of the Js, though she was still shorter than Bea. "Natalie, right? Is there a special man in your life?"

Why is everyone in the complex more interested in my love life than I am?

"Silence means no, Janie," said either Jamie or Jane in a more reserved voice. "Nothing to be ashamed of, dear."

"I'm not ashamed of not having a boyfriend. I have them all the time. Just not right now."

"Hmmm," hummed the elderly trio.

"I have a great-grandson who lives up north," said a J. "He'll be visiting next week. Let's get you two together."

"My nephew's boy lives much closer," said another. "And he's been looking for a friend."

Having been helped in the dating department by

Grandpa on way too many occasions, I needed to stop this ambush in its tracks. I held my palm up. "Hold on now. I've got this covered."

"Okay, dear. But if we don't see a young man around here soon, we'll introduce you to some quality candidates."

Giggles all around, including Bea.

"I'm on the second floor, west side," I said, pushing the conversation in a different direction. "Which units are you in?"

"We have the three-bedroom across from Bea. Top floor."

Impressive. "Well, please keep the noise down; some of us kids need to be in bed at a decent hour."

The J to my right patted my wrist. "Now that we know children are in the building, we'll be more careful."

The old ladies giggled like schoolgirls, with Bea enjoying every moment. Through a mostly jovial discussion, they filled me in on their lifelong friendship. Jamie and Janie were sisters who had lived across the street from Bea and two doors down from Jane when they were in primary school together, until Bea's family moved to London. Jamie and Janie graduated college with business degrees and opened a scrapbooking store that they ran together until recently, when they sold it and retired.

They recalled life events in vivid detail, walking through decades as though they were years and years as though they were days. Each had outlived her husband, a part of the conversation that slowed, but just a little. Shortly after Jamie's husband passed away, they decided to get an apartment together, and Bea suggested the Legends.

"Are you texting while we're talking?" I asked one of the Js, who had her phone out. Actually, they all had their phones out.

"Heavens no," exclaimed the J. "That would be rude. I'm posting this conversation on Post Mortem."

She held her phone up, displaying a picture of me, Bea, and the J on my left. She had modified the picture by sketching my finger picking my nose and Bea's hand covering her mouth.

I shook my head and grinned. "I'm not going to lie; that's pretty cool. But what's Post Mortem? I post to a lot of sites but haven't heard of that one."

Giggles again.

"I'll bet nobody else in this room could modify a picture like that."

"You might be surprised," said the J to my left.

"Seriously, I spent an hour trying to explain Craigslist a few weeks ago."

Two Js looked at me curiously. "Is he the man in your life, dear?" They burst out laughing.

Eventually the conversation slowed because they needed to go shopping. I offered to go with them.

"Should I pull my car around to the front?" I asked.

"We'd prefer to walk."

Uh-oh.

A few minutes later, I met the Js out front—each sitting on a scooter.

Everyone at the Legends who rode a scooter insisted they were going for a walk; some of them hadn't *walked* in years. But a quick look at the Js' scooters told me this would be no ordinary outing. The scooters were snow white, each with a brightly colored flame painted on the side. Headlamps, taillights, and rearview mirrors on each side of a center console that displayed battery life and speed made the scooters look more like tricked-out Harleys than senior citizen conveyances. A license plate on each identified the owner's name and quite possibly made the scooters street legal.

Jamie adjusted her rather plump figure in the seat and smiled proudly. "Our new rides. They came in last week."

Gwen had driven her turtle-mobile at the slowest possible speed and only on the sidewalk. With these scooters, I half expected the roar of an angry engine when the Js throttled back, but the senior citizen crotch rockets jumped forward in silence, and the ladies zoomed down the drive and into the street.

Three abreast, they turned in unison and headed toward the shopping center, zigzagging in a choreographed serpentine movement. I stayed on the sidewalk half walking and half jogging. They paused briefly in the store entry to allow me to catch up, but as soon as I grabbed a cart, they hit the light-speed button and blasted into the store. Jamie turned to the right and Janie turned to the left, crossing each other with millimeters to spare. Jane shot the gap between them in a move that would rival a Blue Angels pilot.

Janie appeared safe in produce, and Jane could do little damage in the meat department, so I tracked down Jamie. Walking briskly and trying to appear as normal as possible, I spotted her in the juice aisle. The plump woman, a few inches shorter than me, was standing on her scooter seat—reaching for a bottle of juice on the top shelf. I arrived just in time to catch the bottle as it fell.

"Had it under control, dear."

"Uh-huh."

"Why on earth do they put those so high that it takes a giant to reach?"

We were interrupted by canned goods crashing to the floor an aisle over. Likely an encounter with one of my kids. Sure enough, some store manager thought that stacking cans of diced tomatoes in the aisle, next to a shelf full of diced tomatoes, was a good idea. While the cans completed their circular dance, the taillight of a white scooter turned left at the end of the aisle.

I was chasing the renegade scooter when Janie caught up to me on my left, dumped a handful of items into the cart, and scooted off. Jane zipped up on the other side and dropped more items into the cart. I looked down the next two aisles, but Jamie had disappeared. I turned back around, and Jane was gone. A glance at the ceiling mirrors showed all three heading to the pharmacy.

I made my way to the three scooters, which were lined up in front of the antiseptic creams.

"I don't remember what the doctor recommended, just pick one," said Jamie to Janie.

"But I forgot my glasses," said Jane. "Can you be a dear and read this?" She handed me a tube of topical ointment. "Does it say anything about pus? How long does it last? Does it require an applicator? Those can be so messy, you know."

"Does it help with odor?" asked Janie. "Really bad odor."

"Don't forget oozing and swelling," added Jamie.

"Maybe you should see where I need to apply it." Jane thrust her foot forward. "Would you be a dear and pull off my sock?"

"But don't touch anything," warned Jamie. "It's a little contagious."

A little contagious?

My head snapped back. No freakin' way was I pulling this lady's shoe off to examine an oozing foot. My facial expression must have conveyed my thoughts, because the ladies laughed so hard they nearly fell from their scooters.

"There's nothing wrong with my feet, dear. We're just having some fun. Hope you don't mind."

I was surrounded by eighty-year-old children.

"Just *kidding?*" I said in the most serious voice I could muster. I turned on real tears. "My aunt died of necrosis last year...It started in her foot, and..."

Silence.

"We didn't know. We would have never..."

I rocked my head. "Seriously, girls, if you want to play on the varsity team, you're going to have to do better than that."

Chapter 25

Exodus from the Great Room

WITH SEVEN DOLLARS in my wallet and slightly less on my debit card, I was rather proud of myself for declining Ramee's request to meet for lattes, but a hot coffee sounded good, and with Grandpa returning from his cruise today, I needed to work out some last-minute details downstairs.

I peeked out the doorway to an empty hall, then turned back to Moose. *Shhhh.* "I'll be back in a little while." Ever since the smoke detector incident, I'd been extra cautious.

I sat with Bea and discussed tag-teaming our approach to disclosing information regarding the cruise. While we were together, multiple residents came to the table to let me know they could hardly wait to see Jimmy when he returned.

I had come to realize many Legends residents did not venture far from the complex, and thus they tended to live vicariously through the exploits of their neighbors. This had lent an air of genuine excitement to any discussions about Grandpa's cruise, the residents buzzing as much as if they had taken the trip themselves.

Bea handed me some actual cruise brochures she had printed. "When the room clears after lunch, place these on a few tables. Return to the room just before four o'clock. That will give you just enough time to explain that James is sunburned and tired before the residents leave for dinner."

The only thing guaranteed to pull this group away from good gossip was a buffet line, making Bea's timing brilliant. Exodus from the great room began precisely at four o'clock, when the flock of white-haired residents migrated down the street to the senior discount buffet at a nearby restaurant.

"The less time I spend talking, the better. We've been planning this for weeks, and I'm still not sure my emotions will hold out."

"You'll do fine, dear. Draw on your memories. It will be good for you."

*   *   *

I kicked off the conversation by telling everyone that Grandpa had enjoyed the trip but was now tired, sunburned, and sleeping. The fact that he wouldn't be coming down to personally share his adventure didn't faze the surrounding seniors. They quickly began talking among themselves about trips they had made to the islands, revisiting their own memories, and answering one another's questions. Our plan was coming together nicely.

"It was a three-week cruise," I said to Millie when I sensed a slight lull, though that might have simply been the afternoon fatigue that often settled on the room. "He just got back today."

Of course, everyone already knew the cruise was for three weeks because Grandpa had been the talk of the Legends since we put him on the fake boat. I then mentioned a few activities featured in the brochure and tossed in random details to personalize it.

"He said the ocean views were beautiful, but three weeks was a little more beauty than he needed. You know Grandpa, he likes to get out and move around. That's why he's always doing things like hiking and fishing and kayaking."

I inhaled a deep breath to allow the bitterness of the previous sentence to fade. *Kayaking.* The whole reason I was having this fake conversation about a fake trip was that Grandpa was gone. Lost on the Saint Croix.

"St. Thomas was his favorite. The ship stayed in port for two days, which gave him time to see the island and take the ferry to St. John."

"That's a national park, you know," came a high-pitched voice from a resident listening in at the next table.

Louis joined the group but remained standing, positioned for a quick exit. Gladys took a chair on the other side, the second time I had seen her in the last few days without Angie anchored to her hip. The table to my left was also full, all ears turned my way. Orval was at the window, ten feet from the nearest person, chatting up a storm.

I glanced at the time. Either the clock was ticking slower than normal, or residents were delaying dinner plans to talk about a trip that had never occurred—my money was on the clock.

"Thank you for the update," said PJ. "Please tell James we'll see him in the morning." The movement of PJ and Louis leaving the room caused a wave of chairs to shift backward and walkers to shift forward as oxygen tanks hissed out the door. Some residents continued to describe their own exploits on the way out. "The water is so salty"; "Chickens are everywhere"; and my favorite, "We were there in seventy-two," reminded me these people had lived full lives.

Bea and I stepped outside, where the breeze carried a late summer chill that brought a bristling memory of my own plunge into the Saint Croix.

"How are you doing?" she asked as we sat together on Thelma's bench.

"I'm good, I think. A lot of people were involved in the conversation by the time they left."

"Yes, but how are *you* doing? You've been so preoccupied with the arrangements that I fear you may not have taken time for yourself."

"It's been a lot of work, but staying busy helps the days pass, and that's what I need right now. It gives me time to accept things slowly, if that makes sense."

I then filled her in on my life story. How my parents disappearing in an airplane accident had left me alone, so Grandpa retired to move closer to me. I talked about parts of my life that I seldom shared because it was too painful to revisit those times. It felt good to add another friend to my short list of confidants.

After the heartfelt conversation, I walked Moose out the back door, and we took our time in the crisp air, knowing that residents would be stuffing themselves at the buffet for another half hour. From the tall grass along the tracks, I glanced back at the door. Angie's glare from the stoop forced us to cross the parking lot to the Manor and hang out there until she grew tired of stalking.

Chapter 26

Lutefisk

WITH ANGIE SEEMINGLY watching my every move, my efforts to mislead residents into believing that Grandpa was asleep, had just left, or was "around here somewhere" had become more difficult. She frequently argued with me in the hall, claiming that she hadn't seen him leave, that his car was still in the garage, or that she had knocked loud enough to wake the dead, but he hadn't come to the door. What little success I had with the lady came from staying out of her sight.

As hard as I tried to lie low, some encounters at the Legends were fate. I returned from the grocery store with a small bag of toiletries and avoided Angie all the way to the elevator—only to run into Louis.

He placed his hands on his waist and looked down at me with his usual smile. "Just knocked on your door to invite you and James up for dinner."

Ugh. "Um, what did Grandpa say?"

"No answer." He cocked his head and stretched out the next word. "*Again.*"

Lying to Louis was not pleasant. "Um, I can ask him

when he gets back, but I don't know if that will be in time for dinner."

"Well, little lady, you find him and bring him up to our place at four-thirty. I'm making my Norwegian specialty."

Four-thirty? My lunch hasn't settled by four-thirty.

"Ooh, I don't think I'll be seeing him that soon. My friends are over at the Manor waiting for me. I'm supposed to—"

"Bring 'em along. Can't have too many friends around at times like this."

* * *

"Change of plans," I said to Ramee and DeAndre when they arrived. "We've been invited to Louis and PJ's apartment for dinner. We'll have to do burgers next week."

"Dang, girl, I was already tasting a thick Juicy Lucy. Biting into a hot fat burger with all that cheese oozing out." DeAndre held his hands to his mouth and devoured an imaginary burger. "Even skipped lunch so I could order the big one."

I was compelled to question the honesty of that statement. "You *never* skip lunch."

"Maybe I ate a little." DeAndre rocked his head in disappointment. "That dude better be making something with mounds of meat."

"He said it's his specialty." I glanced at the time. "Let's go. I could sure use some help tonight. I'm not gonna lie; it's hard handling all these fake conversations by myself."

"Hang in there," said Ramee. "We can do this."

I took a deep yoga breath as we stepped into the elevator, then pushed the third-floor button. Moments later, the door opened to an acrid aroma that smacked us in the face.

"Whoa!" DeAndre pulled his T-shirt over his mouth and nose. "That smell is so bad it's gonna neutralize somebody's

Viagra. It's even worse than the little guy downstairs who blasted me with his nuclear halitosis."

I inhaled a mouthful of the repulsive odor. "Nuclear halitosis?"

"Old-man breath. Everyone around here has it, even the ladies, and until *right now*, I thought it was the nastiest smell in the world."

"It's not that bad," I lied. "The garbage chute is probably stuck open."

Farther down the hall, I began to change my opinion. "This is worse than that urine smell at the Golden Years complex."

"You smelled *urine* in those halls?" DeAndre raised an eyebrow. "Tell me again why we're doin' all this work to keep you here."

Our olfactory senses had almost acclimated to the obnoxious odor by the time I knocked on the Hansen's door.

"Come in, come in," said Patti Jane. "Hello, Ramee, DeAndre. We're glad you could join us."

Hopes of getting away from the stink vanished when we stepped inside and found the rotten smell originating from the stove, where Louis offered a boisterous "Hello."

"Ah, hell no," whispered DeAndre.

"Have a seat. Have a seat," said Patti Jane. "Dinner will be ready any minute."

Louis wiped a sweaty brow. "Did you find James? I want to talk to him about this new sound system we got the other day. He's smart about those things. Got it hooked up, but now the television gives us an echo. Course, that could just be in my head." He knocked knuckles to his head.

"He won't be able to make it," said Ramee.

"I'll look at it." DeAndre went over to the sound bar and started tracing the wires from one unit to the next.

"These things are a lot more complicated than they need to be."

Patti Jane placed salt and pepper shakers on the table, then sat next to Ramee. "James sure stays busy. I don't know how that man does it."

I hated to mislead two of my favorite people at the Legends, but with so much at stake, I didn't have any options. "That's Grandpa."

Ramee drew her head back. *Ah...ah...tsit.* "Excuse me," she said from behind a puffy white tissue that magically appeared in front of her nose, courtesy of Patti Jane.

"I'll make you some tea," said Patti Jane, the palm of her hand already resting on Ramee's forehead. "No fever. Maybe you have a cold. You can't take any chances, dear."

"I'm fine, really." Ramee lowered the tissue to find a lozenge on the table. "I think it was the pepper."

Louis set a cup of tea next to Ramee while PJ wrapped a scarf around her neck and said, "There you go now."

Ramee took one sip and choked. She took a second, longer sip and spread a wide smile.

"Hot toddy," said PJ. "The first sip will knock you back a little if you're not expecting it."

"What's a hot—" I started to ask.

"*Fixed it.*" DeAndre stood in front of the stereo. "You had the surround-sound volume set too high and the woofer too low."

"Woofer?" Louis chuckled. "We haven't had a dog in years."

Patti Jane rolled her eyes. "Thank you, young man. That's been driving him batty, and when Louis isn't satisfied, he tinkers. Been on his knees in front of that unit every day."

DeAndre reached for a frame atop the entertainment center. "Hey, were you really in the Olympics?" He returned to the table with a glass-encased frame, a bronze medal inside.

"Louis won that for canoeing in the 1964 Olympics," said Patti Jane. She squared her shoulders and donned a proud smile. "He was such a handsome man back then."

Louis came up behind his wife and chuckled. "That's her way of saying that I'm not so handsome now, dontcha know."

He put a large hand on Patti Jane's shoulder and gave her a squeeze.

"You *really know how to canoe*? I thought you were kidding."

"This old man raced canoes all his life. Juniors, nationals, Olympics, even the senior circuit. Hung up his paddle when he turned sixty-five."

"It was time, dear." He gave her another squeeze then turned back to the stove, hopefully to kill or dispose of whatever was destroying our nostrils.

As I stared in awe at the medal, I recalled Louis mentioning that he "got out on the water a bit." I had blown him off when he warned me to be careful, treating him like every other old guy who gave me advice. I was certain he was being overly cautious, because he had *never* talked about canoeing. In fact, I now realized he seldom talked about himself at all. He kidded Patti Jane a lot, but always in a positive way that built *her* life stories up, not his own. I glanced at the big man in an apron standing at the stove. As an Olympic medalist, he could be the hero of the great room, but he let her have the attention and even directed it her way, which made his humble "it was time" take on even more meaning.

"I've gone by James' apartment a dozen times," said Louis. He set a plate for each of us, then plated two more for himself and Patti Jane. "Thought he might enjoy my specialty."

I stared at the plate, afraid to take my eyes off of the entrée. "It's so...shiny."

The boiled potatoes and a rolled piece of flatbread appeared edible, but the pile of goop that glistened in the light and wobbled when Louis bumped the table had my full attention. The specimen resembled a translucent version of the pile of butterscotch cookies Moose had left not long ago—but his pile smelled better.

"*Lutefisk.*" Louis explained the dish was a Norwegian specialty.

"Cool," I offered with absolutely no conviction.

DeAndre whispered to Ramee, "Do I use a spoon or a fork?" He looked at Louis. "This must be why you never see a fat Norwegian."

"*Ah*, you're the funny one. Takes some getting used to. Dip the fish in the butter and cream sauce."

Louis forked a pile of glistening goop and dipped it into the melted butter then the cream. He stuffed the dripping morsel into his mouth, closed his eyes, and shared a satisfied smile.

Another whisper from DeAndre. "Can I just eat the butter and cream sauce?"

"It's fermented codfish," said Louis. He tapped the flatbread with his fork. "And the lefse here is a potato bread."

The three of us barely heard him, each strategizing an approach to the meal. Ramee was first to poke the putrid pile. It wobbled in response.

With Louis being so proud of his dish, I was willing to try a small bite. I didn't want to let him down; after all, I would be letting him down soon enough. The glob couldn't taste as bad as it looked and smelled. I dug out a tiny piece of jelly-textured glossy goop and dunked it into the cream and butter. I slipped the dripping glop into my mouth and swallowed fast. It wasn't *that* bad.

Patti Jane watched as we struggled. "It's not my favorite

dish either, but Louis only makes it once a year, so I can endure."

Louis squared his shoulders. "I usually serve it with meatballs."

DeAndre's eyes perked.

"But special for you, I made the lefse. Very Norwegian."

"Meatballs," muttered DeAndre. "You passed on meatballs for *potato* bread."

Louis didn't pick up on DeAndre's disappointment. "Yes, sir. Wanted my guests to enjoy the full tradition of the meal."

After dinner, I insisted on helping with the dishes, which brought a more-than-curious look from Ramee, who had never seen my sink at the Manor empty of dirty dishware.

"Who's up for gin?" asked Louis when the last clean cup was placed in the cupboard.

"Uh, I think we need to go," said DeAndre. "Ramee and I need to get back to...uh...to get back." He whispered to me, "If we start drinking gin, he's gonna put more of that fish on the table."

Louis set a deck of cards on the counter. "Maybe next time."

When the door closed, Patti Jane gripped Louis' hand. "She'll tell us when she's ready."

*   *   *

Back inside the elevator, Ramee held her hand to her forehead. "PJ went a little overboard with the whole 'cold' thing. I had one little sniffle. My head's not even warm."

"That lady must have some kind of medical utility belt." DeAndre hiked his pants up and pretended to pull products rapidly from a make-believe utility belt. "Poppin' tissues and cough drops out of nowhere. Good thing your forehead wasn't warm, or she would've slipped a rectal thermometer in before you even noticed."

"I would have figured that out pretty quick, but one more hot toddy and I might not have minded."

"You're not even old enough to drink those," I said.

"I'm the same age as you are."

"That makes us legal for regular stuff, but I think you need to be seventy-five to drink a hot toddy."

"Hot toddy or not," said DeAndre, "you should have taken her up on the chicken soup she offered for your cold."

"*No!* Nothing chicken." I then filled my friends in on my first introduction to Louis and Patti Jane.

Chapter 27

An Imaginary Friend

SOME THINGS I found myself doing to misdirect and mislead residents felt silly, like putting notes on Grandpa's door. "Came by to say hi, but you weren't here." "Catch you later." "Sorry you're not feeling well. I left soup in the refrigerator." Little phrases with big letters for seniors wandering the hall without their reading glasses. On occasion, I would stand in the parking lot of the Manor and wave toward the Legends in a feeble attempt to indicate a hello or goodbye to Grandpa. More often, I would wave from the side door at the Legends and yell loud enough for third-floor, hearing-impaired residents to eavesdrop, "See you later, Grandpa," or "Don't worry, I'll take care of it." On one of those occasions, I turned around to find Thelma standing silently behind me, an unlit cigarette in her mouth.

"When I was a child, I had an imaginary friend." She lit the cigarette and left a trail of smoke in her wake as she tromped across the lawn. The blades of grass in October were much slower to recover than they were in the summer. Much like me, they had stood strong and tall all year but had finally succumbed to the changing season.

* * *

Through the great room window Bea and I watched Thelma sitting outside in the cold smoking a cigarette and tapping a small electronic Scrabble board. Louis and Patti Jane were sitting in the center of the room filling pillboxes with Glen and Millie. They motioned for us to join them.

"You *can't* be serious," said Glen with enough surprise in his voice that it caught my attention.

"As the day is long," replied Louis. "PJ pulled the plug. It's what her mom wanted, dontcha know."

"Mother insisted she did *not* want to be on life support," said Patti Jane. "She didn't like hospitals at all and hated needles. It was all I could do to get her to have the surgery in the first place. The doctor had told us the bypass was routine and could give her another ten years."

"That's what they told me when I had mine," said Glen, dressed in the usual tan velour, his teeth intact. "*Fifteen* years ago. Scares me to death every time I see my cardiologist. Someday he'll realize I'm five years past due." He raised his eyebrows. "Might try to collect."

He lifted a handkerchief to his nose and blew so hard the breeze dusted my cheek. Bile crawled up my throat.

"The surgery went fine," continued Patti Jane. "But an hour later, something happened. Lights flashed and there were lots of beeps and buzzes. People were moving in and out so fast. Then the doctor came out and said she wasn't going to make it. We waited an extra day, but there was no improvement."

Louis nodded solemnly. "Situations like that help us appreciate all that we have. They also make for very difficult decisions."

"To this day, that was the hardest thing I've ever done."

PJ paused for a moment while Bea and I wiped our eyes; then she looked straight at me and raised her eyebrows.

"Boy was she ever mad at me! Ranting and raving. '*How dare you pull the plug?*' We still don't know what the doctors did, but Mother came out of it."

Louis spread a large grin. "She tore up that do-not-resuscitate form and lived another twenty years."

"When did we do our DNRs?" asked PJ.

"When? Let's see, it was after your mom's bypass. Then she started having chest trouble again the year they did my prostate, right? Had her next heart attack when I had that cyst removed from my backside." He leaned into Patti Jane. "We were both a little scared on that one. You had your foot wrapped when she went in for the second bypass, so it had to be the year your bunion was removed."

The way Louis recalled events based on the year various medical procedures had been performed was fascinating, even though words like "cyst" and "bunion" still turned my stomach a little bit.

"Well, if it comes to pulling a plug," continued PJ, "I'm leaving that up to Louis with no instruction from me." She tossed a loving glare at the big man. "Just you know, mister, if you pull too soon, I *will* come back and haunt you."

"I suppose it's time I sign something for my cardiologist," said Millie, the tiniest woman in the complex. Based on her outfit, she clearly shopped at the same department store as Glen but probably in the children's section.

"Does everyone here have a cardiologist?" I asked, feeling like an outsider to the club. "When am I supposed to get mine?"

Louis bellowed a laugh, "It'll be a long time before you need a cardiologist, little lady. Gotta pass through a lot more troubles before the heart doc comes around. There's the diabetes, the blood pressure, cholesterol, gout, and goiter long before the chest gives out."

"Don't scare the poor girl." PJ patted the back of his

hand. "Those were all your own fault, just like your knee—and nobody gets a goiter anymore."

"Seems like a lot of trips to the doctor," I said while tapping "goiter" into my phone and grimacing at the corresponding pictures. "Grandpa hurt his knee once, but he's never had any serious medical issues."

A hush settled over the table.

Chapter 28

Ground Zero

A FEW DAYS later, I plopped my not-quite-awake body down next to a window in the great room that was covered with frosted snowflake designs courtesy of the frozen dawn. The Anders were sitting next to me at their regular table, where she was reading the morning paper to her husband. I was only half listening, much like I used to do in some of my college classes.

She finished reading about the upcoming Gophers game with Wisconsin and had moved on to another article when Mr. Anders asked, "Who do the Gophers play today?"

"They play Wisconsin, dear. Should be a good game."

"Good game," he repeated softly. "Good game."

Mrs. Anders then read the weather section, another oddity of the Legends that bothered me. Residents could talk about the weather all day long. A fascination that even Grandpa had shared.

Mr. Anders asked again, "Who do the Gophers play today?"

"They play Wisconsin. Should be a good game, dear," she replied as though it were the first time he had asked.

I returned with a fresh coffee and heard Mrs. Anders reading the same headline she had read when I first sat down.

"Who do the Gophers play today?"

"They play Wisconsin, dear. Starts at two o'clock."

From the looks in their eyes, I wasn't sure if he wasn't paying attention to her or if she was so caught up in the paper that she didn't realize he was asking the same question repeatedly.

I made my way to Bea's table. "What's the deal with Mr. Anders? His wife reads the paper to him, but he doesn't even listen. He keeps asking her the same questions over and over. I can't tell if he's ignoring her or she's ignoring him."

"It's no secret, Natalie, though Edna seldom discusses her burden. Carl had Alzheimer's well before they arrived at the Legends. Edna moved him here because they can walk across the street to the doctor and the grocery store." She shook her head slowly. "It's a hard life taking care of an Alzheimer's husband."

I quietly mulled over her words before going back to the Anders' table.

"Mrs. Anders, Mr. Anders, how are you this morning?"

"We're fine, Natalie, thank you. How is your grandfather?"

I offered what had become my standard reply, "Grandpa is Grandpa," then pulled a chair out and sat down. "Mrs. Anders, I would be happy to sit with Mr. Anders if you ever want a little time to yourself. You know, even if you just want to nap or go to the store or something. I have some extra time."

Time that Grandpa, Louis, and a couple of other residents had suggested would be better spent at a second job. Louis had badgered me enough lately that I had started applying for positions, but my heart wasn't really in it.

"Thank you, dear." She followed his gaze out the window. "Carl is such a strong man. He spent his life in construction. He could do anything, build anything, fix anything." She drew in a deep breath and exhaled slowly, her eyes still fixed in the same direction as his. "One day he started to forget things. First his keys or a tie for church or his wallet when we went to dinner. I didn't notice the pattern…until things went bad. Carl answered the phone one day and talked for five minutes. Then he handed me the receiver and said he didn't know who it was." She paused for a long moment. "It was our neighbor who had lived next door to us for thirty years."

Once again, life at the Legends had put me in a position to which I could not relate. Edna was talking about Carl as though he wasn't even there and sharing much more detail about his medical condition than I needed to hear.

"I would like to walk to the grocery store," she said. "The air would do me good."

Twenty minutes later, I was inside the Anders' apartment. Edna showed me to the bathroom and explained what to do if Carl needed to go. Residents often treated me like a four-year-old, but she was the first to tell me where the bathroom was in a one-bedroom unit. She had also laid out a set of clean clothes on the bed, though she expected he would sit on the couch the entire time she was out. Way too much information from somebody who would only be gone for thirty minutes.

I sensed an interesting combination of stress and relief as she closed the door on her way out. A second later, she opened it.

"Forgot my purse." She grabbed the bag and was gone.

Her mantel clock dinged once to announce nine-thirty. Edna had insisted she would be back in thirty minutes, though I suggested she take advantage of the break and maybe have a pastry in the bakery.

"*Agua frio, por favor*," said Carl, catching me totally off guard with a request for a glass of water.

Edna had never mentioned that Carl was bilingual.

"Would you like some cold water?" I repeated in Spanish.

"*Si, agua frio, por favor.*"

I went to the kitchen and filled a glass with water and ice. Carl gulped it loudly, as though he had just come indoors from a long day of working in the sun. He set the glass on the end table and stared back out the window in silence.

I sat in the chair and stared with him, forcibly restraining myself from scrolling through the news on my phone. A half hour of boredom would be good for both of us.

A few minutes later, I noticed Carl's tan sweatpants had turned dark brown around the crotch, which immediately explained why Edna had laid out the clean clothes.

I asked if he needed the bathroom, but his glazed eyes didn't even blink. I repeated the request in Spanish, and he shuffled down the hall and stopped at the door. With his right hand on my left arm, we approached the toilet. Only a few minutes earlier, I had thought Edna was providing way too much information—now I wished she would have explained what to do in this particular situation.

Standing in front of the toilet, Carl gripped my arm tightly with one hand and lowered his sweatpants with the other. A saturated adult diaper with an aroma I was much too familiar with fell to the floor. Carl dribbled what remained in his bladder onto his socks.

It appeared we were finished and I might escape the confines of the small room with little more than a wet mess, but Carl didn't need to go number one; after all, he had finished most of that business on the couch. He stood inches from the toilet and crapped all over himself, the floor, and the lower half of my left leg. I squirmed as much as I dared, but he maintained a grip so firm that I could barely shift out of the way.

Ugh. I now had *his* crap on *my* jeans. At least they weren't new. Oddly, it occurred to me while he let out another wet fart that I didn't have any new jeans.

The sour smell burned my nose but didn't turn my stomach quite as badly as previous encounters with the aroma.

Carl shuffled back from the toilet and stood still, as though waiting for something.

Ugh. I figured out what he was waiting for.

On the counter was a container of cleaning wipes with the lid popped open and the stem of the next wipe ready to grab. Next to the wipes was a stack of disposable bags and next to those, a roll of paper towels. Edna had been through this before.

I pulled a handful of wipes and towels and cleaned Carl's backside and legs. Then I sat him down on the toilet with the lid up just in case he had another round loaded in the chamber.

I slipped his pants off and wiped his legs from the calves down—an intimate activity that put my nose right next to ground zero. I wiped the floor, put the used wipes in the disposable bag, and grabbed another wipe in what felt like a much-too-fluid movement for a first-timer.

We shuffled to the bedroom, he naked from the waist down, me with my eyes locked on the ceiling. With considerable effort, exacerbated by my refusal to look, I tugged a clean pair of underwear over his feet and up to his crotch. Then I pulled the clean sweatpants into place. Just when I had the pants secure, I noticed the bag of adult diapers next to a scale at the side of the dresser. Edna had never come across as someone who needed to watch her weight. The bald wig holder staring blankly at me from the dresser bothered me more than the scale.

I removed the clean pants and underwear, tugged a

diaper into place, and finished dressing the man. We shuffled back to the couch, where he took up his normal position, gazing into the abyss far beyond the railroad tracks.

Back in the bathroom, which had retained the smell, I used more wipes to clean the floor and put the discards into the large diaper pail in the corner. I turned on the exhaust fan, opened the door to the deck, and cracked the front door to air out the apartment, following a routine I had perfected from experience with Moose and his "incidents." I loaded the dirty clothes into the washer, scrubbed my hands so hard the skin nearly came off, and went back to sit with Carl.

The amount of work I had just completed dwarfed any effort I had put into cleaning Grandpa's apartment, including the superficial cleaning I had performed when the smoke detector had scared Moose. Why had I not been taking care of his place at least as well as I just had for this relatively new person in my life?

I rocked my head from side to side, slightly slower than Carl's continuous shake. Grandpa had often mentioned that cleaning the bathroom floor was a good way to remind ourselves to be humble. Another of his remarks I had rolled my eyes at, but cleaning the floor after Carl's mess had indeed been humbling.

A glance at the mantel clock showed ten fifteen when Edna entered the open door.

She dropped her bags to the floor. "I am *so sorry*. I was afraid this might happen."

"It was nothing," I lied.

She scurried through the apartment checking each room, then returned with a look that said she needed to do something but couldn't find anything that needed done.

"I changed him and put his clothes in the washer. Then we sat here and talked. I had no idea he was fluent in Spanish."

She wiped tears from her eyes, which transitioned from guilt to a pride in her husband that she had not expressed in a long time. "He learned to speak Spanish as a farmhand when he was young. Taught himself." She wrapped her arm over his shoulder. "Carl is such a smart man."

"I learned Spanish from my mom. I volunteer as a translator at church every week." *Maybe not every week.*

We both seemed to forget the smell as we talked with and about Carl. When I stood to leave, her hair caught my eye.

"Um, I kind of bumped the plastic head on your dresser. I hope I put it back in the right place."

She squeezed Carl's hand tight and maintained a stoic smile, but her face revealed everything. This tiny woman was taking care of an Alzheimer's husband while she was in a battle for her own life—yet every time I saw her in the hallway or the great room, she smiled and asked how *I* was doing.

Chapter 29

Choices

SOMETHING ABOUT MY time with Carl had touched me deeply. Though Edna seemed relieved every time she left the apartment, she was always excited to see Carl when she returned. It confused me how returning to such a burden could make her happy, but each time she came back, she went straight to him and gave him a special treat that she had picked out. It was usually a piece of chocolate from the confectionary counter at the grocery store, but it always had some kind of intricate design that she would describe to him in the form of a memory they had experienced together. Though Carl had little control over his movements, he always placed his hand in hers the moment she sat down, and their eyes always connected.

I recalled how my dad brought me gifts when he traveled. I would grab the toy and run off to play, never holding his hand or giving him a hug to show my appreciation. Even in his current, seemingly unaware state, it was clear that Carl wasn't holding Edna's hand to show appreciation; he was holding the hand of the woman he loved and she was doing the same.

I couldn't understand a relationship in which Edna had to do literally everything for the man, and she clearly loved him as much as he loved her. The best person to help me understand was Father Diamond, but with the holidays approaching, catching him on a weekday was getting harder, so I arrived at work at 5:00 a.m., a first for me. Getting in at that hour was the only way I could leave early enough to get to the church in time to ask the questions that I needed answered.

"Father, how do people...do it?"

His pleasant smile requested just a little more information.

"I mean, how do people get through life? I've met a bunch of old people lately and it seems like the older they get, the more burdens they have to carry. I can't imagine ever living that long, and I don't think I would want to live through all the things they've had to live through to get that old." Much like Grandpa, Father Diamond seldom offered a prompt reply to my questions, so I continued. "I made friends with an old lady who spent much of her life alone because she was uncomfortable leaving the house. Then her husband died, and her son moved her from the only home she knew into Grandpa's apartment complex where she was all alone again. I have another friend whose husband has Alzheimer's and she has cancer, and she has to take care of him, and she has to take care of herself, and I just don't know how people like her do it. I've even started watching her husband sometimes just so she can get her hair done or go shopping for a few minutes. I just...I just don't know how they do it. I would never be able to live like that."

After another lengthy, thoughtful pause, he said, "I see."

Ugh. Did you and Grandpa go to the same school?

"And you are concerned that these new friends have burdens that appear difficult."

Appear difficult? Did you not hear me?

"Kind of, I guess. I mean, she has cancer, and she takes care of him all the time. I'm only there for a few minutes a couple of times a week, so, like, I know what she's going through, but she has it so much harder than I can even imagine." I took an extra breath to slow myself down. "I guess what I want to ask you is, why would God give her such a burden?"

He again allowed too much time to pass before replying. "Have you asked James these questions?"

I am not lying to a priest! I am not lying to a priest! I repeated the sentence over and over in my head, hoping I could live up to the promise. How should I reply? What could I say to him? What *should* I say to him? I settled for an, "Uh-uh."

"I haven't seen your grandfather for some time now."

I kept my lips pinched shut.

"With age comes experience. With experience comes wisdom. With wisdom comes understanding."

Ugh. I should have known better than to ask a hard question.

He then donned an even quieter, solemn voice. "When I was a young man, I spent a year in a monastery in Poland. We had morning service every day of the week at five o'clock and Sunday service at noon. Service in the chapel provided the only opportunity to hear another's voice. The remainder of each day, every day, was served in silent solitude. Do you know how silent silence can be?" He gazed at the yellow light above the Stations of the Cross. "Yes, I imagine you do."

What do you mean by that?

"During the summer, a prayer bench was available in the garden, where we were encouraged to meditate on our studies. Much of the remainder of the year was spent in solitude in my quarters. A single room barely large enough for a chest of drawers and a cot."

I could hardly handle being alone in Grandpa's two-bedroom apartment. Spending entire days in such a tiny room would cause me to pull my hair out, which judging by the long strands I'd been finding on the bathroom floor, was happening fast enough.

"A single bulb suspended from a cord provided the light by which I would study the Word."

He closed his eyes and took himself back to that tiny room.

"As priests, we learn to live without material pleasures, but such a transition does not come naturally. I came from a large family with brothers and sisters who were seldom described as quiet. Getting used to my accommodations required an...adjustment." He spread a reflective smile. "Though my life had been reduced to a yellow light bulb and four walls, I had a choice. I could reject that glaring bulb and those confining walls, or I could embrace the warmth emitted from the yellow glow and the comforting caress of the close walls."

How do you always know what is going on in my life? Ever since Grandpa had volunteered me at the church a couple of years ago, Father Diamond miraculously showed up and shared stories in an attempt to help me work through struggles I was dealing with at the time. He had shared stories with me after my parents had died, when Moose was sick, and on multiple other occasions. He shared so many relatable stories, it was almost as though he had a direct line to my heart. I glanced at the crucifix on the wall behind the altar.

"What did you choose?" I asked after the silence had gone on long enough to be uncomfortable.

He tilted his head. "The point is to look for those occasions wherein a choice is presented."

By the time I repeated his advice to look for occasions wherein a choice was presented, he was gone.

On the drive home, it occurred to me. His little story was directly related to my life, but once again, he hadn't actually answered any of the questions I asked.

Chapter 30

On the Prowl

FIFTY PEOPLE AT the Legends knew that Grandpa had been back from his cruise for weeks, and many believed they had actually seen him. Some residents would swear they had coffee with Jimmy "just this morning," but Angie was starting to press, and I still hadn't figured out Father Diamond's riddle about my having a choice. As far as I was concerned, my only choice was to get through Angie's upcoming birthday party and then figure things out. Her birthday was two weeks from Saturday, and she had been on a mission to personally invite Grandpa, which obviously wasn't going to happen.

Moose and I had made it outside without being detected only to find Angie on the prowl, lurking behind a thick evergreen. I waved and darted across the street to the pond and then up the grassy hill, where we sat long enough that Angie should have given up. Just to be safe, we returned via a different path, only to find Angie waving in a feigned attempt at being friendly.

"Is James around?" she asked. "I just knocked, and there was no answer."

If you knocked and nobody answered, then why are you asking me?

"He's probably in the shower."

"I didn't hear the water running."

Ugh. Was she putting her ear to the door? Pretty smart, actually, but of all people, this witch was not going to beat me at this game.

"He was probably toweling off or something."

"Well, tell James that I want to invite him to my party. I'll be waiting in the great room."

You'll be waiting a long time.

Angie was definitely a problem that I needed help to fix.

* * *

DeAndre and I met at Ramee's apartment, which was a forty-minute drive from the Legends, but a slice of cheesecake from a nearby restaurant always made it worth the trip, and lately, the travel time provided an excellent opportunity to reminisce on times with Grandpa. The hill overlooking Sliver Lake had been on my mind a lot. Grandpa and I walked up the hill often when he visited me at the Manor. At his encouragement, I would follow him down to the water, where we would circle the slender lake along a shady trail. He always talked the entire way, full of stories about his lake adventures during his youth. I wiped a tear and turned into the restaurant parking lot.

Ramee was so excited to talk about a new team she had been put on at work that neither she nor DeAndre noticed my slightly puffy eyes. Her new team would be spending a lot of time designing a robotics upgrade at a large manufacturing company north of downtown, not far from Platform Marketing, making it easier for us to eat our sack lunches together. DeAndre then described some computer scripts he had been working on to simplify an older code his company used. Greek to Ramee and me, but he was excited enough for all of us. After they brought me up to speed on their new ventures, I filled them in on my increased hours at work and Father Diamond's riddle, which I was still struggling with. I then told them about an application I had submitted for a second job.

The dead silence that accompanied their jaws dropping gave me an opportunity to bring up something more important than the job: Angie's impending birthday party. Patti Jane had given me the scoop on the party plans, which included Angie reserving the great room for the entire day.

"That lady ain't taking no for an answer," said DeAndre. "Grandpa will *have* to make an appearance at that party."

Ramee agreed. "He's right, Nat."

"Then we'll make that happen. Ramee, can your dad pass for James? He's about the same height as Grandpa."

"But that's all he is. My dad's a lot heavier, and he doesn't have any gray hair yet."

I looked at DeAndre.

He stopped chewing a mouthful of steak and mashed potatoes just long enough to stare at his arm and say in a muffled voice, "Those people are old, but they're not blind." He swallowed and added, "The answer is obvious. Your uncle looks just like Grandpa. If he can come to town, we could do this. You know, keep him at a distance, but close enough that even Angie would think she saw him."

Uncle Jerry *did* look a lot like Grandpa. Some residents were still certain they had talked to Grandpa the last time Jerry was in town.

"The party is in that big room, right?" continued DeAndre. "We would all be there watching each other's backs. Maybe even get Bea to help. I'm thinking that when Angie is in one corner of the room, Uncle Jerry could come in with a gift. He could hand it to you or set it on a table or something when Angie is looking; then he waves and leaves. In, out. Zip, zap. He's gone!"

"Zip, zap? I like it," said Ramee. "He shouldn't go more than a few feet into the room, or he could get trapped. If we do this right, she'll see him, but she won't be able to walk across the room fast enough to speak to him before he leaves."

"We can keep her cornered in the back of the room," said DeAndre. "And we'll stall her any way we have to when she tries to move toward Jerry."

We worked through various details and difficulties to cover every base. If Angie camped out at the entrance, Jerry could come in the other door. If only a few people showed up to the party, one of us would get in her way the moment Jerry walked in.

The plan hinged on Uncle Jerry being able to come to town. If he did come, I could also use the opportunity to introduce him to Wayne, who could help spread the word that he too had met James.

It was late when I got home, but Uncle Jerry had never been one to maintain normal sleeping hours.

"Hey, Uncle Jerry."

"That's great-uncle, young lady. What's up? Is everything okay?"

I brought him up to date on life at the Legends, including the new manager, the smoke detector, bringing Bea into the fold, and my stalker. He was happy to hear I had one of the respected seniors on my side. I then told him about Angie's upcoming birthday.

"When's the party?"

Chapter 31

Missed the Mark

EVER SINCE MY visit with Father Diamond, I noticed I had been studying the walls whenever I sat at the kitchen table. I found myself taking deep, anxiety-filled breaths that came with a heavy pressure on my chest. The walls hadn't squeezed the life out of me yet, but without Grandpa's arms to wrap me in a protective hug, how long would it be before they smashed me like a bug?

Ugh. Would I ever lose these fatalist thoughts?

The pressure on my chest was not unfamiliar. Walls at the Manor had also closed in back when my parents died. Some nights those walls closed so crushingly fast it was suffocating. I would sit straight up in the middle of the night with my chest heaving, trying to refill lungs that felt as though they had been squeezed empty. In the weeks after my parents died, I wanted to move away from Sliver Lake completely, because the memories were so painful. But it was my parents who had set me up in the apartment at the Manor. They had taken care of my every need for my entire life, then, when I needed them the most, they were no longer around. I didn't have a choice. With my parents gone, I couldn't afford to move, so I had to continue living at the Manor. Not long afterwards, Grandpa came to town, and it was his presence that soothed my transition to life without parents. But who would soothe my transition to life without Grandpa?

What on earth could Father Diamond have meant when he was talking about choices? What choices could I possibly have? I was stuck at the Legends. Grandpa never had any choices, because he was taking care of me. Edna didn't have any choices, because she had to take care of Carl. The more I thought about it, the more I realized Father Diamond had *missed the mark*.

I rolled my eyes at yet another phrase Grandpa used to toss out. I brushed a tear from my cheek. I missed him so much. Grandpa had always been there for me. He taught me so many things about life—about how to get by on my own.

Regardless of what Father Diamond said, with some things there were no choices. The only choice I could afford was to live in my car, but that was a ridiculous idea. What I needed to do was get off my butt and do what Grandpa had taught me to do—to get to work.

Get to work. I repeated the thought in my head. I suppose *work* was a choice I could have made better, but with Grandpa around to help with things, the easier choice was always to ask him for money. I had chosen the easy path over the hard path because the easy path was…well…easier.

"Duh! Dummy."

Moose twitched his ears.

I did have choices; I had just never thought of them as choices. *Choosing* to work more would have increased my income and given me a choice in my living arrangements. But I had never thought of work as a choice. I'd had a job at Platform Marketing for a long time. Sure, my hours had been cut, dramatically at times, but that wasn't my fault. I still had the job. I was still employed, and that was how I was brought up: to always have a job.

I spent the next hour listing opportunities that had presented themselves over the last couple of years. Each opportunity on my list required a choice, and not surprisingly, my choice was always the easier path, a path in which Grandpa usually had to subsidize in some manner. The more I thought about it, the longer the list grew, but the items were much like my job: things that never seemed like something I had a decision in. I ate out much too often, rationalizing restaurant prices by telling myself I needed to eat. I paid for coffee all the time, and not just coffee but eight-dollar lattes because I had to be the one to add vanilla and an extra espresso shot. I rationalized coffee shop coffee as a *need* rather than a *want* because I needed to stay awake at work—something that hadn't been a problem in months, because I was going to bed at a decent hour. Louis had repeatedly shared his opinion on paying for coffee, which was almost exactly the same as Grandpa's. "The best tasting coffee is free coffee." Somehow those words resonated more clearly now that Grandpa was gone.

At the end of a full page of choices, each one having a corresponding excuse, I realized Grandpa was the one who had the real choice. He didn't have to move up here from Texas when my parents died. At the time, he claimed that retiring in lake country had always been a dream of his, but I knew how much he loved the desert. He chose to take care of me when I needed help. Had he stayed because I still depended upon him?

I leaned back and thought about residents at the Legends. Edna had a choice. She could have put Carl in a home. I recalled when she confided in me that she had always wanted children but wasn't able. Now, at a time in her life when cancer might have been her greatest concern, she was blessed with Carl, who needed her as a child needs a mother. She had described her time with Carl as more than special.

PJ had a choice. She grew up wanting to be a nurse and had earned a college scholarship to the nursing program down south. But in her family, the girls were not allowed to move away until they were married; thus, college was not an option. She chose to abide by her mother's rules, and as a result she met Louis, and her life couldn't have turned out better.

Even Orval had a choice. He could have given in to the ridicule and whispers around the complex and remained holed up in his apartment, but he chose to spend his time in the great room surrounded by people he didn't even talk to.

Suddenly it all made sense. All these people had choices, and each had chosen the path that helped someone else. And although those choices seemed hard and even impossible to me, I was beginning to see that the reward far outweighed the cost.

Chapter 32

Cool Dude

THOUGH I ACCEPTED that I did indeed have choices, I struggled to identify what my real choices were under the current circumstances, which included Thelma's recent "imaginary friend" remark. I was a little worried about just how much the lady knew. Thelma had never been unkind or suspicious, but I found her to be a little strange. She seldom left the apartment except to smoke, which made it extra difficult for me to sneak past her. As often as Moose barked and scratched at the door, she had to have heard him, but she never said anything, which gave me another reason to believe the peculiar remarks she made were ominous. Adding to my insecurity, this morning I could feel Thelma's eyes on me when I left the apartment.

A biting morning cold from a whipping November wind made for an unpleasant walk to the bus stop, my preferred choice of travel from the suburb to downtown when the roads were icy, but at least in the frigid air, I didn't worry about running into residents, except for Angie.

Fortunately, work was busy enough to keep my mind off my problems at the Legends. Near the end of the day, the boss called an urgent meeting with all staff to discuss efficiency techniques related to employee time management, a discussion that would have been directed at me a few months ago, but I had been *pulling my weight* lately.

I rolled my eyes at yet another of Grandpa's phrases that had stuck in the back of my mind.

Twenty minutes of information took the boss an hour to deliver—a point I would have brought up had he not already made me late for the bus.

I turned the corner just in time to be blasted by a plume of diesel smoke as my mass-transit carriage pulled away from the curb. Though the next bus would arrive in a mere fifteen minutes, my anxiety about arriving home late began to swell. Following my regular routine, I could often predict where Angie would be waiting, but if I arrived late, my stalker could be anywhere.

The anxiety turned out to be well-founded but misplaced. Angie was nowhere to be seen by the time I got home, but Moose had knocked over Grandpa's shiny metal trash can and scattered garbage around the kitchen.

Ugh. The can hitting the floor had to have bellowed loud enough to be heard in the hallway and certainly by Thelma.

I grabbed the broom and dustpan from the pantry, swept the mess, wiped the floor, then took Moose for a fully restrained walk across the street. I left him back in the apartment with strict orders to be quiet, then went to visit Stephanie.

"I can't do this, Steph." I paced back and forth in front of her desk. "It's not like it was when I lived here at the Manor. You used to walk Moose for me if I got held up at work and was late getting home. The apartment was a disaster tonight. Moose spread trash everywhere! You wouldn't believe the mess." I described the shredded paper, plastics, and other debris that had been strewn about and then mentioned the metal can that had rolled in a half circle.

"Which I assume is still on the floor."

"Nah. I cleaned it up, wiped down the floor, and took the trash bag to the bin." I shrugged. "Probably should have taken it to the bin this morning."

She gave me a serious curious look that had both of us wondering about my reply.

"Maybe I could go over and let him out on days that you work late," offered Stephanie. "It wouldn't be that often, and it's pretty easy for me to get out of here for ten minutes."

"That won't work at the Legends. Walking Moose can take twenty minutes, even longer sometimes, because I have to sneak him off the property without anyone seeing, especially Angie. Think about it. How would you explain to that witch why you're returning Moose to Grandpa's apartment?"

"Then what are you going to do?"

I smothered my face with my hands and pushed out an exasperated breath. "*I don't know.* I just need a break sometimes. Between stress at work and the Legends, I just need to decompress somewhere quiet."

Her eyebrows popped up. "The movie room! You can come over here and hang out in the movie room. Nobody's ever in there. There's a couch, and it's quiet and everything. This new manager doesn't get as upset with dogs as Ms. Glass used to, but we should still be careful. I can text you when everything is clear, and you can slip in."

"And I can bring Moose with me!"

The next evening, Moose and I kicked back on the leather couch in the Manor movie room. I was scooping noodles from a Yang's Chinese take-out box, and Moose was catching pieces that I tossed his way.

Stephanie stopped in to see us. "What smells good?"

I handed her a white box and a plastic fork. "Sweet and sour pork."

She sat on the arm of the couch and said, "My mom's favorite. Are you feeling any better today?"

"I'm not gonna lie, Steph, I needed this break. Nobody over here is stalking me. I'll bet this secret room has dropped my blood pressure ten points."

"Blood pressure?" she asked quizzically.

I shook my head. "That's what's happening to me! I mean, the people over there are nice and everything, but all their conversations are about old-people things. They talk about surgeries and diseases like we talk about clothes and shoes. Everyone sits around the tables popping pills or taking their blood pressure or checking their A1C levels."

Her eyes requested another explanation.

"That's for diabetes—and I should *not* know that! It's so weird. I'm freakin' twenty-four years old, and I can tell you what a good BP is for my age and what my HDL and LDL values should be. Living at the Legends is totally messing with my mind. Six months ago, I couldn't spell HDL!"

"Relax, girl." She held out the sweet and sour pork. "Trade me."

I handed her the Mongolian beef.

"Any soy sauce?" She gestured to the bag while she shoveled a forkful into her mouth.

I passed a packet. "Careful. It's all salt."

Stephanie spread a light grin.

Ugh. "Why do I care if it's all salt? What's wrong with me?"

"Aw." She patted my thigh. "Our little girl is growing up."

*   *   *

Working and hiding out in the Manor movie room had made me somewhat of a ghost around the Legends. I still managed to talk to Bea and sit with Carl now and then. Edna made sure he pottied before I arrived, thus there had been no further aromatic incidents.

It didn't take long for the movie room to also start feeling confining, so one evening I went to the store after work and bought a plush lap blanket to cover my legs during my evening work hours.

"That's pretty," said Steph when she entered the room.

"Just picked it up." I held a corner out for her to touch the soft fabric.

She cocked her head just a little. "We have blankets in the cabinet."

"But this is so soft, I just—" I released a sad exhale. "I don't know what it is, Steph. I haven't told you this, but sometimes I find myself buying things that I don't even need, and Lord knows I can't afford it. And when I get home with the new stuff, I start to cry."

She moved closer and put her hand on my shoulder. "Impulsive buying might be a side effect of something else. I hate to say it, but that sounds a little like depression. Don't worry, it's a natural part of the process."

At Stephanie's suggestion, the following evening I skipped my after-hours work routine in the movie room and invited Ramee and DeAndre to the Legends to play cards—an invite that made them nervous because our age group never plays cards.

"You're shitting me," said DeAndre after I filled him in on the Anders incident. I had left out the chemo details, thinking that Edna's medical condition was personal, though why chemo was more personal than Carl crapping himself, I wasn't sure.

"Dang, girl, I could never do that."

"Sure you could. It was one of those things where you do what you have to do. It must be really hard for Edna, though. I remember Gwen talking about her husband and how she had to do everything for him toward the end. She never complained about anything, but it was clear she had no time to herself. That's why I sit for her pretty often now." I winked at DeAndre. "And if there's a mess to deal with, you can come and help."

He squirmed. "I ain't helping with that."

While I was shuffling the cards, DeAndre moved to the window, attracted by flashing red and blue lights in the parking lot.

"That's Mrs. Anders, the lady I was telling you about. I hope nobody broke into her car. She doesn't need any extra problems."

"Let's go see what they're doing," said Ramee.

Two officers were talking to Edna when we walked up.

"*Natalie*," said Edna with a ghostly fear in her eyes. "Carl's gone. He walked off. He just walked off."

"Do you know the missing man in question?" asked the officer.

"Yes, sir, they're friends of mine. He has Alzheimer's. I'm sure Mrs. Anders told you. Have you started looking for him yet?"

"Momentarily. We need to ascertain the situation first."

I reached for Edna's hand. "*What happened?*"

"I fell asleep on the couch, and he was gone. I was only asleep for fifteen minutes, and he was gone."

"We'll find him." I turned to the officer and spoke too quickly for him to interrupt. "I need you to start searching. Carl is about eighty, and he walks slow. He can't be far. I'll go to the office and check the video to see which door he exited. Ramee, DeAndre, come with me." We dashed away before he could reply.

Estrella was talking to Thelma at the front desk when we came frantically around the corner. I quickly explained the situation, and she led us to a room in the back where four video screens each displayed multiple camera views. She replayed the videos, starting with the front door. Bingo. We got lucky on the first try with a clear shot of Carl walking away from the complex in tan sweatpants and a light

T-shirt. When he was almost out of the camera view, he turned to the right.

"Thanks, Estrella."

"Ramee, you go to the cop and tell him what we just saw. Then check inside the grocery store and around the parking lot. DeAndre and I will go out the front. It's been almost thirty minutes, but he moves slow."

Ramee sprinted back down the hall, and DeAndre and I burst through the front door. I angled off toward the residential area behind the shopping center. In seconds, DeAndre and his gazelle legs were out of sight down the street that bordered the grocery store.

It was cold and dark, and Carl didn't have a jacket. I ran as fast as I dared, my footing tenuous on the icy side-walks. I did one lap around the pond across the street, where multiple benches were situated for people to enjoy the area when it wasn't frozen. Benches that Carl might sit on if he walked past. *Nothing.* On the far side of the pond, I followed the path all the way to the grassy hill that overlooked Sliver Lake. From the hilltop vantage, I could see much of the neighborhood, but no Carl.

A text chirped from Ramee.

> He's not in the store. I'm heading down the main street.

Another chirp, this one from DeAndre with a picture attached.

> This the dude?
> That's him!
> We're walking back now. Cool dude.

I texted Ramee and asked her to run back and tell Edna that we found him, then I caught up with DeAndre who was so cold his body was shaking—his jacket hung on Carl's shoulders.

"*Buenas noches*, Carl. *Muy frio.*"

"*Si, muy frio.*"

A car pulled up alongside us, and the window crawled down.

"Get in," said Thelma. "You'll catch your death of cold."

She drove us back to the Legends, the red ember of her cigarette making sweeping arcs with each spin of the steering wheel.

Edna and the two police officers were waiting at the front door. With tears in her eyes and one hand firmly gripping Carl's arm, she hugged each of us.

Thelma disappeared in the commotion.

Chapter 33

First Snowfall

SPENDING SO MUCH time in the Manor movie room had kept me away from everyone, including Bea, so when she invited me upstairs for tea, I jumped at the offer. She filled me in on the Js' current antics while she filled the teapot, and I filled her in on our preparations to fully roll out the job we had set for Grandpa a few weeks ago at Digitronics Plus 2. Excitement over the cruise had lasted longer than we expected, which allowed us to delay broadcasting Grandpa's new job around the Legends, but now we were ready. The company already had a James Thomas on staff, so if Angie looked him up, she would see his name and hopefully not dig any deeper.

I stayed away from the great room the next day to allow subtle hints from Bea to float among the residents. Upon my return a day later, I grabbed a cup of coffee, and taking care not to bump into any short, bald-headed men, worked my way to Bea's table.

"How does James like working again?" asked Louis as I walked past him and PJ.

"I think he likes it. His hours are weird right now.

Something about a lot of training on the computer, so I haven't seen him much lately."

"Used to work at Digitronics myself," he said matter-of-factly. "Real good people, dontcha know."

My stomach fell so fast it made my legs wobble. We had spent so much time stressing over every aspect being believable, because any mistake could put me out on the street, and the first person to ask about Grandpa's job *used to work at the same company*. What if he still had contacts at the company and tried to call Grandpa? He had been looking for James for weeks to give him more meat from that ridiculous raffle he kept winning. If Louis called an old friend at the company and asked for James, all our effort setting this up would be wasted. While I considered all the ways this could go badly, I noticed Louis pretending to count on his fingers.

"Busted my hump for thirty-five years driving the interstate every morning before the sun was even up. Rain or shine." He grinned. "But usually snow, dontcha know."

I wasn't sure what hump he busted, but my plan was about to be shattered—that much was certain.

"Louis never called in sick," said PJ. "Not once in thirty-five years."

"Thirty-five years," I muttered dejectedly. That was enough time to know every person at the company.

"That was back when you worked even when you didn't feel too much like working, dontcha know. Back when we appreciated having a job. Today's kids, like our grandson, jump from job to job pretty often."

PJ gave him a look. "He does just fine, Louis."

"Oh, I'm not complaining. Might take the same path myself if I was starting again. And Lord knows our grandson is smart as a whip, that one."

I still hadn't figured out how *fast* a whip was, so I thought I'd clear this up now. "How smart *is* a whip?"

He slapped his leg extra hard and bellowed, "Think she might have something there. Maybe that's setting the bar a little low."

What bar, and what does a whip have to do with the bar?

"I'm just sayin' I could see myself calling in sick nowadays. Back in the day, if you were sick, you still came to work but kept your distance a bit."

"Um, so...when did you work there?" I asked, bracing myself for the expected reply.

"I worked there when it was just Digitronics. It's Digitronics Plus 2 now. Escaped in ninety-nine."

"Did you say ninety-nine?" *Whew!* Everything about that place could have changed since then. My stomach returned mostly to its rightful position.

"They gave me a nice watch when I retired." He raised his wrist to exhibit the gift which was quite possibly an antique by now. "It's a real good watch." He paused for a moment to remember the past.

"What did you do there?" I asked.

"Louis was in accounting," said PJ. "He could type numbers into a comptometer faster than anybody, and he zipped his fingers up and down that ribbon of paper to find whatever number he needed."

I released a sigh that Louis evidently interpreted as confusion.

"Sometimes I have to remember what year this is. I started on a comptometer, but we moved pretty quick to a ten-key adding machine. It's just like a calculator, I suppose, but these were mechanical for a long while, until they went electric. The calculation printed on a roll of white tape, kinda like your receipt at the store. My early machines had a hand crank to total the numbers. Those were about the size of a breadbox and weighed a good ten pounds. By the time I left, of course, we were using the computer."

He leaned back and reflected on his career. "Saw a lot of changes over a lot of years."

I slipped away when Louis directed his animated conversation about vintage calculators to Glen, whose mouth was contorting as he sucked breakfast remnants from his teeth.

Halfway to Bea's table, Janie grabbed my elbow. "Can James get me a discount on the new release of that *Senior Snipers* game? It came out yesterday."

Jamie added to the request. "And can he get me one of those wireless ear thingies for my phone? I'm going to start wearing those instead of earrings. Kind of a 'two birds and a stone' thing."

Both of them asked loudly enough for the entire room to hear, leaving me to wonder whether Bea had brought them into the fold or they really wanted that crap.

"Uh, sure. I'll ask him." I moved on to Bea's table. Her perch at the head of the room was my only safe haven at the complex outside the confines of Grandpa's apartment walls.

I slid my chair close to Bea and whispered, "I think I messed up. We built an entire social media presence around Grandpa working at Digitronics Plus 2, and I just found out that Louis used to work there. What if he tries to call Grandpa? Or what if he asks one of his friends about him?"

Bea patted the back of my hand. "Let tomorrow worry about itself."

Father Diamond had said the same thing recently in a sermon that he had preached about another sermon. "Does that mean I shouldn't worry about it until it becomes a problem?"

"Exactly, dear. You did your best, so don't go worrying yourself about it."

"I'll try not to." I glanced at the clock on the wall. Moose was upstairs waiting impatiently to go out. Before I left, I had to ask, "Hey, Bea, what's a breadbox?"

*   *   *

Moose and I returned through the side door after watching the seniors shuffle down the street to a special brunch they had all been talking about. Angie and Gladys were in the middle of the pack. The weather outside was chilly and clear, so the snowfall inside the Legends caught me by surprise. Not a traditional snowfall, and one that would never have occurred at the Manor.

Over the last few weeks, the cold of mid-fall mornings followed by almost warm afternoons had brought an increase in elderly sniffles. Legends residents, who regularly forget their glasses, sweaters, socks, and sometimes teeth, never seemed to forget to blow their noses. With all that extra wiping, tissues tended to drift like autumn leaves, and residents never bent over to pick them up, possibly for fear of being unable to return to a vertical position.

I dropped Moose off at the apartment and followed the tissue trail all the way downstairs to the great room, picking up dozens of white puffs along the way. The great room was even worse, half covered with white tissues flattened by the rush-hour scooter traffic that had left the room in a hurry for the discount brunch.

I stuffed my pile of tissue into the trash can and returned to the apartment. I needed to put some serious thought into preparing for the week ahead—a week of critical activities that would undoubtedly determine how long I would be staying at the Legends. Though I appreciated Bea's remark about not worrying, I couldn't shake the haunting thought of being kicked out if anything went wrong with the plan that so many friends had helped put together.

Having finally implemented Grandpa's fake job should have given me more relief than I was feeling. We had put a lot of effort into researching companies, selecting one that fit Grandpa perfectly, and building a social media profile to make it appear that he had found his dream job. A job that didn't exist and didn't come with a paycheck. Two things that I desperately needed. Had we put half of that effort into searching for a job for me, I wouldn't be stuck hiding in the apartment to keep residents from seeing too much of me. I would be at an office somewhere, earning a full paycheck.

I curled up on the couch next to Moose and stared aimlessly at dead hands on the mantel clock that I had come to despise.

Chapter 34

Never Steered Me Wrong

THE NUMBER RINGING my phone was the third call I had received from Digitronics Plus 2. The first call woke me up at six, followed by a call at seven that had also caused Moose to stir, and now this one at eight. *Ugh.* Ignoring the caller was not working. Had they already figured out I was using their company as a fake employer of Grandpa? Had Louis called Digitronics yesterday after I had left him?

I grimaced and answered, "This is Natalie."

"Natalie," came a friendlier-than-expected voice on the other end. "I've been trying to reach you all morning."

And I've been trying to avoid you all morning.

"My name is Brett Cummings. I'm the human resources manager at Digitronics Plus 2. Are you familiar with our company?"

More than you know.

"Um, yes. I know you do some electronics stuff and digital-interface systems."

"We do indeed, and a lot more. In fact, we're in a growth mode now as we position ourselves for a larger share of the market, and that's what I want to talk to you about. We're looking for some young guns to join our team. People who can help develop advertising platforms that will move us forward in this very dynamic environment."

He paused a little too long, prompting my most professional, "Uh-huh."

Brett then spent ten energetic minutes describing in a much-too-cheerful voice the details of the organizational structure and current marketing strategy employed by Digitronics Plus 2, which he abbreviated as DP2. He worked his way systematically through every question an applicant would ask about a position, though I had never applied for a job at the company. He wrapped up his sales pitch with an overview of the employee benefits package that included five days of sick leave and fourteen days of annual vacation, both of which were better than what I received at my current job.

"So, what do you say?"

I was able to hold in the next "uh-huh."

"Let's do this," he said after my prolonged silence. "Come by my office tomorrow at eight o'clock. I'll introduce you to the team, and if you like what you see, we'll get you started immediately."

"I, um, certainly, Mr. Cummings. I'll be there."

"Excellent. Louis said you'd be a good match for us, and he's never steered me wrong in the past. I'll see you then."

My hands were shaky when I hung up the phone. *Louis!*

*   *   *

I washed the sleep from my eyes and slipped out the back with Moose, who took care of business on our way to see Stephanie at the Manor.

"I think I start a new job tomorrow."

Steph closed the nail polish bottle and giggled. "You *think* you start a new job? Don't you have to apply somewhere in order to get hired?"

"I know, right? But this guy Brett Cummings called me a few minutes ago. He told me all kinds of stuff about DP2 and then asked me to come over tomorrow morning."

Stephanie's face turned serious. "Are you sure that wasn't some kind of spam call? I mean, even the name sounds fake. DP2? You can't meet up with some strange man who calls you at random."

"That's what's so weird, Steph." I filled her in on my visit with Louis and his career at Digitronics, which was now DP2. I explained how worried I had been all night, thinking that Louis might try to track down Grandpa at the company.

She grinned through my entire ramble.

"It sounds like you finally got that elusive second job."

Moose tugged at the leash, so I let him free to sniff the Christmas tree in the corner of the quiet foyer.

"I don't have time for two jobs! I barely have time for one job."

Stephanie gestured to the wall clock. "Which you were supposed to be at thirty minutes ago."

I left Moose with Stephanie and dashed back to the Legends, where I took a quick shower, dressed, and was driving out of the garage in Grandpa's SUV just as Angie was entering.

Ugh.

At the end of a surprisingly full day of work at Platform Marketing, the boss pulled a dozen of us into the conference room and explained that the company had secured a large contract sure to keep all of us busy. To help us adjust to the added workload, we would be allowed to complete some work remotely, provided the work was measurable in terms of production and hours spent on the activity.

It sounded as though he didn't trust staff to be as efficient at home as we were at the office.

To test the new system, I brought four hours of work

home, which would allow me to spend the following morning meeting with Brett at DP2 before going back to my office.

Between interruptions from Moose, knocks on the door by residents looking for James, and cooking enough food to prep meals for the week, I ended up spending six hours on the four-hour task I had brought home. Clearly, working remotely would need to become more efficient.

I packed enough lunches to last the rest of the week, then did the dishes and walked Moose. We were in bed before nine o'clock, which had become relatively common, and I was already awake when the alarm went off at seven. After a quick shower, I took care of my morning duties and made it to the DP2 office with ten minutes to spare.

"Ms. Thomas, it's nice to meet you." Mr. Cummings shot his hand out and continued talking in the same energetic, cheerful voice he had used on the phone. From his burgundy leather office chair behind his large desk, he briefed me on the history of DP2, the operations conducted at the headquarters facility, and its clients and products. We continued the conversation while he toured me through three floors of the office and manufacturing complex. We then walked across the street to their distribution center, where he described the product lines in even greater detail.

The enormity of the operation was more than impressive. The corporation dwarfed any company I had worked for in the past, but the way Mr. Cummings explained everything made me believe that I could handle the increased responsibilities.

I left DP2 through the human resources department, where I completed all the necessary paperwork to start my new job Monday morning.

The drive from DP2 to Platform Marketing was only eight minutes, which gave me just enough time to wolf down the sack lunch I had prepared. I worked six hours in the office and brought two hours of work home, which I completed while working and eating another prepared meal in the Manor movie room with Moose.

I noticed Stephanie from the corner of my eye as she came in, but I was in the middle of a management briefing that would be presented first thing in the morning.

"Just a sec, Steph."

I finished typing two more sentences, then pulled my head back from the laptop and read what I had typed. It wasn't quite the way that I wanted to describe the current marketing campaign, so I deleted what I had written and tapped out a revised paragraph.

After a few minutes, Stephanie tapped my shoulder. "I've never seen you this focused."

"It's just that my Platform Marketing manager likes the work I've been doing, so this management brief needs to be the same high quality, and it's not quite there."

She held her smile long enough for me to catch the tail end.

"Do you want me to walk Moose for you?" she asked.

"That would be so great."

"I have another idea if you'll stop pecking those keys for a second."

I glanced up, then finished the next sentence.

"Now that I'm not jumping between the Golden Years complex and here, I could keep Moose at my place for a couple of weeks, if that would help you out. I mean, I know you two have never been apart, but it wouldn't be for too long."

My fingers stopped. "Oh, Steph, that would help *sooo* much. I'm running a little ragged here, and to tell you the truth, it's a little weird that I'm not pulling my hair out." I shrugged. "I kind of feel like I've got everything under control, even working two jobs. But if you watched Moose for a couple of weeks, that would take away a lot of my stress at the Legends."

"Done." Steph grabbed his leash and led him down the hall.

I was so focused on the management brief that I kept writing for another hour before realizing I hadn't given Moose a goodbye hug.

Chapter 35

Feathered Fowl

WITH ME WORKING two jobs, the days leading up to Angie's birthday flew by faster than snowflakes in a windy winter storm. Jerry arrived two days before the party, and we got straight to the business of how he would make an appearance in the great room without anyone realizing he wasn't Grandpa.

I showed him the gift I had picked up for Angie on my way home from work.

"A birding book?" He snickered.

"A lot of these people like to watch birds. Evidently, when you reach a certain age, a desire to focus on feathered fowl kicks in." I nudged his shoulder. "I'm surprised you haven't started yet."

"Oh, I like to watch birds—when they're in season." He cocked an imaginary shotgun and pulled the trigger.

Next, I handed him the Caribbean shirt and hat that Ramee and DeAndre had picked out. "Hope these fit."

"I ain't wearin' that, so it doesn't matter if it fits." Another snicker.

"But you have to! The hat will cover your face so that

nobody gets a clear look. We picked this shirt to give residents a visual reminder about the cruise, because you *can't* stop to talk with anybody."

He snarled. "If I see one picture of me posted anywhere, I'm coming back with my bird gun."

"Keep your gun holstered for now, cowboy. We have a meeting with the apartment manager, and don't forget, Grandpa chuckles. You've got that snicker thing that—"

"I hear you." He chuckled exactly like Grandpa.

For weeks I had misdirected, misinformed, and otherwise convinced people that they misunderstood without ever having shown Grandpa's face to anyone. The meeting with Wayne would be the first live test, so I briefed Jerry on everything I could think of to ensure there would be no mistakes. If he slipped up, I would be out on the street before nightfall.

We were both quiet in the elevator to the first floor. Jerry's confident demeanor reduced my anxiety with each step down the hall to the office. Uncle Jerry could handle anything. Thoughts of Grandpa calling him for advice on how to fix things at the house came to mind. Grandpa wasn't afraid to get his hands dirty, but he didn't always know what to do and often relied on Jerry's expertise. I took a deep breath and released it with renewed confidence as we neared the office area. This meeting would be a piece of cake.

We turned the corner and found Estrella sitting at the front desk. *Ugh.* How could I have forgotten to mention Estrella and my volunteering at the church? I had shared those details with Wayne when we first met. Surely, he would bring that up in the discussion. The future of my living arrangements was on the line, and I hadn't even considered who would be manning the front desk. *What else had I forgotten?* My stomach sunk to a new low.

"Good morning, Estrella," I said nervously. "This is my grandpa Jer—um, James, um, my grandpa. We're here to see Wayne."

She extended a hand. "Good morning, Mr. Thomas. It is nice to meet you. Natalie has mentioned you at the church. You know, she is the reason I have this job."

Her explanation was a bit of a stretch. I had introduced Estrella to somebody at the church who thought they knew of a job opening. I had no idea she would be working at the apartment.

Jerry beamed a smile that almost looked real. "I'm so proud of her work at the church."

How do you know about St. John's?

"Is Wayne in?" I asked, my voice rising an octave.

"Yes, I will tell him you are here."

When she went down the hall, I whispered to Jerry, "I forgot to mention Estrella."

"Don't worry."

It seemed like a lot of people with nothing at risk had been telling me not to worry lately.

"I can handle being James for a day. Of course, I'll have to dumb myself down." He chuckled a little too long, clearly practicing.

Estrella returned with Wayne.

"Mr. Thomas, it's a pleasure to meet you."

"James. Call me James," replied Jerry as I sank into the shadow to hide my nerves. Having never seen this side of Jerry, I had no idea what to expect.

"I've been wanting to have this meet-and-greet since I took over management of the complex, but you were on a cruise at the time. Did you enjoy it?"

"Actually, the trip was a little too long. You know how it is. Three weeks sounds great, but toward the end, it's just too long to be away from home. At least for me—some people can pull it off. Spent an extra couple of days in New Orleans before the ship left. It's such a great city, right, Natalie?" He looked at me.

I had never been to New Orleans. Either my

sometimes-crazy uncle didn't know this, or he was intro-ducing Miss Direction to sidetrack Wayne.

"Birthplace of bananas Foster," I replied, citing a sliver of trivia picked up from a food channel. I exhausted the rest of my knowledge of the city by saying, "And the cemeteries are above ground."

"Speaking of cemeteries," said Jerry, "remember those catacombs in Paris?"

I was fairly certain Jerry had never been to Paris, but I had traveled there with Grandpa and Grandma a few years ago.

I cringed a little for effect, but mostly because I was worried about the surprise details Uncle Jerry was adding to a conversation we had rehearsed. "I'll never do that again," I replied. "What about you, Wayne, do you travel much?"

"Travel? Not at all, but it sounds like you two get around. I don't know if a three-week cruise would be too long or not, but I'd sure like to take one and find out for myself." He sounded a little envious. "At this stage of my career, it's tough to get off for two weeks. Three weeks would be impos-sible. We don't get much paid time off here, and every time I need to run an errand, it comes out of those hours."

"We all have to pay our dues," said Jerry. "Early career is the hardest part."

"I know what you mean, Wayne. I get an extra week of vacation after I'm at this job for three years. I can't wait for that to kick in, because whenever I take Moose to the vet, they dock my vacation hours."

Dang it! I bit the inside of my lip. The last thing I had wanted to do was remind Wayne about my dog.

"The time goes by fast enough, young lady. No need to rush it," said Jerry, sounding a lot like Grandpa.

"Well, Wayne, it was nice to meet you." Jerry stood and extended a hand. "Stop by for a cup of coffee."

Thanks, Uncle Jerry. What am I supposed to do when he knocks on the door next week?

We exited through the front door and headed straight to the car to avoid unwanted encounters in the hall.

"That was amazing, Uncle Jerry. You were great."

"Thought I'd have some fun with it. You did pretty good yourself."

"How did you know about my volunteering at church?"

"Seriously? Where do you think James came up with the idea to volunteer you?"

I tossed a curious look. "*You* told him to volunteer me?"

Another snicker. "Ha! Dad, that would be your great-grandpa, signed us up as permanent members of the church volunteer team when we were a lot younger than you. He did it to keep our hands from being idle. Of course, James and I did as little as we could get away with initially, but that stuff kind of grows on you."

"I know what you mean."

"I still show up every Saturday to groom the church grounds. My yard is a mess at home, but the church landscape looks pretty good if I do say so myself."

The next stop was the motor vehicle department, where Jerry handed the clerk the vehicle title, registration, and Grandpa's passport. The lady barely looked at the passport picture. In twenty minutes, we were back in Grandpa's car, the title of which was now in my name. We then closed the account at Grandpa's bank, again using the passport for identification. Jerry looked at me as the teller went back for a form that needed to be signed.

"It's just easier this way," he said in a soft voice.

The fourteen hundred dollars in the account was almost enough to cover the auto insurance bill that was due on his SUV. I could hear Grandpa saying, *"If it's free, I can't afford it."*

Back in the car, Jerry glanced at me from the driver's seat. "I miss him too," he said solemnly.

We were both quiet all the way back to the Legends.

"You'll have to work through this at your own pace, but he wouldn't want you to be sad for too long, kiddo."

Again, he sounded a lot like Grandpa.

I had recognized most of the emotional stages that I'd already worked through. Denial was the obvious first stage. Guilt had come and gone multiple times. Guilt for giving him the kayak trip that I had won. Guilt for not telling him I loved him the morning he left. Guilt for not appreciating him enough over the years. There was no bargaining stage, and I was never angry that he was gone, but I had been stuck in the depression stage much too long, lost in a hollowness that seemed to have no way out. Uncle Jerry was right: it was time for acceptance. It was time to move forward.

When we returned to the apartment, Uncle Jerry helped me move my things into Grandpa's room.

Chapter 36

Angie's Party

BY THE TIME Angie's party arrived, I just wanted to get it over with.

"You have to get me a set of keys to the back door," said DeAndre with way too much energy for my pent-up nerves.

"Why would you need keys to the back?"

"'Cause there's too many old people around the front door. Ramee and I got stuck behind some lady whose extra-wide walker blocked half the hall. Then she ripped one right in front of us." He sputtered a cough. "I think I inhaled some."

"It was pretty bad," added Ramee.

"*Pretty bad?*" DeAndre pulled his head back. "That was a walking squirt. I might have even stepped in it." He checked his shoe.

"Be nice. Nora has only been here for a couple of weeks. She's a little big, but sometimes that's hereditary, you know. And besides, she's very nice. Every time I see her, she's smiling."

"Probably because she released a silent toot." He shook

his head. "I'll be thinking about that lady's backside all day."

"You like whose backside?" asked Jerry, coming down the hall from the bedroom.

DeAndre's eyes bulged. "That's a good look for you."

"You want to be buried in it?" replied Jerry with an almost convincing glare. "I got a shovel in the trunk."

I nudged DeAndre in the side. "Lucky he likes you. Anyone else and he would have just gone for the shovel."

Jerry looked down at his Caribbean shirt and smirked. "Now I know why they drink so much rum in the islands. You gotta be drunk to wear this."

I inhaled a nervous breath and pushed it out. "Is everyone ready?"

Ramee slipped down the hall alone to see how many people had shown up for the party. She returned with a cup of punch and a report that there were enough people between Angie and the door that Jerry would be safe.

My stomach twisted a knot. This was it. My future at the Legends rested on whatever happened in the next five minutes.

Ramee, DeAndre, and I left Jerry in the apartment and headed to the party. When we reached the door to the great room, I stopped.

"What's wrong?" asked Ramee.

"It all comes down to this. If we get caught, Moose and I will be kicked out." The thought of being surrounded by four blank walls in some cheap apartment kept me from turning the handle.

"Nobody's gonna get caught," said DeAndre. He put a warm hand on my shoulder. "And you could always stay with me."

Ramee put a hand on my other shoulder. "Me too."

I turned the knob.

We entered the great room quietly and surveyed the

layout. Immediately to the left of the door was the cake table with a half-sheet vanilla cake in the middle. A tub of the local favorite, Kozy Shack tapioca, sat on either side of the cake, and at the far end of the table was a plate of Louis' lefse next to a jar of lingonberry jam. The gift table was behind the cake table, much farther from the hall entrance than I had hoped. Jerry would need to enter, walk past the cake table to the gift table, set the wrapped birding book present down, and walk out before Angie could hurdle a lane of aluminum walkers and intercept him at the door.

The silver-haired cougar had her back to us while she chatted with residents near the window, giving us the perfect opportunity for the drop-and-dash.

I fired a text to Jerry. My lips moved as I counted the seconds in a nervous whisper. "Twenty-nine, twenty-eight, twenty..." My eyes bounced from the door to Angie faster than they had the last time I watched a tennis match.

Thirty seconds passed—no Jerry. One minute passed, then two minutes. Still no Jerry. My body tensed when the door finally opened, but it was just Millie and two other residents I knew only by sight.

Angie moved toward the new arrivals.

We moved to intercept, taking our preplanned positions directly in front of her. "Happy birthday, Angie. These are my friends DeAndre and Ramee."

"Nice party," said DeAndre. "Thanks for having us."

The door opened again. In walked a Caribbean shirt, but Angie was way too close.

DeAndre shifted left to block her view, then raised his voice. "I don't see any other people our age. Do you have any young friends?"

Angie craned her much-too-long neck to see around him. "Um, uh...of course I do. Excuse me."

Jerry was halfway to the gift table. On cue, he held up

the bag for Angie to see, waved, and turned to leave—but Patti Jane blocked his exit.

Angie muscled her way between DeAndre and me.

"Can I hold that for you?" Ramee flung her empty sleeve forward, wrapping it halfway around Angie's waist.

Angie stared briefly at the sleeve then returned her focus to Jerry, who was still in conversation with Patti Jane. She half shouted, "Jimmy!"

My shoulders slumped. The charade was over. What had I been thinking, bringing Jerry into town to pretend he was Grandpa? Devising an elaborate plan just to deceive these people was never going to work. Legends residents weren't stupid.

I took a step toward the outside door, where I could sit on Thelma's bench and hang my head. The last place I wanted to be was surrounded by these nice people when they realized I was nothing but a fraud.

A cane came out of nowhere and blocked Angie. "The toll for the birthday girl is one hug." Louis lowered the cane and wrapped his free arm around Angie. "Happy birthday, Angie. You don't look a day over—" He spread an ear-to-ear smile and bellowed a laugh. "I'm just funnin' ya."

She busted loose but only made it one step before another set of arms wrapped her up.

"Happy birthday, my dear." Bea had made her move with precision.

Angie wriggled away. "Thank you, Mrs. Barrington, but I need to—" She skipped past without finishing the sentence and lunged desperately for the door just as Jerry stepped out. She grabbed the handle before it latched.

My stomach, which had been flip-flopping with every near miss, fell back to my feet.

Angie pushed the door open and nearly collided with Jamie, Janie, and Jane, whose scooters were parked in a semicircle blocking the door. The ladies were babbling incessantly with hellos, happy birthdays, and questions about the cake, each grabbing Angie's hands and refusing to let go.

The poor woman finally realized her attempt to see James was in vain. Her anxious smile was replaced with a genuine sadness that reminded me of how I had felt not long ago.

Wayne stepped up behind the Js. "I believe this is a no-parking zone. Might have to haul you off to the big house for a violation of this magnitude."

"You can haul me to your big house anytime," replied at least two seductive voices.

"Hello, Natalie. I just saw James in the hall and was talking to him about cleaning the carpet. He suggested I schedule it with you."

That's what took Jerry so long!

Angie whipped her head around. "You saw *James*?"

"He just left. I watched him get into his car."

"Are you certain it was James?"

"Well, I would think so. I spent an hour with him yesterday talking about his travels. The man gets around, but today is your day, Angie, and this is for you." He handed her a gift bag with a bottle poking out the top. "Sparkling cider." He offered an apologetic shrug. "The stronger version isn't allowed."

"Thank you, and thank you all," said Angie, the crispness gone from her normally self-assured voice.

By the time she set the bottle on the gift table, her perky façade had returned. She corralled a few residents and began talking about her wonderful daughter, who would have come but for...

I tossed a smile to Bea as we left. The party could not have been scripted any better, and Wayne was all the proof I needed that Grandpa had attended. Our complicated scheme had quite possibly shut Angie up permanently.

We regrouped at Yang's, where we yammered about every tense moment as though we were giddy teenagers. The plan had worked to perfection even though Jerry hadn't shown up on time. But we couldn't have done it without Louis, Bea, and the Js. Bea had been Jerry's idea, and she had cringed when he suggested the hug in our practice round. None of us knew how Louis or the others figured into the plan, but we were grateful for the help.

We finished eating and were ready to leave when Thelma stopped at our table. I was so excited when we arrived at Yang's that I hadn't checked to see who else was in the room.

"Hello, Natalie." She smiled, then looked at my uncle. "And you must be Jerry. Word gets around, you know." She held out a hand.

I stumbled over the simple introductions. "These are, uh, my friends...Ramee and, uh, DeAndre."

"I've met Mr. DeAndre. I trust everything went well."

She left us sitting there with our jaws on the table.

"What was that all about?" whispered DeAndre, a little late with his cautious voice.

"If she knows, then who else knows?" asked Ramee.

My throat closed a little tighter with each resident's name we listed who might know that I was living at the Legends. Bea was the only person I had told, but Louis had stopped Angie with his cane. If Louis knew, then Patti Jane surely knew, and neither of them had an inside voice. If they had ever mentioned my situation in the great room, then everyone might know. I had initially thought the Js arriving right when Jerry left was a coincidence, but after we talked it over at Yang's, we were all pretty sure they were part of the plan—but whose plan?

*   *   *

Jerry left the following morning after loading me up with groceries, something he insisted upon even though working two jobs had my checking account balance looking better than it had in years. As I watched Jerry drive away, Stephanie arrived with Moose. She was leaving town for an extended vacation prior to the holidays, so she brought Moose to the apartment, slipping in the back door.

I wrapped my arms around my furry friend, whom I'd missed so much. In the short time that Moose had been gone, my stress had virtually disappeared. Not once had I worried about being seen, because "watering Grandpa's plants" was a perfectly reasonable excuse—an excuse that was always more complicated when I had a dog at my side.

"Um, is that you, girl?" asked Stephanie.

"You wouldn't believe how relaxed I feel. It's like I caught up on a year of missed sleep."

"I believe it. Did you know Moose doesn't like fireworks?"

"Uh-oh."

"The kids down the street must have been practicing for New Year's Eve, because they lit stuff off every night." She shrugged. "I could hardly get upset because we've done our share, but I've never seen a dog that barked so much with every boom."

I dropped Moose off in the apartment, then went upstairs to see Bea and give her a stuffed teddy bear.

"This is for you. Something to practice your bear hugs for next time."

"Thank you." She wrapped an arm around my shoulder and led me inside. "But I believe that was my last bear hug."

She set the bear prominently on the velvet bench in her entryway, an amenity not offered on lower floors. "From here, he can keep watch and warn me when my young neighbors are scheming again."

"Thanks, Bea. I kind of feel bad though, you know."

"I understand. You're faced with a difficult situation. One which requires difficult choices."

Again with the choices.

"So many residents were at the party, and Angie was having such a good time until we showed up. I think the only person I didn't see was Orval."

"Not on the first Saturday of the month," she said matter-of-factly.

The look on my face told her I didn't understand.

"You and he talk so often that I assumed you knew."

I shook my head in confusion, prompting her to continue. "Orval goes to the cemetery on the first Saturday of the month to visit his wife and daughter." She took a breath and closed her eyes. When she opened them, they were glazed with tears. "His wife and daughter were killed in a car accident almost fifty years ago. Orval was driving when they were hit by a train. Automatic crossing arms weren't on that particular track, and he never saw it coming."

The lump in my throat was so big I couldn't swallow. "I...I had no idea."

"Orval is a brilliant man. A physicist, actually. He lost himself in his work after they died, and he seems even more lost since he retired. He is quite conversant, as you know, and a most pleasant man."

"Is that what you were, a physicist?"

"Not exactly."

Chapter 37

Do It Alone

IN ANTICIPATION OF a late night at work, I stopped in the great room for an extra cup of coffee before I left for the day. Early morning visits to the room were usually quiet because residents needed to "work out more kinks and cricks in the winter," as Grandpa had put it some time ago. But this morning, one table was partially full.

I waved to my friends as I filled my cup.

Louis' voice carried louder than usual in the mostly empty room, where he and PJ were sitting at the far end with Bea. The boisterous man with the jocular smile had never spoken badly about anyone. I, on the other hand, let complaints fly like wild turkeys and usually enjoyed good gossip, though Father Diamond had reminded me in a recent Sunday sermon that neither of those personal traits were beneficial to my spiritual path. So this morning, I was a little curious when I heard Angie's name being tossed about.

An extra-long yawn forced itself out as I pulled a chair back from the table. "Good morning."

Greetings from my friends were followed by a quiet lull

in the conversation. For a moment, I thought they might be holding back on the juiciest parts until I realized they were all chomping on bran muffins, a half-empty plate of which was sitting in the middle of the table.

PJ swallowed and said, "Angios have been nothing but trouble for Louis."

"Angio?" I asked.

"Angio is our abbreviation for angina and angiogram and angioplasty," replied PJ. "Louis has had the pleasure of getting all three."

"That angioplasty, well, she can be such a pain in the crotch." Louis chuckled.

Bea rested her hand on her chest. "I've had a few angios myself." She slid the plate of muffins my way. "That's why we're having a healthy snack this morning."

"The sudden pains are the worst," said Louis. "Had one of those sharp ones come about midnight a few years back. I knew when it hit that PJ would be taking me in for an angio something. That pain knocked me clean out of bed, dontcha know."

"It was a struggle just to get him to sit up on the floor," said PJ. "I was ready to call an ambulance, but then he popped a nitro pill and was fine in a few minutes."

Louis pulled the chain around his neck, revealing a silver vial hanging on the end. "Don't leave home without it," he said with a mild chuckle.

"I don't get it." Confused eyes reinforced my statement.

"I'm sorry, dear," said PJ. "I suppose this is more of an adult conversation."

"She means an *old* adult conversation," added Louis. "*Really* old. That angioplasty is a procedure they use to clean out all that cholesterol I stuffed into my arteries. I call her a real pain in the crotch because that's where they enter with the probe." He slapped his hand on the inside of his thigh. "They slide some kind of fancy doohickey into your vein and go all the way up to the heart." He rocked his head. "Now, what doctor do you think figured that out? Seems to me there are a lot of closer ways to get to the heart."

Bea grinned at the large man. "I prefer the cardiologist use a *catheter* rather than a *doohickey*, and with me, they enter through an *artery* in my leg, not a *vein*."

Louis shrugged.

"The catheter is quite fascinating," said PJ in her medical advice voice, which I had come to trust. "It has a balloon on the tip that inflates to clear the blocked artery. While the cardiologist is in there, he can position a stent or two, or however many you need, to hold the wall of the artery open. That allows the blood to flow better."

Louis placed a hand on his chest as though he were about to sing "The Star-Spangled Banner." "Had that done a few years before my bypass. When the doc gets the balloon where he wants it, he puts in a stent that looks like a tiny piece of chicken wire and holds the artery open."

Uh-oh. Here come the chickens.

He leaned back and said, "Now there's another one that makes you think. What farmer was sitting on the porch one day saying to himself, 'If I made that chicken wire really tiny, I could stuff it into an artery and save a man's life?'"

Bea rolled her eyes, not for the first time in the conversation. "Chicken wire is a little different than a platinum alloy mesh, Louis."

Louis held up his hand, fingers spread. "Five stents, and they never let me keep the balloon."

"*Five*," repeated Bea. "I have no desire to own those bragging rights."

"Oh, they took them all out when they did the bypass," he said. "I'm as good as new today." He toasted PJ with the bran muffin. "Thanks to these and a wife who cares enough to keep me in line."

They continued talking about medical procedures and terms that seemed to apply to people on the threshold of death. I thought it fitting that the scariest words started with "Angie."

As I headed out the door, my mind drifted to Grandpa, who never knew any of those procedures.

*   *   *

Ramee's text at six o'clock pulled my eyes from the computer screen for the first time in hours.

Dinner at Riverside BBQ in one hour.

I had worked at Platform Marketing from six until two and still had at least another hour at DP2 before I finished my latest priority task. The work I was doing had been so captivating lately that I often found myself leaving the office after everyone else had gone home; thus, her timing for dinner at the downtown venue worked perfectly.

By the time I arrived, Ramee and DeAndre had secured a window table with a spectacular view overlooking the river. We spent the next hour eating, talking, and drinking iced tea. We had so many refills that each of us excused ourselves multiple times to make room for the next glass. I returned from the powder room to find my friends laughing uncontrollably. DeAndre was, for the *millionth* time, reliving my first experience with Carl, complete with graphic depictions of the bathroom adventure.

"Don't lie, Nat," said DeAndre. "You peeked, didn't you?"

They laughed harder.

"You're sick, dude. I just ate."

More laughter.

I looked DeAndre in the eye but couldn't keep a straight face. "You want to go there? Okay. I'll give you details that'll keep you up nights. You want to know what you're going to look like in sixty years? You're going to have elephant skin sagging halfway to your knees. Wrinkles so thick they have their own wrinkles. The gray hair…"

DeAndre held his hands up in surrender. "*Ah, hell no.*"

He jabbed his fingers into his ears. Ramee grabbed my left index finger and stuck it into her right ear. Then she put her left index finger into her left ear. Anybody who saw us about then would have sworn that it wasn't iced tea on the table.

My vibrating phone interrupted our teenage antics.

"Natalie, hello. This is Deputy Peterson."

Deputy Peterson? He had always insisted I call him Marshal.

"Uh, hi, Marshal." I gestured to Ramee that I'd take the call outside. "I haven't heard from you in a few weeks."

"And I'm sorry about that, Natalie. We've been so busy that I wasn't able to keep in touch. Not that I had anything to update, but I should have at least called on occasion."

"That's okay."

"How have you been? Are you getting along okay?"

Am I getting along okay? I had been so busy keeping Moose and myself a secret at the Legends that I hadn't actually asked that question. Over the last weeks and months, our advanced scheming around the Legends had become an effective coping mechanism that kept my mind from wandering to sad places. Lately, I'd been crying a lot less, which was a good sign. Another good sign was that I'd stopped blaming Grandpa for things I encountered that he used to handle, like a huge spider in the bedroom that had refused to leave on its own when I opened the door to the deck. A swift brush with the broom took care of that problem visitor. Tonight I was out to dinner with my friends, and we hadn't started talking about Grandpa yet, which must have meant that I was getting along reasonably well. Still, "I think so," was the best reply I could come up with.

"This isn't just a friendly call to ask how you're doing," said Marshal. "Natalie, this is one of the worst types of calls I have to make, but I need to inform you that we've closed the case on James Thomas, your grandpa."

Closed the case? That was bad, right? That meant there was no hope of finding Grandpa, right? That meant Grandpa wasn't going to show up some night and give me the hug I'd been longing for, right?

"Are you still there?" asked Marshal.

"Um, yeah, I'm still here. I was just thinking about a few things."

"I hate to have to tell you this over the phone, but I knew I couldn't get into town for at least a couple of weeks and didn't want you to wait any longer. Obviously, nothing has turned up, and after a period of time, we're forced to close our files. It was your Uncle Jerry who persuaded us to keep it open a few months longer than we usually would."

An image of Uncle Jerry persuading the uniformed officers crossed my mind, complete with the intimidating vocabulary I was quite certain he had employed in that conversation.

"I guess I've been expecting this call. Is there anything I need to do?"

Marshal spoke for a few minutes, but after he explained that I had no actions to take, I lost track of the words. With a sullen face, I returned to Ramee and DeAndre and filled them in on the conversation, which included Marshal working with Uncle Jerry on the death certificate; the last formal detail.

We split at the door when we left. I walked down the sidewalk in the opposite direction stopping in front of the same boutique window where only a few months ago Grandpa and I watched a keychain carousel perform its unending circular dance with a small black dog keychain chasing a poodle keychain on each rotation—the same keychain that Chip had found in the river.

I rubbed a chill from my arms. Moments ago I was surrounded by friends, and though I hadn't actually expected Grandpa to return, at least the door in my mind was open to the possibility. Now that Marshal had firmly closed that door, I felt very alone. I wanted Grandpa to come back. I wanted my friends to come back. I wanted Andy to come back. The reflection of my face in the glass was as clear as any mirror. I looked exhausted. I looked alone, and it occurred to me that if I was ever going to get myself together, I would have to do it alone. The games were over.

*　　*　　*

Though dinner with my friends had kept me out later than usual, I was still up early on Saturday morning and had finished my chores an hour before I needed to drive to the church, so Moose and I walked to our hill and gazed at the rippling water. After a few moments reflecting on the times I had sat on the same hill with Grandpa, listening to his stories about sledding and fishing and life, I led Moose to the water's edge and bowed my head in prayer. I placed a wallet-sized photo of Grandpa on the water's surface and watched the breeze push the picture away from shore until it was out of sight. Marshal had his closure, and now I had mine. An hour later, I was placing Sunday Missals in the pews at St. John.

After setting the last Missal in the corner of the back pew, I turned around to find Father Diamond standing behind me.

"Thank you for your help this morning. It's always nice to see our younger parishioners so involved."

He sat down and gestured for me to join him.

The prolonged silence prompted me to speak first. "I think I could start helping on Tuesday evenings, if there's anything you need. Maybe I could teach a catechism class or something?"

"As much as it warms my soul to see parishioners helping every day, it is equally important not to overextend oneself in the service of the church."

My surprised look prompted clarification and a chuckle that was a little softer than Grandpa's.

"I can always use another teacher, but I didn't sit here this morning to solve my troubles. I sense something is troubling you."

How do you know these things?

I released a heavy sigh, then filled Father Diamond in on everything from Grandpa's kayaking accident to Angie's party and explained how the game I had started by fooling residents had turned into a trap with no way out. After I described my makeshift memorial at the lake, my shoulders felt ten pounds lighter. Father Diamond's face had remained placid throughout, though I glimpsed a hint of a smile during my description of the hand wipe incident with Gwen.

Again, he allowed the silence to linger while he appeared to mull over my predicament. "You feel as though you are in a trap with no way out. In God, there is always a way."

I offered a hushed "Uh-huh."

The weight on my shoulders began to return until his eyes caught mine.

"Such a complicated situation for someone so young."

He looked over at the light shining above the Stations of the Cross almost as though he were drawing strength from the warming glow. I felt the same warmth and sensed powerful advice coming my way.

"The solution to your problem is within your problem. Trust in the Lord."

My eyes wanted to roll after he left, but something held them fixed on the light.

The entire drive home to the Legends, I kept repeating, often in a sarcastic tone, "The solution to your problem is within your problem." *What the heck did he mean?*

Chapter 38

Others Know

MOOSE BEHAVED SO well at his annual checkup on Monday that I stopped to get him a pup cup on the way home from the veterinarian. Following my new strict regime of no unnecessary purchases, I ordered nothing for myself, which had me feeling a little prideful as I exited the drive-thru, but only momentarily, because at the end of the block, four turkeys fluttered from the curb into the middle of the road where they stopped to glare at me. I hit the brakes, which threw Moose's pup cup to the floor. Rather than bark like mad at the ugly birds, he dove to the floorboard in search of the remaining whipped cream cup. By the time I pulled Grandpa's SUV into the Legends parking lot, my nerves were frazzled and I still had to avoid small drifts of snow on the way to the short ramp into the garage.

I preferred driving my smaller SUV, which I kept parked outside at the Manor, but once or twice a week I drove Grandpa's. A somber thought, of which I'd had many lately, passed through my mind: how long would I refer to this SUV as Grandpa's?

Halfway to his reserved spot, I saw two gray-headed

individuals in the next row and noticed the movement of another individual a few cars farther down. A cringe coursed through my body. I had been lax in devising excuses for my presence at the Legends ever since Angie's party and had nothing formulated for this trip with Moose. I could only hope that nobody would see us.

My *ugh* brought Moose to attention.

"Of all the stupid luck."

A dome light came on in the car two spaces away from Grandpa's spot. Angie stepped out with a familiar glare and stared as I pulled in.

Having seen Angie in the garage on only one other occasion, I had led myself to believe that she didn't drive often. She stalked, strutted, and strolled the grounds constantly in search of Moose and me, but I'd seldom seen her in a vehicle. My gut sank, but the façade needed to be maintained rain or shine, depressed or not, at least until I figured out how *the solution to my problem was within my problem.*

I screwed my game face on and climbed out of the car.

"Isn't that sweet?" I whispered sarcastically. "She's waiting for us. Maybe you could give her a little chase around the garage."

With a bag in each hand, Moose on the leash, and keys hanging from my teeth, I headed to the stairs. The elevator was a better option, but I didn't want to wait next to Angie until the elevator arrived, and being in a confined space with that woman was not a good idea.

"I see you're driving James' car now."

"Every once in a while," I replied in the muffled voice of a person with keys in her mouth. "He usually takes the train to work. Doesn't need the car much."

"I haven't seen James in some time."

Her expressionless face reminded me of Ms. Ass, another witch like Angie but one that I would thankfully not be seeing around the Legends again.

"He was at your party." My keys fell when I reached for the doorknob to the ground floor.

"I haven't *spoken* to him," she replied with a bitter edge in her tone.

Once again, I feigned an exhausted voice—which didn't sound very convincing. "Join the club. I doubt I've seen him twice since your party either. I don't know where he gets all his energy. He seems to like the new job and has made a lot of new friends." As a last resort, I finally pulled out the largest weapon in the arsenal. "Including a lady that he has dinner with almost every night. I've been wanting to grill something for him, but between the cold weather and his schedule, we never seem to get together." I had been lying so often and for so long, I didn't give it a second thought when a story needed fabricated but deep down, the lies still bothered me. Once I figured out the solution to my problem, I'd have to schedule an extended session with Father Diamond in the confessional, but right now, I was struggling to see how his cryptic wisdom about choices and solutions to problems could clean up the mess I'd made of things.

She was still on my heels in the lobby.

"Where *exactly* does he work?"

The bags were heavy, and Moose was tugging on the leash. I needed to put the groceries inside and walk him before he hiked his leg right in front of her.

"Digitronics Plus 2."

"Yes, that's what his social media page indicates, but as you know, that is a large company. What store does he work at?"

"He's not at a store, Angie." I feigned an "*obviously*" look. "He's corporate. He manages something related to digital electronics." I wasn't about to tell her that I worked at the same place—a detail I hadn't even shared with Louis, and he was the one who got me the job.

I adjusted my grip on the bags. "I need to drop these in

his apartment and get home, Angie. I'll talk to you later."
I started walking.

She followed.

"But where exactly does he work? What does he do?
You know, my daughter works in electronics. She would
like to talk to him about it."

Of course she does. Your daughter does everything—
except visit.

"Don't know what else to tell you. I haven't been to his
office."

I unlocked the apartment door, stepped inside, and
closed it behind me in a single motion. I immediately peeled
my jacket off and set everything on the table, then went out
the back with Moose. In my haste to get Moose outside and
on the way to the Manor in time for Angie to see us walking in that direction, I had set my keys and phone down
together with the bags—and locked myself out.

I barely had the energy to push out an *ugh*.

We made our way around the complex with Moose
sniffing and marking every bush at a much too leisurely
pace, considering that my jacket was on the table inside the
apartment.

At the barbecue grills, which glistened with ice crys-
tals, we peered through the window. Lights were out in the
locked great room. A twist of the knob on the fire pit timer
brought forth flames that were just high enough to take
the chill off. I sat on Thelma's bench and pulled my arms
in tight to fend off an icy breeze. Moose joined me on the
bench; his head on my lap provided enough extra warmth
that I ignored his dripping nose. Twenty minutes passed
before I noticed movement inside the great room. The lights
flicked on. PJ approached the coffeepot.

I tapped numb knuckles lightly on the glass.

Evidently the frozen snot on my nose and the dusting of
ice in my hair surprised her. She rushed to the door faster

than I had seen any old person move at the Legends. "Come in. Come in. You'll catch your death of cold."

A phrase I expected regardless of who opened the door.

As my body warmed, a chill coursed through me, bringing goose bumps and an uncontrollable shake that also chattered my teeth.

"I...accidentally...locked...us out."

"You poor dear. Let's get you some coffee. Sit right here. I'll bring you a cup."

We sat at the corner table opposite the window, Moose at my feet.

"Wrap your hands around this. It will help."

She handed me a cup and gave me a moment to soak in the warmth.

"How have you been, dear? I know it's hard, but you can talk to me if you're ready."

I wasn't sure exactly what she meant. Patti Jane and Louis were two of my favorite residents, but I had never confided in them, though I suspected Louis knew something. I kept my group of trusted friends small because the risk was so high, but I desperately wanted to trust PJ and get everything out in the open. The chill returned, bringing with it an image of me sleeping in my car on a frozen winter night.

"It's not a big deal. I've locked myself out before."

Patti Jane looked at me with the same aged wisdom I used to see in Grandpa. Was the gleam from the light, or was there more to my friend? I looked away.

"Well," she continued in a soothing voice, "it's hard living alone. If you ever need anything, our door is always open."

A tear crawled down my face and curled into the corner of my lip. "How did you know?"

She took a sip of her coffee. "That wasn't James at the party."

Duh! I could have slapped my forehead. How could I have forgotten that she spoke with Jerry at the party?

"But this has been going on for some time now," she said. "Many months."

For the second time that day, I found myself explaining what I had done, why I had done it, and how sorry I was for everything. I then described my conversation with Father Diamond and his advice that the solution to my problem was within my problem.

"I think he's right," said PJ.

This time I allowed my eyes to roll, though discreetly.

Patti Jane kept Moose at her feet while I went to the front desk to get a spare key. When I returned to get my furry friend, the look in my eyes must have told her how worried I was that the secret was out.

"Louis and I have been rather taken with you, Natalie. When you started helping Gwen, I was touched by how caring you are for your age. You see, Gwen and I were quite close. I've been fond of you ever since you started taking care of her. You were simply being a friend with nothing in it for yourself."

"I wouldn't say there was nothing in it for me. I got a really good friend out of the deal."

We talked about Gwen and how I had buried her next to Robert under the apple tree. A perfect ending to a perfect love. We found ourselves smiling at various stories we each shared, including the first time I took Gwen shopping. It was nice to hear new things about my special friend. I didn't talk about Grandpa, and she didn't ask. That conversation was for another day. I left with the knowledge that I had another confidant at the Legends and the words "Don't forget to gargle with warm water and salt" following me down the hall.

I stared at Grandpa's door before I opened it, contemplating what life would be like when I was no longer allowed to enter. If Patti Jane and Louis knew, then certainly more residents were aware of my situation. Possibly a lot more. I would need to figure out the solution to my problem pretty soon, and it was becoming clear that nobody was going to offer an actionable plan.

The click of Thelma's doorknob caused me to look in her direction as she poked her head into the hall. "You can call me when you lock yourself out." She pulled her head back inside just as fast as it had come out.

* * *

Though it seemed many residents were aware of my living conditions, I still clung to the hope that enough people were in the dark that I was not yet in imminent danger of being evicted. To reinforce my visitor status to those who weren't aware of my permanency at the Legends, especially Angie, I brought home some marketing swag from DP2 and left the bag in the hall for an hour to allow residents walking past Grandpa's door to see it. I also set a DP2 coffee cup on the dash of the SUV where Angie would be sure to notice it, and on Saturday morning, I carried a cloth DP2 bag to the great room, where I found Orval sitting at his usual table talking to his coffee or the window. His oxygen tank was on one hip, and his shopping bag was hanging from the crossbar of his walker. Without asking, I joined the little man.

Over the last few months, we had developed an interesting relationship in which he treated me like family, and I felt awkward but obligated to carry on the role.

"Your bag is looking a little worn, Orval. Here, take this one."

He accepted the bag with a smile and an extra quiver of his lower lip. He then reached for his old bag, much like Gwen used to reach for her purse in the basket of her scooter. Bent, arthritic fingers with nails in serious need of a clipping took four tries to secure the strap, each attempt performed with the same deliberation as the last. He finally pulled the bag off the crossbar and poured the items onto the table. An asthma inhaler, a pair of extra-large, extra-wide, extra-dark sunglasses that he probably should have worn on our walk to the store last summer, wads of used tissue, a bottle of lotion, and a square plastic alarm clock complete with an irritatingly loud second hand. A final shake released a seven-day pill pack, a wallet, and a flip phone.

For a talkative man, Orval was not much of a conversationalist. He began filling the new bag while resuming a story he had often told in our odd encounters. A story I thought had ended at the front door of the complex upon our return from the grocery store last summer. After just enough detail to get me up to speed on a train passing through Omaha, the small plastic clock, which was not much bigger than his flip phone, knocked me back with a gong almost as loud as Grandpa's mantel clock.

"Whoa! That'll wake you up."

No reply. But the remark drew a smile, directed either at me or at the yellow tablet he fished from the pillbox. He popped the pill into his mouth, tossed his head back like a pro, gulped one swallow from the water bottle, and continued the story.

When he paused to inhale a deep breath, which required three stages to complete, I took the opportunity to add to the conversation. "I drive through Omaha when I visit family in Texas."

His fingers stopped filling the bag but continued to vibrate. Eyes that normally drifted from side to side zeroed in on a flock of dust specks hovering in a sunbeam. When his mind eventually returned to the Legends, he said, "Not Omaha. Don't go there, Natalie. Nothing good happens in Omaha. Not in the dark. Not by the trains. *Don't go to Omaha.*"

At least he heard me, something I questioned often in

our conversations. My promise to never travel to Nebraska seemed to relieve his odd anxiety.

He opened the wallet, unfolded a string of pictures, and set the accordion arrangement on edge.

I tasted the salty tears before I realized they were streaming down my cheeks. My eyes never left the black-and-white photos of his wife and daughter as I reached for the wad of used tissue. The little girl looked exactly like me. Her round face. Her dark hair in a long bob. Bright eyes and a smile with dimples that kissed each cheek, just like my dimples.

"Her name was Natalie too," he said with much less quiver in his voice than usual.

His eyes caught mine, possibly for the first time ever.

"I need to keep her memory alive. You of all people here surely understand. She was so young. Her entire life was ahead of her, just as so much of your life is ahead of you." His eyes drifted to the window before returning to me with renewed strength. "I often find myself in conversation with my little girl. She replies as though she is here with me."

He released the saddest wheezy chuckle I had ever heard.

"People think I'm losing my mind. I hear what they say, but I'm simply talking to my daughter."

"I'm so sorry, Orval. I didn't know. Seeing me around here must make you feel so sad."

His eyes perked and his quivering lips smiled. "On the contrary, my life has been wonderful since the day I first bumped into you. I know you're not *my* Natalie, but you're as close as I'll ever be. I've found that talking to my wife and daughter keeps them present, where they belong. It's been so long. Memories and photos fade no matter how hard one tries to maintain them. Your presence has brought color to my memories—bright, happy colors."

The surprisingly coherent conversation was both heart-breaking and uplifting. It had never occurred to me that simply being present could mean so much to someone. We talked until the plastic clock gonged again, prompting him to reach for the pillbox.

While he took his medication, I glanced around the room, which was still mostly empty. The great room had become so familiar to me, so comfortable. A place where I sat and visited with people that I had come to know well. People I considered family. I imagined the grandmotherly Bea smiling toward me from her perch, often providing guidance. I imagined Louis as the great-uncle, with his boisterous laugh, together with his partner in life, Patti Jane, always concerned about the health and well-being of others. Thelma and Orval would be the peculiar aunt and uncle who you knew would be there if you ever needed them. Even Angie and Gladys were part of the family—the distant cousins you would never want to live without but have trouble living with.

Orval snapped the pillbox closed loudly, bringing my thoughts back to the table. He reached out to hang the bag back on the walker.

"I gotta ask you, Orval, why do you use the walker? I mean, it's a little slow. Everyone else here has a scooter."

With a dimpled smile as big as his little round head, he replied, "Because I can, Natalie. Because I still can."

As I stood to leave, I leaned in for a hug which produced a familiar crinkling and waft of urine, no longer noxious.

*   *   *

Back in the apartment, I sat on the couch with Moose and stared at the walls I had been so desperate to protect. It occurred to me that the walls had in fact been protecting me for the better part of a year. I had started this adventure thinking of Legends residents as nothing more than old farts who were easy to trick. But these people were family, and aside from Uncle Jerry, my only family, yet I was still trying to trick them every day. Had I continued to lie and deceive just to stay at the Legends? Was I treating these people so unfairly just to save rent? Working two jobs and employing a little discipline—another lesson from Grandpa that had somehow crept in—had my finances in reasonable shape. Moving wouldn't be easy, but I had moved plenty of times.

The truth of the matter was that I didn't want to move, because I couldn't afford to lose any more family. But what was it costing me to stay? What was it costing them?

*   *   *

Convincing people that Grandpa was living at the Legends and I was not, when in fact I was living there and he was not, had begun to turn my stomach, but not quite enough for me to make an adult decision and stop all the nonsense. Grandpa's job at Digitronics Plus 2 didn't exist. The cruise had been contrived, and the excuse that I was taking care of his apartment was a total farce—Grandpa didn't even have plants to water. For months, I had been worried about Angie finding me out and telling everyone, but I was beginning to think that she might be the only resident who didn't know.

Moose and I sat on the balcony to watch a rare cloudless winter sunset. There was a sadness in the evening hue, as though the somber reds and oranges understood that happier yellows had left and would not return until spring.

Thelma's crisp voice from the balcony next door broke the silence. "What can you spell with the vowels I and U and the letters T, G, and L?"

I had been waiting for an opportunity to play Scrabble and impress her with my vocabulary. My brain quickly assessed the options.

"*Guilt!*" I replied excitedly. "Wait, that's only five letters."

"It's a very difficult game for someone so young. It may be time to show your letters."

Chapter 39

Got a Minute

I SPENT THE evening searching for apartments, which turned into a reality check that I wasn't prepared for. Massive changes in the economy had shot rents to record highs. As flush as my savings account was, I still needed at least another month to have enough money to move, and if I could get by for another month, then I should just extend that through winter and move to a new apartment when the weather was nice. I somehow convinced myself that lying to the residents was the only thing I was doing wrong, so if I stopped lying, everything would be okay while I maintained the charade a little longer.

I started avoiding the great room altogether and changed my commuting patterns to stay out of sight. The new plan was largely successful and resulted in fewer pangs of guilt because I seldom looked into the eye of another resident—but it was a lonely plan.

On the walk home from the bus stop after work, I ordered takeout at Yang's and caught Wi in her typical talkative mood. She first filled me in on her lunch rush fiasco, then described in way too much detail all the things her husband had done on his day off. I thought about how nice it would be to have a day off. A day without worry over my life, my dog, my apartment, my finances. *My dog!* I had spent thirty minutes listening to Wi while Moose was in the apartment, probably howling to be let out.

I picked up my pace and took the most direct route back to the apartment—through the front door of the Legends. While I wiped my snow-covered shoes on the metal-grated rug, a suspicious voice found my ear.

"Good evening, Natalie."

Ugh. "Hey, Angie."

"I haven't seen James in months. Where have you been hiding him?"

Her pinched lips reminded me of Ms. Ass.

I feigned disgust, but it was a weak effort. "He came to your party, and you don't even remember." Actual disgust settled in my stomach after the first lie I had told in two weeks rolled off my tongue without hesitation.

"You want me to *believe* that I saw him. That was quite an elaborate performance you managed to pull off. I might have been impressed if the joke were not at my expense." She glanced at the lone Chinese take-out container dangling from my fingers. "Dinner for one?"

"Yep."

"It's been dinner for one every time I see you. Does James *ever* eat at home?"

"Not since he started seeing Janice." A name I made up on the fly and would have DeAndre add to Grandpa's social media profile as soon as my nervous fingers stopped vibrating long enough to send a text.

"Janice? I don't believe I know her," she said with even less conviction in the made-up name than I had conveyed.

"I mentioned her to you when we were in the garage. He met her at work."

"How convenient. Now he has another reason to be away."

"Look, Angie, between his job and his new lady friend, I don't see him much either. I'm just here to water the plants and clean up the place a little before he gets home, then I have to do the same thing at my apartment. I'm kind of pressed for time."

I couldn't blame her for not believing me. I could hardly even listen to my lies anymore. Father Diamond's words resonated in my ear, *"The solution to your problem is within your problem."* Ugh. *My problem is Angie.*

Patti Jane walked up from behind. "Missed you Saturday, dear." She put her hands on my shoulders and gave me a little squeeze. "James took us to a restaurant by the lake. Said it was one of your favorite places. Will you be joining us next time?"

Whoa. I was not used to people helping out as much as they had been lately.

"Uh, I thought dinner was *next* week." I shook my head in disappointment, but as with the rest of the conversation, it was a weak effort.

"Janice is such a doll," said Patti Jane.

"Isn't she?"

Flames in Angie's eyes melted the rest of the snow off of my shoes. Her lip twitched. "I see you have another on your side."

Thelma approached from the hall. "Don't you have something better to do?" she said firmly. "Leave this girl alone for a change. Do us all a favor and mind your own business."

Angie huffed and left.

*   *   *

"What are we going to do, Moose? We can't keep pretending that residents don't know."

His snout didn't move, but his eyes glanced up with a look that said, "What do you mean, *we*?"

I sat at Grandpa's table and thought about the first day we toured the unit. The high ceilings had not only provided space, they provided a feeling of openness. Warmth from the early spring sun had poured through the windows that were now touched with winter frost. The new-apartment smell had long since faded, and the once-shiny appliances had dulled to match the winter sky. The apartment was full of Grandpa's furniture and Grandpa's things, which were no longer haunting reminders of what had happened but pleasant memories of times past. It was his apartment, but it felt like my home. A home I had kept relatively clean since the smoke detector incident. I had never lived any-where so nice—but at what price?

The truth was closing in on me. Bea, the Js, Patti Jane, Louis, and Orval all knew. I was also convinced that Thelma knew much more than she let on. Such wonderful people, and they were all lying for me, abandoning a moral foundation they had spent a lifetime building.

I picked at my food, sharing more than usual with Moose, before taking a long walk outside. I no longer cared about the wind or the snow or whether Angie saw us. I had a lot to think about. Life at the Legends was coming to an end.

My somber mood hadn't improved by morning when I took Moose out. Angie was lurking in the parking lot. Her cold look chilled me to the bone even more than the icy air.

Work was slow until shortly after lunch, when the phone rang.

"This is Natalie."

"I spoke with James at Digitronics Plus 2. He's thirty-six years old, and he *does not* live at the Legends. The man had no idea what I was talking about. I've already informed the Legends management."

It was Angie. I was busted.

"I'm at work, Angie." I hung up the phone.

I couldn't focus the rest of the afternoon, and the bus ride home only made me feel worse. I took the last empty seat, which left standing room only for the dozen additional commuters who followed me onboard. The heater, as usual, was warmer than necessary for a load of people bundled in what would be considered ski apparel anywhere else in the country. A rather large man stood in front of me with his hindquarters inches from my face. The garlic he evidently ate at lunch sweated out of him and wafted my way. The teenage girl to my right on the leg-against-leg bench seat was talking on the phone to her boyfriend. Her tricolored hair fell loosely onto her shoulders, and she wore more makeup than I use in a week. Evidently, her mother had never taught her how to use an inside voice, which made me an unwitting eavesdropper of intimate details discussed in a cryptic language that seemed to omit every third word.

My dejected walk from the bus stop to the Legends gave the chilly air time to temper a splitting headache, which had been exacerbated by exhaust fumes that entered the bus every time the back door opened. I leashed Moose as soon as I entered the apartment and headed to the grass at the Manor. Angie watched our every move from the window, which sapped all the energy from my *ugh*.

We returned unaccosted and had lukewarm leftovers for dinner, with Moose eating most of my portion. We curled up on the couch, where I scrolled through my phone searching for photos of Grandpa and me, Grandpa and Moose, and selfies of the three of us. I had hundreds of pictures of food, friends, and my furry canine. The paltry number of pictures that included Grandpa was disappointing and would never provide the lifetime of memories I would need.

I played the last video I had taken of Grandpa. A clip of him at the sink, dishing out constructive ridicule of my ability to get a dirty plate all the way to the counter but not into the dishwasher. I fell asleep to the sound of his voice.

*　　*　　*

After tossing and turning all night, I awoke with a mission to make things right. The lying stopped today. After work, I would tell residents in the great room the truth about Grandpa's accident, Uncle Jerry, and my living at the Legends. But first, I needed to tell Wayne.

I dressed for work and stopped at the office on my way out only to find an empty desk and an Out of Office sign on Wayne's door. Maybe he had taken that vacation to New Orleans. I plopped down in the chair, grabbed a pen, and wrote him a note.

"Wayne, I would like to schedule a meeting with you at your earliest convenience."

I rocked back in the chair and stared at the words. Did I really need to leave a note when I could just stop by after work? And if he was in New Orleans, he would probably be gone for at least a week. My commitment was still losing the battle with my intentions.

I crumpled the note, tossed it into the bin, and exited through the front door. As I turned toward my bus stop two blocks away, I saw Angie sitting alone on a bench. I bit my lip and slowed my pace. The game was over.

"Hey, Angie. Got a minute?"

Chapter 40

A Moment of Self-Respect

"I AM SO sorry, Angie." The words felt good and were hopefully a first step in returning my long-lost self-respect.

The woman on the bench had made a terrible first impression when I met her at the entry table. Snippy remarks, fake smiles, and her detest of dogs had turned me against her from the beginning. But I had known for a long time that I had never given Angie a chance. My childish contempt and irrational fear that she was somehow a cougar on the prowl for Grandpa had been utterly ridiculous.

She interrupted before I could continue. "Please, no apology is necessary."

What? I've been a jerk for months, and *no apology is necessary?*

Angie and I sat on that bench for an hour. She had suspected something was up early on, and by the time the leaves had turned, she was quite certain. My living at the Legends had never actually bothered her. Being the butt of every joke and the only resident who supposedly didn't know what was going on was what had gotten under her skin. The main reason she moved to the Legends was to build a new family after her husband passed away, but residents had maintained an arm's-length relationship because they didn't trust her, largely because I never trusted her. A lack of close friends had left her lonely and caused her to skip various events and social opportunities. Events I had avoided to keep a low profile, she had avoided because residents treated her...differently. Like someone who couldn't keep a secret. The only way she knew how to cope, to maintain her sanity, was to paint a scowl on her face and move forward.

Though her voice carried no animosity or anger, the words shattered my brief moment of self-respect. What had I done to these people? What kind of misery had I put this woman through? Because of me, she had missed opportunities to make new friends in her new home. She had spent the last nine months feeling even more isolated than me.

I lowered my head. "I'm the reason they don't trust you."

"That's not important."

Again with the nice. Yell at me. Please!

The more we learned about each other, the more I came to understand that Angie could be snooty and snide, just like I can be rude and obnoxious, but below the surface, we were not very different. The bony-fingered woman sitting next to me had pulled plenty of capers in her day. Her description of them as "capers" narrowed the timeline of those activities to something on the order of three decades before I was born. But the birthday party was her lowest point. A day she had looked forward to, a day to celebrate with her friends and daughter, had turned into a public humiliation that she was forced to endure with a smile. When she saw how many people were involved, she realized that everyone was keeping the secret from her. A revelation that created even more isolation, and to make matters worse, her daughter never showed.

That brief feeling of self-respect curdled in my stomach. On what should have been a joyous day for this woman, I had embarrassed her, then met up with Uncle Jerry and my friends to gloat over our success. We had left Angie in the crowded room surrounded by people who were part of the charade, all singing "Happy Birthday."

Angie needed to talk, and I needed to let her. Other than with Gladys and a couple of shut-ins on the ground floor, she seldom had meaningful conversations with residents. When the conversation turned to her daughter, so much of what she said sounded like Gwen talking about her son.

Three buses had come and gone while we talked. I was going to be late to the office, but that time could be made up. This time was much too important to miss. When Angie left, my thoughts turned to Gwen and how her son had been too busy to be bothered by his mother, much like Angie's daughter was too busy to visit. I flashed a prideful smile as I thought of all my visits with Grandpa. A tiny bit of self-respect returned. At least Grandpa had a granddaughter who cared. He had left this world knowing he was loved.

I stepped onto the bus and negotiated my way past a woman with a brown dog leashed to a red assistance harness. My mind drifted to my best friend, Moose, as I found a seat. I thought about how scared I was when he got sick. How I almost lost him when he got into the chocolate. Twice he had ended up at the vet. Twice Grandpa had paid the bill. How many times *had* Grandpa paid my bills? My rent? My car? Had I really treated him just like Gwen's son had treated her? Or like Angie's daughter treated her? Were Grandpa and I close, or had he just been convenient? That tiny bit of self-respect was ground into the floor like the mud under my shoe.

I arrived at work over an hour late with a feeling that I had been punched in the gut. Though the long talk with my new friend had eased my stress over an imminent eviction,

I was now burdened with guilt for having tormented Angie and having treated Grandpa as my personal ATM. Three hours later, I had barely completed an hour's worth of work, which wasn't fair to the company. I rolled my eyes at how easily Grandpa's little sayings entered my mind, then emailed my boss that I would be taking the rest of the day off because I wasn't feeling well. A truthful excuse, something I had promised myself began today.

The cramped seats and smelly bodies didn't bother me on the ride home, because my mind was elsewhere. I was almost twenty-five years old. *It's time to grow up.* Something Grandpa had often insinuated in subtle conversations or through his life-lesson lectures. I'd heard the phrase around the great room when residents talked about their children and grandchildren, but I couldn't remember Grandpa having ever actually said, "It's time to grow up."

I stepped from the bus and looked skyward. *Maybe a little tough love would have helped me learn the important things.* The bus pulled away from the curb, belching a plume of diesel smoke that forced me to smile. *You're right. My thick head wouldn't have accepted that either.*

My walk from the bus stop was slow, deliberate, and full of thought. Though Moose needed a walk, I needed to fix things first.

I entered the half-full great room, which was abuzz in low-key conversation. Orval looked up from his coffee and quivered his lips in a hello. Bea smiled from her table and offered a supporting nod. *How do you always know?* Louis and PJ sat at a middle table with Angie, Gladys, Glen, and Millie.

Louis motioned me over. "Here's our girl."

I stepped up behind him and placed one hand on his shoulder and one hand on Angie's shoulder. The solution to my problem was indeed within my problem—Angie.

"Is this seat taken?"

Chapter 41

Just When Things Get Better

THE NOTE CLIPPED to my door was visible as soon as I entered the hallway, but every door had a note, which indicated the issue was more likely maintenance-related than Moose-related. I read the page as I turned the key.

"We are proud to announce the new General Manager of the Manor/Legends Complex. Please join us in welcoming Ms. Christine Glass as the leader of our management team. We ask that—"

The paper slid from my fingers to the floor. I had barely mustered the courage to tell Wayne the truth upon his return. Legends residents were willing to plead with him to allow me to stay until I could find a new place. How could I sit across from the warden, who had shown no mercy for my minor infractions at the Manor, and explain to her that I had been lying for months?

I picked the note up and read it again just in case I was losing my mind or something else was wrong with my head that would be easier to deal with. The last few lines explained that Ms. Glass had scheduled a meet-and-greet in the great room, complete with cookies and tea. In an effort to get to know each resident personally, she would schedule appointments with every tenant.

Any hope of leniency evaporated. I pushed out one of the deep sighs that had become common lately. It was good that I had decided to come clean, because I didn't have the strength or desire to continue this charade on the warden. Obviously, I would miss the meet-and-greet, and I would delay the face-to-face meeting as long as possible, but that could only last a week or so. The realization that my time at the Legends had truly come to an end sent a shudder down my spine.

I opened my laptop and searched for apartments. Again, the search was in vain and did nothing to lift my spirits. Units that were immediately available were expensive, run-down, and generally located in areas where I wouldn't be able to walk Moose after dark. The Legends was gorgeous. The location was perfect. Everything I needed was only a block away. Most of all, I had friends here. Maybe not anyone who would hike the hill that overlooked Sliver Lake with me, except the Js, but these people were true friends.

I exhaled a deep sigh and looked from wall to wall. Surprisingly, the room didn't feel as tight. The walls weren't closing in. Father Diamond's words came to mind. I did have a choice, and I was finally choosing to do the right thing. "It's been a good ride, Moose, but all good things come to an end."

For some reason, I still felt as though I was accepting my fate without a fight, but as I thought about it more, I realized I had been fighting for most of the year.

I called Ramee and talked for an hour. She understood how exhausting the fight had been and had seen the toll it had taken on me. She agreed I should come clean with

Ms. Glass and offered to let us stay with her for as long as it took to find another place.

*   *   *

I tapped three times and waited for Bea to open the door. The Js were sitting in her living room engaged in chatty conversation until the look on my face quieted the trio. Fake flowers on the coffee table brought to mind the day Grandpa moved into the complex. At the time, I had looked at the old residents as feeble geriatrics and couldn't imagine Grandpa ever being that old. Now I would give anything for him to have the opportunity.

"I'm glad you're all here. It's been tough living with myself lately, and now everything is closing in on me all at once—but that's okay, because it's my fault that I'm in this situation. It's all my fault."

A gentle silence fell over the normally loquacious group like a soft snowfall. I had come to understand this as the wisdom of age. They knew I needed to clear my conscience.

"This was supposed to be fun. Just Grandpa and me pretending that I was visiting until I landed a new job and could afford my own place. My whole life, I've been getting in over my head. Living at the Manor was great, but I couldn't afford it. Instead of being responsible for myself and getting another job, I was always asking Grandpa to help with rent. And it's not just that. Every time something went wrong, I blamed somebody else. The apartment manager, a neighbor, a friend, even Moose, but it was all my fault. Living at the Legends was a privilege, but I didn't realize it. I've had a special opportunity to be surrounded by friends who have taught me a lot about growing up and being responsible. It's up to me to make things work in this life, just like all of you have had to do for so long. You know, I've never heard anyone in this place complain, except Angie, and even *that* was my fault."

I sucked in a deep breath and exhaled a year's worth of stress. "I want to be the person who looks back with no regret, and right now, I regret that all of you have had to cover for me. It's not right, and it's time I put an end to all of this."

Chapter 42

Read the Contract

THE EARLIEST APPOINTMENT I could get with Ms. Glass was after work the following day. My stress had eased considerably, because I'd resigned myself to the outcome regardless of the impact and had even started filling boxes in preparation for the instant eviction. I was giving up a free luxury apartment even though I hadn't been officially caught by the manager, but having to worry about every move I made and every word I spoke each time I entered or left the apartment was just too much.

"Come in, Natalie," said Ms. Ass in a pleasant tone, probably soaking in the thrill of the kill. "Please, sit down. We need to discuss your grandfather's arrangements."

Arrangements? What would she know about arrangements? I knew I was busted. I knew everything needed to be moved out—and what industrial-strength lubricant had she applied to curve those permanently pursed lips into a smile? A smile that didn't even look cynical, though she wouldn't know any other kind.

As I sat down, I noticed pictures on her desk of residents from other complexes she had managed. Photos of tenants receiving awards for best balcony garden, prettiest walker, and best-decorated door for various holidays. Sadness replaced bitterness as I reflected on my time at the Legends. The real friends I had here. All the things I had learned, like the term "octogenarian," the capacity of an adult diaper, and that milk sometimes ends up in the pantry. Who was going to take the Js shopping? Who would sit with Mr. Anders?

Who was I kidding? These people would all be better off without me. For decades, they had gotten along on their own. When Grandpa and I started this, he said it would be fun to try, and I guess it was at first, but we never talked about how hard it might be to end. I couldn't allow these seniors to compromise their integrity any longer.

"It's okay," I replied quietly. "I know what you're going to say."

"I'm not sure you do, sweetheart."

Sweetheart? Why was she trying to make this so difficult for me? Deservedly so, but I hadn't conned her—just everyone else at the Legends. Maybe it was because she finally had me right where she wanted for so long—on the doorstep with a high-heel shoe aimed at my butt.

"It's time I explain something that I was asked to keep secret long ago. You see, Natalie, I knew James very well. We met in Texas and were friends for more than twenty years. Very good friends."

I was only half listening because I knew the conversation would end with my eviction, but as she spoke, I began to think it might be more appropriate to refer to her as Ms. Glass.

"When you first applied for the apartment at the Manor, we were full. Not a single vacancy and none expected for months. Of course, we always have the showroom apartment for prospective tenants to view. That was the unit you saw and eventually moved into. Jimmy told me how much you loved the complex, so I just had to rent to you. It was the least I could do for a man who had been with me so long and seen me through some of my own hard times."

My thoughts transitioned from combative to curious. "If you were such good friends with Grandpa, how come you never spoke to me when I said "hi," and how come I was fined for every little thing?"

"That requires a little explanation as well. You see, your grandfather knew that you could barely make the rent but that you would indeed make it. He always loved how you dedicated yourself to anything you felt was important. From your volunteer work at the church to Moose to your exceptional cooking skills and the care you've shown many of the residents here at the Legends."

She paused to dab her eyes.

"But James made me promise to make you follow the rules of the contract to a T. He wanted to be sure that you understood the importance of reading contracts before you signed because that is so important in life. I explained to him that we can penalize residents with fines for just about anything, and that was okay with him. If it was ever an issue, he would take care of it."

She paused again.

My clothes were packed upstairs, but I was less certain where they or this conversation were headed.

"He asked me not to discuss our relationship with you. Nothing was really secret, but you know how he was; your grandfather wanted you to succeed without his help because he was so proud of you when you did. Of course, he was *always* proud of you. Regarding my reserved greetings, I must say, it was difficult to see you around the complex because each time I wanted to smile and chat. I was afraid if I ever started talking, I would blurt everything out. I'm quite the babbler, as you can now tell."

She had that right. This was the most I had ever heard

her speak, and I was still uncertain what the heck she was trying to say, but she was sounding genuinely nice.

"I'm sorry I wasn't able to be more pleasant in our interactions at the time. I hope we can be friends now."

"That would be nice, but I don't know where I'm going to end up after the dust settles." *Ugh.* Did I really just toss out one of Louis' phrases?

"Well, that's one of the things we need to discuss because you have some decisions to make. Your grandfather suspected you wouldn't read his apartment contract. That's the reason I asked you to bring it here today. As his leasing agent, we had agreed on a few terms that neither of us wanted to think about at the time but both knew were important. Please open your contract to page eight. Notice item fourteen states that in the event of a death, any funds previously paid are nonrefundable."

"But there's an exception at the bottom of the page." I pointed to my copy. "What does this mean?"

"You read the contract? James would be so proud. Yes, there is an exception, negotiated by your grandfather and handwritten in the space at the bottom of the page."

I had read the contract last night and again this morning but didn't think it mattered. I was still not sixty years old and had entered the office certain that Ms. Glass would have something up her sleeve to void any clause in my favor.

I read the clause aloud. "With regard to item fourteen, maintenance funds have been prepaid in full for three years from the date of the contract. As these funds are nonrefundable, in the event of the Owner's death, it is agreed that Ms. Natalie Thomas may reside in or sell the apartment."

I looked up for clarification. "What exactly does that mean? I can't sell an apartment that you own. Estrella had checked Grandpa's file and told me that rent was paid for three years, but she never mentioned maintenance funds."

"The Legends leases and sells units. James bought his

unit and paid in full. So it is really exactly what it says. If you want to live in the apartment, it is yours, and for the next two or so years, all maintenance costs are paid in full. The parking spot in the garage is yours as well, which I'm sure you'll agree comes in handy in the winter. Estrella must have been looking at something else."

"Um." I raised my eyebrows. "This all sounds too good to be true. Are you sure it's okay? I mean, it's the *Legends*. I'm not sixty, and I have Moose."

"Ah, yes, Moose. I have two dogs at home." She pulled another piece of paper from the file. "This is a memo your grandfather drafted when he purchased the unit. You'll see this has been initialed by myself in agreement. It specifies that one dog which provides *service-like* capabilities is allowed in the unit. We linked the condition to service animals for legal reasons, but the language is soft enough that Moose quite easily fits the definition. So, yes, the apartment is available to you *and* Moose if you should choose to stay. And I must say on behalf of myself and the other residents, we would be happy if you did."

"And everything is okay? I mean, what about Angie?"

I had made nice with Angie, but that didn't mean she would accept me as a neighbor.

"Ms. Chambers? I've already met with her. She made a point to tell me how helpful you are around the complex. You know, her daughter moved her into the Legends and hasn't been back since. Can you imagine how your grandfather would have felt if you never visited him? Most of the people here don't have half the relationship with their children as you had with James."

"So, she's okay with everything?"

Ms. Glass smiled. "Angie has no problem with you residing at the Legends. She does, however, have an issue with her icemaker, which she asked I make a top priority, and I will do that because it's my job. You know, every time this phone rings, it's a problem. Calls come in at all hours, day or night, for plumbing leaks, noisy neighbors, beeping smoke detectors, and backed-up toilets. Anything you can imagine. Nobody ever calls just to tell me that the coffee was great this morning."

"This is seriously too good to be true. I came in here thinking you were ready to kick me out."

"Everything is perfectly legitimate. Even if another manager was in charge, the contract would be interpreted the same."

She smiled with the warmth of a friend. "And as you've heard me say before, 'We must abide by the terms of the contract.'"

Grandpa had thought of everything. I missed him so much. Living in his apartment would be wonderful and would help me transition to a life without him.

"You know his saying, right?" I asked.

We chorused, "*If it's free, I can't afford it.*"

I wiped my eyes. "You don't know how true that's been since the day I moved in. I've spent so much time and money and stress trying to convince people that Grandpa was living here and I was not, when all along, I was living here and he was not. I came in this morning to tell you the truth about everything because it wasn't worth the trouble. The apartment was free, but I couldn't afford it."

She gave me a long hug and insisted I stop by the office often.

"I will. I definitely will."

On the way out, I grabbed Grandpa's mail—my mail—from the box. The top envelope was a Christmas card from Andy—he was moving home because he missed me too much. I walked on clouds all the way back to Grandpa's unit. My unit. The rest of the evening was spent worry-free, visiting residents in the great room, texting friends, and unpacking boxes. When I reached to turn out the kitchen light before bed, I glanced at the mantel clock. It was time. I wound Seth Thomas for a full seven days and fell asleep to the rhythmic ticking, just as I had all those nights I slept on Grandpa's couch.

In the morning, I took Moose out the nearest door, no longer needing to be discreet. I grabbed a cup of coffee in the great room, said good morning to my neighbors, and headed to work. At nine o'clock, I dialed the Legends.

"Hello, Ms. Glass. I'm just calling to say the coffee was great this morning."

Acknowledgments

First and foremost, thank you to my wonderful wife, who is the first to see every manuscript. As my frontline editor, you find and correct the most embarrassing mistakes. Your dedicated work ethic keeps me focused. Thank you to Dora Walker, Mary Baligad, and Debbie Baligad, whom I trust to provide honest critiques as you review draft manuscripts that can be so difficult to navigate. To my brothers Jim, John, and Jerry, thank you for positive reinforcement along this journey.

Thank you to Chris Aas for providing excellent suggestions that improved the story particularly with the local vernacular and Scandinavian-influenced traditions that abound in the upper Midwest. Thank you to Dr. Joe Schelling for taking the time to review, edit, and improve another book. Thank you to the editors and staff at Elite Authors for again providing excellent edits. Thank you to Julie Frederick for your diligent and thorough editing which made this a much better product. Thank you to Damonza for another excellent cover. Lastly, I thank you, the reader, for making it all the way to this page. If you liked *If It's Free, I Can't Afford It*, be sure to check out *Ghost of the Gray* and *Crack in the Red Ice*.

About the Author

J. Jones is married with three children. After an eclectic career that included writing numerous technical documents, he retired and put his pen to work in the fictional arena. *If It's Free, I Can't Afford It* was inspired by the author's daughter when they were leaving her apartment one day and she joked about renting a unit in the cheaper, brand new, seniors-only complex across the street. Thus, a seed was planted for a story that would be years in the making. If you enjoyed Natalie's adventures, check out other works by J. Jones, including *Crack in the Red Ice*, his best-selling *Ghost of the Gray*, and the soon-to-be-released *Synthetic Lithium*, available at Amazon, Barnes & Noble, and Apple Books or through the author's website at **https://www.amazon.com/author/ghostofthegray.**

Made in the USA
Middletown, DE
20 January 2024

48215400R00161